VAMPIRE

"You get them where they live and breathe. I was trying to figure out what was totally horrifying."
—ROBERT RODRIGUEZ, DIRECTOR, *From Dusk Till Dawn*

"Vampires are sexy, as opposed to other great monsters.... They're beautifully dressed, they come into your bedroom."
—JOEL SCHUMACHER, DIRECTOR, *The Lost Boys*

"The book is one of the most original pieces of Gothic horror fiction since Bram Stoker's *Dracula*.... It's a wonderful book and the themes are terrific; it's a vampire story written from the point of view of the vampire, which had never been done before. The minute I read it, I had to do it."
—NEIL JORDAN, DIRECTOR, *Interview with the Vampire*

"The vampire is always presented as someone who is living a heightened existence, and that is very seductive. He also is someone who is able to satisfy all of his cravings."
—ANNE RICE, AUTHOR, *Interview with the Vampire*

"People have been fascinated and intrigued with vampires for years and years, and they love this story."
—GARY OLDMAN, ACTOR, Dracula in *Bram Stoker's Dracula*

"I saw him as a very decisive, charming, heroic, erotic figure—irresistible to women, unstoppable by men—a sinister but aristocratic nobleman. He also had a tragic quality to him—the curse of being immortal by being undead."
—CHRISTOPHER LEE, ACTOR, Dracula in several Hammer Films

ATTENTION: ORGANIZATIONS AND CORPORATIONS

Most HarperPaperbacks are available at special quantity discounts for bulk purchases for sales promotions, premiums, or fund-raising. For information, please call or write:
Special Markets Department, HarperCollins*Publishers*,
10 East 53rd Street, New York, N.Y. 10022.
Telephone: (212) 207-7528. Fax: (212) 207-7222.

FANGORIA® VAMPIRES

Edited by
ANTHONY TIMPONE

HarperPrism
An Imprint of HarperPaperbacks

HarperPaperbacks
A Division of HarperCollins*Publishers*
10 East 53rd Street, New York, N.Y. 10022-5299

If you purchased this book without a cover, you should be aware that this book is stolen property. It was reported as "unsold and destroyed" to the publisher and neither the author nor the publisher has received any payment for this "stripped book."

Copyright © 1996 by Starlog Group, Inc.
All rights reserved. No part of this book may be used or reproduced in any manner whatsoever without written permission of the publisher, except in the case of brief quotations embodied in critical articles and reviews. For information address HarperCollins*Publishers,* 10 East 53rd Street, New York, N.Y. 10022-5299.

ISBN 0-06-105666-9

HarperCollins®, 🔥®, HarperPaperbacks™, and HarperPrism® are trademarks of HarperCollins*Publishers* Inc.

Cover photographs: © 1987 and © 1968 Warner Bros. Inc.

First HarperPaperbacks printing: November 1996

Printed in the United States of America

Visit HarperPaperbacks on the World Wide Web at
http://www.harpercollins.com/paperbacks

❖ 10 9 8 7 6 5 4 3 2 1

CONTENTS

ACKNOWLEDGMENTS

Many people helped make this book possible, especially the entire Starlog staff, *FANGORIA*'s managing editor Michael Gingold, John Douglas, John Silbersack, Karen Muratori, Eric Eskenazi, Michael Updegraff, Margaret Grohne, Jeff Walker, Tom Weaver, and all interviewees (including casts and crews) featured in this book.

INTRODUCTION

ANTHONY TIMPONE

CHILDREN OF THE NIGHT . . . nosferatu . . . bloodsuckers . . . the undead . . . *vampires.* They are our most enduring monsters of literature and film. Their status as both nightmare figures and enchanting seducers enthralls countless audiences and readers, generation after generation. While other fright figures fall out of fashion for decades at a time (when was the last time you saw a big-budget mummy movie?), vampire films and novels are as eternal as the fiends themselves. But why?

Vampires are way cool. They wear great clothes, have lotsa money, never have trouble finding dates and, except for the tight confines of your average coffin, live in splendid, comfortable abodes. They rule the night life and live forever. During the daytime, they can catch up on all the sleep none of us ever get, or watch videotapes and play Nintendo all they want until dinnertime. Not too shabby. Most guys would love to be vampires; most girls want to sleep with them.

Whereas vampires used to be wealthy counts pining for lost loves in musty, Gothic castles, today they come in all shapes and sizes. Anyone can be a vampire, everyone has been one. Vampire cops, vampire detectives. Vampire punks, vampire rockers. Vampire priests, vampire sluts. Vampire celebrities, vampire gangsters. Lesbian vampires, gay vampires. Psychic vampires, blind vampires. Vampire dogs, vampire cats. Even vampire motorcycles!

Since the English publication of John Polidori's now-forgotten novel *The Vampyre: A Tale* in 1819, vampire fiction has become a genre practically unto itself. In 1897, Bram Stoker made his bloodsucker breakthrough with *Dracula*, a novel that has never gone out of print in one hundred years. Modern readers have found their blood fix in the works of one-woman industry Anne Rice, whose dark hero, the vampire Lestat, has stalked through an ongoing series of best-selling *Chronicles*, beginning with *Interview with the Vampire* in 1976. Rice imitators are legion; not a month goes by without a new vampire novel or short-story collection haunting bookstores, with only endless serial killer opuses offering any real horrific competition (can a vampire serial killer book be far behind?).

Vampire mythologies, personalities, philosophies and physiognomies have been dissected and explained in detail, *ad infinitum*, by Stoker's descendants. We now know why they feed, who they vote for, and where they do their shopping. No (grave)stone has been left unturned.

Vampire movies have kept audiences spellbound since the beginning of film, with the silent German classic *Nosferatu* (a thinly disguised *Dracula* adaptation) making the strongest initial impression in 1922. In 1931, Hungarian actor Bela Lugosi entered immortality in the lead role of Tod Browning's now-dated but essential *Dracula*. Besides successful stage runs and the Universal pictures from the thirties and forties, the Stoker perennial has been brought to the screen innumerable times since, most memorably in a series of Christopher Lee/Hammer films (1958–1973) and an opulent version of the story directed by Oscar winner Francis Ford Coppola in 1992. While horror films have been risky business at the box office in the last decade, fang flicks rarely lose. Since 1985, *Fright Night*, *The Lost Boys*, *Bram Stoker's Dracula*, *From Dusk Till Dawn* and Neil Jordan's sumptuous take on *Interview with the Vampire* have left moviegoers screaming for more.

The bloodsucker boom is not solely a literary and cinematic phenomenon. There have been vampire board games (Ravenloft, Vampire: The Eternal Struggle), TV shows (*Dark Shadows*, *Forever Knight* and, most recently, Fox's vampire soap *Kindred: The Embraced*), model kits (Necroscope, based on Brian Lumley's multiple novels), comic books (indie hits *Vampirella*, *Purgatori: The Vampires Myth*, DC's *Vamps*) and even breakfast cereals (sugar bomb kid favorite, Count Chocula). Rarely has so much green been spent on so much red!

The pages of *FANGORIA* magazine have chronicled the bloodsucker bonanza in detail, visiting the sets of vampire movies and television shows, profiling their talented stars and creators. The following collection of articles is a time-capsule journey behind the scenes of the most popular vampire films of all time. Our writers will also tell you which books obsessed us the most, and you'll even meet the *real* Dracula, one of history's most notorious madmen. Perhaps after reading this collection, you will have a better idea of why vampires continue to hold us in their grasp, hypnotize us with their eyes, and make us beg for more. The fangs in the night are upon us, seeking to feed. Enjoy!

ON-SET WITH *FROM DUSK TILL DAWN*

ANTHONY C. FERRANTE

AS THE R-RATED RED-BAND coming attraction trailer appears on a television monitor in director Robert Rodriguez's office, a low voice intones over black: "Now the most controversial of the year." Suddenly, fast-paced guitar music cranks into high gear as the image of a knife slamming down on a biker's hand and blood splashing onto a table fills the screen.

"Remarkable," the voice continues, announcing a critic's quote from *The Village Voice*, followed by someone getting their neck chewed off as easily as someone peeling an orange.

"Sensational," adds the voice, followed by its source, the *New York Daily News*, while KNB EFX artist Greg Nicotero dies violently.

As more quotes follow (including "Electrifying" and "A Great Movie") in the same gratuitous fashion that has become a staple of that never-ending promotional treadmill, you start to realize there's something suspiciously wrong here. Not every major publication is going to be in unanimous agreement over a horror film. That's like

Roger Ebert, Gene Siskel, *and* Michael Medved all agreeing that *Friday the 13th* is a swell movie for small kids to watch over and over again.

Naturally, before anyone gets too content, the mugs of Quentin Tarantino and *ER's* George Clooney appear, shooting off a round of bullets at the camera as they pay homage to a certain *Pulp Fiction* scene featuring Samuel L. Jackson and John Travolta.

Finally, the screen goes black and the title *From Dusk Till Dawn* comes into view. The sound of a soothing music box tinkles in the background and the tag line "Our gift to you at Christmas" slowly fades in.

This is the type of trailer horror fans have been waiting for, but this clever little promotional reel never played at a theater near you—Rodriguez simply designed it as a crowdpleaser to entertain the film's crew.

"I'm trying to make the strongest picture I can, but I know there will probably be another version that will have some additional stuff," says the enthusiastic Rodriguez, who acknowledges that bloody good intentions sometimes lead down that hellish road to the ratings board. "I didn't get the [alternate] coverage because I didn't have the time. When you're making one movie, you have to deal with that movie, and you can't be concerned with what someone else is thinking about. If nothing else, we will release another version on laserdisc, but we've colored the blood differently for all the creatures, so we might get it past the MPAA."

Cutting together raw footage in his spare time is one of many unique ways that director Rodriguez is setting himself apart from any other filmmaker working in the business today. At twenty-eight years old, Rodriguez is enjoying an autonomy in Hollywood reserved only for top directors; he not only edits his own films but serves as camera operator as well. He earned this right, however, because his $7,000 debut *El Mariachi* proved to

Hollywood that you don't need to spend millions of dollars to make a kick-ass movie.

While Rodriguez has firmly established himself in the action genre, horror fans will relish the powerhouse combo on *From Dusk Till Dawn*. In addition to Rodriguez at the helm, costar Tarantino also concocted the script (from a story by KNB partner Robert Kurtzman) that follows a group of characters who find themselves trapped in a biker bar near the Mexican border, only to discover that it's infested with some very beautiful women with very deadly bites.

"If you do a horror film with a big budget, the studio will just water it down—nobody will see what you did," says Rodriguez. "They usually take out all the good horror stuff because they feel it will be too strong. We're trying to push the envelope here. It's like we're doing a down-and-dirty B-movie and attempting to elevate it to A status. That's all we're aspiring to be. If it gets higher, then great. If not, it will still satisfy fans who like this sort of stuff."

By all indications, Rodriguez isn't pretending just to curry favor with fans—he's one himself. And anyone who saw what the director did with the $7 million Columbia afforded him for this past summer's action epic *Desperado* will certainly be confident that with an $18-million budget, a healthy ten-week shoot, Miramax/Dimension Films as distributor, and Hollywood names Harvey Keitel and Juliette Lewis acting alongside such genre faves as Tom Savini and action hero Fred Williamson (not to mention Cheech Marin as a character named Chet Pussy), *From Dusk Till Dawn* will be unlike any horror film fans have seen in some time. Think *Evil Dead II* meets *Pulp Fiction*, and you'll be in the right ballpark.

"There are more effects than we've ever done for one film on this," says KNB's Howard Berger. "In five weeks, we've delivered about five or six mechanical puppets, eleven body suits, over 150 individual makeups, and on top of that tons of blood gags and transformations. And at the same time we were shooting 1st unit with Robert, we were also shooting a bunch of optical elements on 2nd unit, so there was so much—it was never-ending."

One of the most surprising aspects of the *From Dusk Till Dawn* set is its very low-key, relaxed nature. The attitude on this film is more akin to shooting an epic in your backyard with your friends—but with several million dollars instead of your leftover lunch money.

The predominant bar set is also an indication of the film's unabashed status as a true horror movie. Called The Titty Twister, this Mexico border town dive is decorated in haphazard style, mixing a classic Aztec look with a few modern accoutrements, including patches of bright neon. Thus, many of the walls are made of what resembles the remains of ancient stone ruins, while the floor is drenched in day-old, sticky fake blood.

"We spent two weeks on the line from the script, 'The biggest barroom brawl you've ever seen,'" says Savini, who plays the biker Sex Machine and is doing his own stunts. "Here you had a hundred or so people fighting all at once, with the topless dancers flying down from their alcoves and attacking people. There must have been fifty stunt guys out there. It was extraordinary."

Some individual moments of this big brawl are being played out on set on this midsummer afternoon. KNB artist Gino Crognale is getting his chance to be munched on camera by what have become affectionately known as Butt-Ugly Vampire Chicks. This one in particular is a horrendous-looking, *Evil Dead II*-inspired creation nicknamed The Mouth Bitch who pulls Crognale's head down to her stomach, where a huge maw is waiting to bite off his head in a subsequent series of shots. First, though, he is tongued by the creation—so for take after take, the oversize appendage, drenched in methylcellulose,

French-kisses Crognale until his own face is covered in slime.

According to Berger, this monster was one of a few that Rodriguez sketched out to give the KNB team an idea of the direction he was going for. "Robert's an artist, and his drawings are super-duper cartoony, but it was great to go off from that," Berger says. "His style is like Dr. Seuss with VD. They were really weird, so with our own illustrator, John Bisson, we devised something that we could practically create. We all loved this mouth monster—it looked like a weird Martian creature with a stomach. So what we did was keep the essence but created it in a way that could be practically done and also be scary. It ultimately turned out to be my favorite in the movie."

The evolution of this new breed of lethal women is part of Rodriguez's attempt to scare the male contingent of the audience, since very often they're the hardest ones to get a jolt out of in a horror movie. "Since a bar is usually where a guy's worst nightmare of picking up a girl who he thinks is beautiful but turns out to be really ugly occurs, we came up with this idea of Butt-Ugly Vampire Chicks," the director says. "So a guy will be sitting there, and a real pretty girl will come up to him and start lap dancing, and then she'll turn around and be a horrible monster, with a gaping stomach wound, sores, pus, and tongues. Most guys can't get scared in horror movies these days, but if you show something like this, they'll get freaked out. You get them where they live and breathe. I was trying to figure out what was totally horrifying."

The shoot goes smoothly as the various elements that comprise this horrific monster moment fall into place. Rodriguez operates the Steadicam (having done so on his previous films), which keeps the set lively and fast-paced; the director averages an unprecedented thirty to fifty setups per day. As for Crognale, he actually appears as if he's enjoying his moment of horror movie immortality, offering an impressive scream each time The Mouth Bitch proceeds to bite down on his head.

"This is a movie where we've been working constantly," says Berger. "The thing about Robert is that he moves so fast, we can't keep up. We're always a step behind him. He'll already be onto his next setup, and we'll be walking in with our next effect—as opposed to most other films, where you're waiting for the directors to be ready."

Ultimately, KNB has been a step ahead all along—since there would not have been a *From Dusk Till Dawn* if it weren't for the perseverance of coproducers Kurtzman and John Esposito. Back in 1989, Kurtzman had conceived the story for *Dusk* to be developed as his directorial debut. "The inspiration was *Assault on Precinct 13* and *Night of the Living Dead*, as it was for many before us," Esposito says. Looking to go way over the top and make a no-holds-barred horror movie with cameos by every genre favorite in the business, *From Dusk Till Dawn* began to seem feasible once Kurtzman and Esposito paid a little-known writer named Quentin Tarantino $1,500 to pound out a script from the story outline.

"That script financially released Quentin from ever having to hold down a regular job again," explains coproducer Elizabeth Avellan, Rodriguez's wife. "So this movie is real symbolic for him. It wasn't much money at the time, but it was just the right amount he needed so he could continue writing and make movies."

The script then sat around for years collecting dust as Kurtzman and Esposito watched it become an on-again, off-again project, but as Tarantino slowly crept into the mainstream, first with *Reservoir Dogs* and then *Pulp Fiction*, financial backers started to take interest. "We developed a love-hate relationship with the project," admits Kurtzman. "Over the years it did take its toll on us. The worst part was that the same readers who said the script was one of the worst things they had ever read were calling it brilliant right after Quentin hit."

The closest *From Dusk Till Dawn* came to seeing production was around the time the *Tales from the Crypt* team was looking to start off their film franchise with the project. After languishing for a time in development hell, however, Kurtzman became disillusioned with the process, especially when the script began slowly turning into standard *Crypt* fare.

"*Tales from the Crypt* has a specific formula, and they wanted us to establish that this was a supernatural film early on, and they wanted more comic elements," says Esposito. "They wanted more straight comedy, as opposed to Quentin's style, which is ironic. His criminals don't tell jokes. You laugh at the truth in the situation."

Kurtzman adds, "We always intended it to be two movies in one. We wanted to do this psycho thing at the beginning, and then halfway into the movie it does a ninety-degree turn and becomes a vampire film. Most people who were interested in the film didn't want the two movies. They either wanted a vampire movie or an action movie." (Ironically, the second *Crypt* film, *Bordello of Blood*, based on an old Robert Zemeckis/Bob Gale script, has a very similar storyline to *Dusk*.) Once the *Crypt* deal fell through, Kurtzman realized it was time for him to step down from the project as director and move on to other endeavors with Esposito (*The Demolitionist* now marks his directorial debut). Meanwhile, Tarantino had suddenly become the hottest thing in Hollywood, and since *From Dusk Till Dawn* was the only remaining script of his that hadn't been produced, a feeding frenzy began. It soon evolved into his own next project, so he immediately contacted Rodriguez, whom he had spoken to about the script a couple of years before.

"Quentin said he would rewrite the script if I would direct it, and I said I'd direct it if he rewrote it," Rodriguez recalls. "So this became our next project, and we wanted to do it really quickly and not spend our whole lives on it— and also have it out by Christmas." [The film unltimately opened in January '96]

The essential story remains the same, as the criminal Gecko brothers (Clooney and Tarantino) take minister Jacob Fuller (Harvey Keitel) and his daughter and son (Juliette Lewis and Ernest Liu) hostage in their Winnebago. Hiding out in Mexico at The Titty Twister, they think everything will be OK, but soon realize their troubles have just begun.

"There's a sense of morality to my character," explains Clooney, who has completely shed his nice-guy image from TV'S *E.R.* to play the crewcut, tattooed Seth Gecko. "See, Quentin is very amoral. He rapes and kills and is basically like Lenny [from *Of Mice and Men*]. He touches pretty, shiny things and breaks them, and I go around saying, 'Don't do that.' I'm opposed to killing anyone unless we have to—only if they get in my way. I'm the bad guy, but I'm not really *that* bad."

The addition of Lewis to the cast even prompted Tarantino to beef up the role, according to Avellan. "He said, 'I have to rewrite this and make it worthy of her,'" Avellan recalls. "She's been really great, too. We've seen Juliette as the saucy wench, and now she's playing the sweet little girl. She looks like she's seventeen or eighteen years old. Robert even says she has great screams. Very few women can scream like that. Maybe Jamie Lee Curtis."

Rounding out the Fuller clan is Liu, playing the young adopted son who would do anything to get out of the bar alive—even sell out his family. "When he came in, Robert's first comment was that he was so much like Quentin," says Avellan. "He was like a little Asian Quentin Tarantino. When he finally got on the set, it was great watching him go into this bar with all these topless dancers because he didn't have to act. He was mesmerized. This was his first movie. I told his mom not to worry—'He'll never find a bar like this in his whole entire life. He'll never want to go to another one—he's been to the best.'"

Ultimately, the most ingenious bit of casting was saved for last—the team of Savini and Williamson as Sex Machine and Frost. "A lot of people were pitching big mainstream stars for those roles, but we really wanted to satisfy the horror fans," says co-executive producer Lawrence Bender. "Besides, these guys are great. Tom does his own stunts, and Robert had him do this whole Jackie Chan-inspired sequence. And Fred is so cool. He's got that cigar, and he looks like he's going to beat the shit out of these vampires in a way only Fred—the Hammer—could do. They just totally fit into this movie."

Ironically, the roles almost ended up reversed, according to Savini, who was busy in Pittsburgh putting the finishing touches on his book *Grand Illusions II* and only had time to do an audition tape for the filmmakers. "This is the kind of thing where you hope you don't suddenly wake up and you've been dreaming," says Savini. "When I got the script in the mail, I read Frost and thought he was good, but when I read Sex Machine, he was a terrific character. So I sent them a tape based on Sex Machine's lines. When they saw it, I was told both Robert and Quentin were laughing out loud and loved it. Originally, Sex Machine was this big hulking type like Fred, and Frost was this little guy. After the tape, they changed the body types and gave us each other's role. So there's a Hollywood story right there. I got a part by auditioning not for what they sent me but for something else. It's one of those things where someone takes a chance and then it happens. So pinch me, I'm dreaming."

For his fans, Savini speculates that Sex Machine has some lineage from his character Morgan the Black Knight in George Romero's *Knightriders*. "From what these guys have been telling me, I look the same as I did back then, so I really feel this is where Morgan ended up," Savini says. "I have my chaps, my motorcycle jacket, and my motivation. I also have a whip and this great codpiece—when the flap opens up, there's a chrome cylinder gun that pops out and flips up. I've blown a few vampires away with this, firing from the crotch. They're calling it the crotch rocket."

Much like John Travolta nabbing his role in *Pulp Fiction* based on Tarantino's affinity for the actor's body of work, the same held true with Williamson in this film. According to the actor, Tarantino's encyclopedic knowledge of the seventies included almost all of the films Williamson had done. "He knew the key dialogue from each film I made and how I said it, which was impressive," says Williamson, who reveals that Tarantino first met him back in the early eighties at a gas pump.

"We were at the same service station, and he was on the other side of my pump and recognized me," Williamson recalls. "He was a little bit nervous to make himself known to me or ask if it was really me. Then he got up the nerve to say, 'Aren't you Fred Williamson?' and he was naturally waiting for a certain kind of response that would be indicative of my screen presence and reputation. He was waiting to be defeated or overwhelmed, and I said to him, 'You got it.' Quentin said that was the ultimate response that a big hero like me could have given him, and from that point on he assumed I was a real action star and not just a make-believe one."

Never having done a horror film before, Williamson still views his character within the action context, since he feels he has to live up to the type of character he's cultivated over the years. "I know what my fans expect from me," he says. "When you see Fred Williamson on the marquee, there's not going to be any singing. I'm not going to tell jokes. I'm going to be doing what I'm noted for, namely being a tough guy who's smooth and suave.

Even though I'm in this kind of picture, I'm still maintaining my character by not doing anything that's going to prostitute or assassinate the character I've worked so many years to maintain."

Though the possibility of reaching a new generation with this film might be an incentive for some actors, Williamson says he did *Dusk* for the fun of it more than anything else. "I make three or four movies a year anyway, so I don't think I'm concerned about losing any generations," he says. "I'm having fun out here and it's a good time for Quentin, so why not make it a good time for me? I make action films that cross over in all media, ages, and colors. A foot in the mouth translates to a foot in the mouth all around the world. And I'm not prejudiced. I kick white people and black people. I kick anybody in the mouth who's a bad guy in my films."

And, he says, *Dusk*'s monsters warrant the same kick in the mouth. "They're still evil, so they translate into bad people, and bad people get the same wrath whether they're vampires or humans," Williamson deadpans. "I do find it tough to do this in a serious way. You have to play for the lightheartedness of it, but you also have to play it straight. We've been spiking the vampires through the hearts with pool cues, and I found a way to spike them through the heart with pencils which still gives me my action hero status."

With all these disparate elements coming together at once, *From Dusk Till Dawn* is shaping up to be a very dense movie, which Bender affirms will be a little under two hours. "It will definitely be longer than a regular horror film because it has all this character stuff," he says.

Back on set, it's apparent that the film is in the right hands from a horror fan's perspective. Rodriguez loves every aspect of the special makeup FX, constantly coming up with new ideas on how to make scenes more interesting and never one to carelessly ignore the usually taboo dictum of "more blood."

"I love horror films, and I always wanted to do one right," Rodriguez concludes. "The real horror films are the low-budget ones that try to please horror fans and go for the throats—the ones where you don't know what's going to happen next. You know they'll do anything to scare you. We thought that if we made this one and did it through a company like Miramax that would leave us alone, we would be able to get away with murder. So they've given us the creative freedom. Plus, the KNB guys have been great. They're like, 'Hey, we can make you a *Blade Runner* gun, we'll just pour up the mold and paint it up for you.' Where were these guys when I was growing up? We would have become best friends. And every time I see them in their area on set, I'm like, 'Man, you guys have the best place over here. I wish I could hang out here with you. Damn, I have to go direct now.'"

FROM DUSK TILL DAWN:
An Interview with
Quentin Tarantino
and Robert Rodriguez

ANTHONY C. FERRANTE

"TWO AUTEURS—ONE VISION" might be the best way to describe the unholy filmic marriage of *Desperado*'s jack-of-all-trades director Robert Rodriguez and red-hot *Pulp Fiction* filmmaker Quentin Tarantino. In the thick of the downtown Los Angeles summer heat, the two friends are plugging away at *From Dusk Till Dawn* (Rodriguez directing, Tarantino scripting and starring), a good old-fashioned bloodbath kind of horror movie with big money and an A-list cast (George Clooney, Harvey Keitel, Juliette Lewis) mixed in with familiar genre faces (Tom Savini, Fred Williamson, and KNB's creature creations).

"This movie won't be easy to categorize," beams Rodriguez. "It's just like *Pulp Fiction*—it's a bizarre film. And it's something horror fans haven't seen and probably won't see at this level ever again."

It would seem an impossible dream that these filmmakers would link up for one of the most eagerly awaited genre films of the year (they previously collaborated on the anthology *Four Rooms*), but with *Dusk*, they've managed to convince Miramax's Dimension Films division to plop down $18 million for a balls-out shocker—with the big bonus of total creative control. "We're doing this independently," notes coproducer Elizabeth Avellan, who is also Rodriguez's wife. "Miramax isn't bothering us—we're allowed to just do it. That's how *Pulp Fiction* was for Quentin. There's a certain trust they have. Being left alone and free to do what they want is how Quentin and Robert were able to get where they are. They worked at their craft and did their first movies for nothing. Miramax appreciates that, because [studio honchos] the Weinsteins came out of nowhere, too. So they're like, 'Let them do their thing and they'll come up with something cool for us.'"

Nonetheless, the producers are no doubt well aware that the results will certainly be much more gratifying for the average Fango fan than for Dimension's marketing department, especially if the heavily blood-drenched floors on set are any indication. "They keep watering down all kinds of movies, especially horror films, so we're trying to push the envelope," says Rodriguez. "In a horror film, you're supposed to get what you pay for, and get what you deserve."

While promises can, and very often are, broken by filmmakers (especially in an unpredictable climate where studios are wont to sell their horror movies as "psychological thrillers"), the powers that be behind this film are trying to ensure that its effectiveness will not be sabotaged. Part of this involves Rodriguez's multifaceted talents; in addition to producing and directing, he's also serving as the film's Steadicam operator and editor. Add to that Tarantino the Untouchable, and *Dusk* might be the break the genre needs to regain its edge.

"I love the way the film is structured," Tarantino says. "The first half is closer to *Silence of the Lambs* in that it's a real serious, intense thriller, while the second half turns into this big, wild carnival of horrors like *Evil Dead II*. In fact, the second half is very much influenced by *Evil Dead II* in the sense that there's humor and one damn thing after another coming at you."

On the second to last day of principal photography, it's clear that the two filmmakers complement each other, yet are also a study in contrasts. Rodriguez is living up to his reputation for staying busy as he waits for a complicated makeup effect to be rigged by KNB's Greg Nicotero and Howard Berger. Instead of relaxing in his director's chair, the fidgety director keeps himself occupied by playing with a prop guitar.

"The guitar keeps me calm—I would never have had time to play one on my other movies," says Rodriguez, who is notorious for knocking off fifty to seventy setups a day on his prior pictures, *El Mariachi*, Showtime's *Roadracers*, and *Desperado*. "Things that have to do with horror effects take time—you have to wait for the monsters."

Meanwhile, Tarantino (who has wrapped his acting role but is on set to shoot a videotaped introduction to the *Pulp Fiction* laserdisc) is talking up a storm and having fun with the cast and crew. Hyperactive is the operative word as he carries on the type of movie-absorbed conversations that would have probably gotten him fired from his early job at a video store. Outside his trailer, he chats with a couple of crew members about special "director's cuts" he used to make of movies he really liked (such as editing together the "exposition-heavy," watered-down TV cut and the incomprehensible theatrical version of the overlooked 1982 shocker *The Sender* into a largely complete video edition). "I'm just waiting for some kid to send me a homemade tape of *Pulp Fiction* that tells the story in chronological order," Tarantino quips to his small audience.

Later, in his trailer, Tarantino waxes enthusiastic about

finally having the chance to deliver a real horror movie, which has been his goal for some time now. "The virtue of this film is that it's like a big-budget drive-in movie," he beams. "That's what's good about it—it's an exploitation film. It's not *Bram Stoker's Dracula*—and there's nothing wrong with that. It's just not this high-class thing. It's not even a serious take on the horror genre. It's a movie to drink beer and to watch and hoot and holler. We've kept that tone, even though we're doing it on a much bigger scale."

Tarantino lives up to the description of being "the first director who's a rock 'n' roll star" when, a few moments later, a couple of young female visitors knock on his trailer door requesting an autograph. He agrees to comply after the interview and then offers his observations about the current state of horror. "We feel there's actually a big audience out there for horror that hasn't been showing up because the movies have been weak," he says. "*Species*, with its big opening, proved to some degree that that audience exists, but the problem is it has become a ghettoized genre. There hasn't been a really good low-budget horror film in a long time, especially with a theatrical release. They're all going straight to video, which cuts out fifty percent of their effectiveness right there."

The main problem, Tarantino feels, is that the big studios have created a monopoly on the horror market by churning out "mainstream" fare that doesn't have any faith in the genre's audience. "They're trying to make horror films for people who don't go to horror films, which turns off the fans automatically," he says. "Studios are scared of the word 'horror,' and we're not. This is a horror film—a rip-off-your-head-and-drink-your-blood horror film."

On the set, Tarantino's promises are not proving empty, as carnage is getting ample play; numerous special FX gags that were pushed to the end of the shoot due to

time constraints are being shot. On a normal movie,
these scenes would have simply been cut, but Rodriguez
knows the importance of delivering the goods and is
sparing nothing to film every gruesome thing he can—
even if it means going over schedule a couple of days.
"We just keep shooting all this cool stuff," the director
says. "It's been long hours and a lot of shots. It's probably
going to be a two-and-a-half-hour movie. Everyone's
character kind of grew and got more stuff to do. I will
have to cut it down, though there might be an epic-
length laserdisc."

Savini has been one of the benefactors of this growth
of character. Playing the quick-witted biker Sex Machine,
the actor/makeup guru began with a couple of lines and
ended up as the film's unstoppable Jackie Chan type. "I
knew we would go to hell if we put Tom Savini in the
movie and didn't do anything with him," says Rodriguez.
"So I started thinking of all the things we could do with
him, and when he said he'd do his own stunts, we had him
flipping off pool tables and other things. Now he's Mr.
Badass. He has a bigger part than anybody else in the last
half. Savini won't die; he keeps coming back, and horror
fans will love that. Every time you try to kill a piece of
him, another one turns into something else."

Currently shooting on the set of The Titty Twister
(the film's Mexican bar), a vampire "rat" version of Savini
is fighting off star Clooney. One of the film's most
impressive and threatening KNB creations, it attacks,
bites, and does all sorts of horrible things to the actor
throughout the afternoon. On the video monitor, the
scene plays beautifully; the cable-controlled/animatronic
creation provides a show-stopping set piece.

"Shooting horror stuff is the same as shooting the
action—it has to be energetic, like *Aliens*," says
Rodriguez, who moves around the stage from the "rat"
setup to various 2nd-unit shots that include everything

from a deep-focus closeup of a crossbow, Sam Raimi style, to a vampire getting hit with a balloon full of holy water. "The faster you move, the better the movie looks anyway," the director continues. "In *Desperado*, I'd reload the gun and start shooting again. Here we reload the goop and the monsters."

The teamup of Hollywood's two most wanted directors began back in March 1993, when both were working on the Sony Pictures lot—Rodriguez prepping *Desperado* and Tarantino developing *Pulp Fiction* (then a TriStar project). "We were both working late at the office and decided to go out to eat," Rodriguez recalls. "I was telling Quentin how I liked shooting in Mexico, because there are no rules over there and you can have more freedom. People can run through the streets with guns in your movies and no one will question it. Then he said he had written a horror movie that was set in Mexico."

Rodriguez ultimately read the script, but it was tangled up with various producers and unavailable. A year and a half later, the producers were interested in Tarantino becoming involved with the film again, and he said he would rewrite it only if Rodriguez directed it. The deal went through quickly, and the film went into production. "We got very excited about it and wanted to do it fast—we didn't want to spend our whole lives on it," says Rodriguez. "We wanted to go and shoot the hell out of it rapidly. We originally wanted it out by Halloween, but most of the actors were not available right away, so we had to wait."

Though Tarantino had the option to direct the film, he always saw it as a script for somebody else, and when it became available again he thought Rodriguez's "quick poppy style" could make it work. "Years would pass, and from time to time I pulled the script out, read it and thought, 'This is really cool,' but I didn't have much hope for it," Tarantino admits. "It would be so easy to do

badly. They could get the wrong guy, which would probably be the case, and he wouldn't understand it or just
make it cheap. And I didn't want to do it. If I could do it
real quick, like in eighteen days, I would have, but it's so
special effects-heavy I couldn't."

The script's structure is also important to Tarantino,
who is used to breaking down and reinventing genre conventions. *Dusk* starts off as an archetypal Tarantino film,
revolving around two psychopathic brothers—Seth and
Richard Gecko (Clooney and Tarantino)—who go on a
cross-country killing spree and kidnap a minister (Keitel)
and his family along the way. Once they hole up at The
Titty Twister midway through the movie, the story suddenly takes a turn for the horrific when they discover that
the bar is host to stripper vampires.

"Harvey Keitel asked me, 'Quentin, do you think this
is going to work when all of a sudden the movie flips over
and becomes another movie?' and I thought, 'Yeah, I
think it will,'" recalls Tarantino. "What I told him,
though, was, 'You don't have to worry about this. You
will still be in the same movie you were before. The characters just have to deal with it and rise to the occasion.'
None of these people are expecting to be in a horror
movie, so when everybody turns into vampires in the second act, it's just as much of a surprise to them as it is to
the audience."

While many producers over the years tried to bring the
horror elements to the forefront in the first half (particularly when the film was slated to go before the cameras as
one of the *Tales from the Crypt* movies), Tarantino felt content to leave the structure the way it was, and instead
focused on beefing up the characters in the rewrite. "Every
time I tried to deviate from the original structure, it
wouldn't work," he notes. "That was not the problem.
That was one of the strongest things about it. The problem was that most of the characters were one-dimensional,

so I made them three-dimensional and meatier. They were clichés before; they were fun clichés, but they were still clichés, so I gave them more human heart."

While Tarantino's influence lies in the dialogue, Rodriguez was allowed to embellish the horror elements. The major vampire attack scene, for instance, was intended as the world's longest bar fight, and now, at the end of principal photography, it's safe to say Rodriguez has achieved just that. "This is a rare horror film in that it's steeped in Mexican lore," the director asserts. "We really wanted to come up with monster concepts that got away from simply being fangs, because Mexican vampires are much different from other legends. They're more brutal. They would sacrifice people to the sun to keep it going during Aztec times and rip people apart to get more blood out. It's a real ritual. So we came up with this concept that they had turned an old temple into a bar, just to entice customers over the centuries for sacrifices."

Though Rodriguez affirms that there will be a nod to famed Mexican horror wrestler Santo in the film, the extent of his presence is minimal (if you pay attention to the bar walls, you may see faded photographs of the wrestler pasted all over, alongside such other wrestling stars as Andre the Giant). "Everybody said we have to have Santo in there, so we have a burial site for him in the film, and in the bar's back room there's a bust of him," says Rodriguez, who reveals that he's received plentiful fan mail suggesting he do a Santo movie.

According to the director, one of the more interesting challenges of *Dusk* was working for the first time on something he didn't write. But even after being present to defend his work, Tarantino admits that Rodriguez usually got his way. "Robert's a bully," Tarantino says. "He's the best bully I've ever seen, though, because he doesn't do it by picking on you; he does it by being nice to you."

The one place Rodriguez expects to get bullied himself, however, is with the MPAA. Despite everyone's assurance on set that *From Dusk Till Dawn* will get by the ratings board relatively unscathed, it's pretty obvious from the constant horrific activity that there will definitely be some concessions made. "We can't do an NC-17 because this is going out with a big two-thousand-screen release," says Tarantino. "I'm not worried about cuts, though, because I have a good relationship with the MPAA. We're going to have to go back a few times, but one of the things I've learned is that I usually get them released exactly the way I want them to. Again, my films are different from Robert's. Nevertheless, when you're as intense as those films are to start with, yeah, you cut this and cut that, but you still have a strong movie at the end of the day. It's still got real impact. You see a film like *Hard Target* and go, 'Wow, that's a lot of shit.' It doesn't look like they cut everything out. Fans may go, 'Oh my God, the good stuff got cut out like in *Friday the 13th Part 2*,' but that won't be the case with this. The good stuff will still be in there."

Both self-confessed Fango fans (Tarantino started with the hard-to-find *Motel Hell* issue #9, and Rodriguez shortly thereafter), the duo can each recall incidents where friends told the budding young filmmakers that one day they'd be featured in its pages. "I've always liked the magazine and felt inspired by it, because it made me want to make movies," says Tarantino. "Whereas someone would read *American Cinematographer* and get all excited, I would read *FANGORIA* and feel the same way, because the heroes were the directors. People would write in saying, 'Joe Dante is God,' and the directors and makeup effects artists were the real horror stars of the time. It was no longer star-driven—it was the people behind the scenes who drew in the fans."

Both filmmakers would like to continue in the genre,

and Rodriguez has a head start with a script for *Predator 3* he's finishing up for 20th Century Fox. "I started writing it a few years ago when *Desperado* was postponed and my agent got me the gig," recalls Rodriguez, whose story involves a group of humans traveling to a Predator planet. "I didn't really finish it, though. I would call it *Predators*, and it's more along the lines of *Aliens*—there would definitely be a bunch of them. If I do finish it, I probably won't direct it; I just want to do my own stuff. They own it. I'd rather create something of my own. Then you participate in the profits and control it a little better instead of watching them market a bunch of goofy stuff."

As for the immediate future, Tarantino's slate is filled only with acting gigs, including a turn in the Spike Lee movie *Girl 6.* "I would totally like to be involved in another horror film as either a writer, director, or actor, but I have nothing on the burner," he says. "I have nothing after this—I'm finished for now."

By contrast, Rodriguez's job is just beginning as he goes into a round-the-clock editing whirlpool in order to complete *From Dusk Till Dawn* in time for its opening. "On a normal Hollywood movie, there's usually an editor working on the movie from the moment they start shooting," he says. "So there would have been an editor working on this movie for ten weeks as of now, but I'm the editor and I'm just getting ready to start. I will be eleven weeks behind by next week and have about four weeks to edit the movie where most people have twenty. So we will be cutting it close."

While *Dusk's* delivery date may have been somewhat flexible, the due date of Rodriguez and Avellan's first child certainly wasn't. They are the proud parents of a brand-new baby boy, Rocket Valentino Rodriguez. "Every time my baby cries, I'm planning to record him with my little digital tape recorder, put his voice into the computer, and morph it to make it a monster voice," says Rodriguez with a grin. "Kids make such horrible high-pitched sounds and he's going to be crying all the time, so why not put the kid to work the moment he's born? Give him a strong work ethic and get him his first paycheck before his feet even hit the ground."

INTERVIEW WITH THE VAMPIRE:
Tom Cruise Speaks

DAVID McDONNELL

WITH THE SUN BEATING DOWN on a Colorado Saturday, the vampire spoke at noon. And he was greeted by thunderous applause.

Of course, the man in the dark blue sweater and black pants wasn't—isn't—really a vampire. He's an actor, one of Hollywood's hottest talents with a list of credits that includes Rain Man, Born on the Fourth of July, A Few Good Men, Legend, Top Gun, *and* Risky Business. *He's Tom Cruise, and he portrays the vampire Lestat in Neil Jordan's film version of Anne Rice's* Interview with the Vampire. *The fact that Cruise is playing a bloodsucker is actually less remarkable than his very presence at Denver's StarCon, a science-fiction convention. Until recently, such a formidable celebrity wouldn't be caught, well, undead at an SF con. But Cruise is here, charming and thoughtful, to answer questions from the audience.*

FANGORIA: Your casting as Lestat produced a storm of controversy, eliciting negative comments from

Anne Rice herself. Now Rice has seen the film, come out in favor of it, and praised your performance. How has this controversy and her turnabout affected you?

TOM CRUISE: I spent five months working on the character, and I was really surprised by the controversy and by Anne Rice coming out [against the casting]. I was excited about playing the role, yet I could understand [her feelings]. People have an image of who they think you are, and really can't see what another individual is capable of. I was lucky that Neil Jordan felt differently, but I was very hurt, because the controversy just kept going on and on. But [producer] David Geffen sent her the video, and she was very pleased with the movie.

Originally, Anne didn't think I was right for it; she was trying to protect these characters that she created and loved. These are fascinating, complex characters that come from her imagination. They mean a great deal to her, and I respect that. But I also respect the fact that when Anne *did* see the movie, and she saw how her material was handled, that she had enough grace and class to acknowledge what Neil and all the other actors had accomplished. That meant a great deal to me.

FANG: How familiar were you with Rice's books before doing the film?

CRUISE: I had actually read *The Vampire Lestat* a few years ago. Then I read the *Interview* script, and then the book. And I had both books on the set with me every day, underlined and paper-clipped—they were my bibles in playing Lestat. But I haven't read the other books.

FANG: What attracted you to the role of Lestat?

CRUISE: When I choose a character, it's really from the gut. I like to feel I have something to contribute to the role or to the project. And I've always *really* loved vampires. For an actor, you read these scenes [in a script] and you want to play them. I loved actually playing those scenes. I had such a great cast to work with, and a very, very fine director. When you challenge yourself in different areas, you can't help but grow.

I work very hard on every movie I do; I don't know why I haven't figured out an easier way to do it yet. I spent five months working on this film, and reading the books, reading aloud from classical novels. We spent a tremendous amount of time perfecting everything: the behavior, the hair, and the makeup—on which Stan Winston and his guys did a great job.

FANG: What aspects of Lestat's character did you find most difficult to convey on-screen?

CRUISE: When you're playing a character, it's far more interesting to see someone who loves a great deal. If there's a scene about two characters who don't like each other, there's no complexity to that. When two people care about each other and have problems, that's life. So one of the real problems I had was that when I was on the set, people talked about how evil Lestat was—"God, he's so scary." For an actor to have that translate to the screen, you *can't* just act evil. People don't just act evil. Maybe there's an enjoyment in suffering or a deep loneliness that communicates itself in other ways.

Also, I had always felt that Lestat has a very acerbic, wicked sense of humor. I was trying to find how to communicate that humor. So you really have to make the character come to life and show how he deals with his own pain and anger. Stuff like that was a lot of fun to play.

Reading *Interview with the Vampire*, it's all told

from Louis's viewpoint. There are little sentences that give you an indication of who Lestat was, and his own personal loneliness, his own compassion, his own needs. To create a whole, fully realized character, you have to block all that stuff out and find what it is that's going to communicate in a scene. I hope that answer made sense; it made sense to *me*.

FANG: Did you find preparing to play Lestat more difficult than past roles?

CRUISE: I spent over a year on *Born on the Fourth of July*. Lestat was certainly on a par with that, for the demands physically and in every other area. I'm not one of these actors who carries a role home with him, but you can't help it when you're playing a character like Lestat; you can't just close your trailer door and that's it. When I'm making a movie, I can't help thinking about it all the time. Thank God I've got a family; otherwise, I would be an incredibly boring person just thinking about my scenes and my movies.

FANG: What's your interpretation of Lestat's character?

CRUISE: I think that Lestat really is capable of a tremendous amount of love, but he's also incredibly lonely. There's the scene where Lestat is trying to get Louis to drink the blood. He wants a hunting partner, he wants someone to share his life, and realize how great it is to be what he is. He tells Louis, "In the Old World, they called it [vampirism] the dark gift, and I gave it to you." Lestat truly feels that way about it. And I think he's very frustrated with Louis, and disappointed in Claudia, because they don't realize that. He feels betrayed by them. Lestat just keeps choosing the wrong people; he's very misunderstood.

FANG: In the novel, it doesn't seem like he has any love to show anyone.

CRUISE: No, but you must understand, when Claudia dies, he weeps. He's devastated. And he saves Louis from the fire; he doesn't let him die. From Louis's viewpoint, there is a brutality, but Lestat *is* a vampire. It's like the lion made the deer a lion, and then the lion wants to be a deer. For me, that's what's incredibly fascinating about the book—it's ambiguous, leaving enough hints that it causes conversation. People have their own ideas about it and identify with different characters.

FANG: Hypothetically, given the chance, and now that you've had a small taste of it, would you ever accept the "dark gift" of vampirism?

CRUISE: No.

FANG: This movie is subtitled *The Vampire Chronicles*. And of course, there are several other Rice novels that could be filmed. So, what about a movie of *The Vampire Lestat*?

CRUISE: I just want to get through this one. I don't think I could handle talking about the next one just yet. We'll see how *Interview* goes. But I'm sure the studio would love to do another one.

FANG: Out of all the films you've made, what's your favorite role?

CRUISE: I always find that a hard question to answer, because it's always the last experience that you feel to be the best. When you look back, there are a few keystone moments in a career. I'm only thirty-two. I've been doing this for fourteen years. But *Interview with the Vampire* is certainly an experience that I will *never* forget. I missed playing Lestat when it was over. As challenging and difficult as it was, I really enjoyed it. So today, I would have to say it's *Interview with the Vampire*.

INTERVIEW WITH THE VAMPIRE:
Neil Jordan on Directing

MARK SALISBURY

IN A CUTTING ROOM in London's West End, Neil Jordan, writer/director of *The Company of Wolves* and 1992's Oscar-winning *The Crying Game*, is supervising the editing of his adaptation of Anne Rice's popular novel *Interview with the Vampire. Interview*'s release is still five months away at this writing, but Jordan, a pleasant, soft-spoken Irishman, is hard at work on a movie many thought would never reach the screen.

A filmmaker and novelist with a remarkable track record for tackling complex, sensitive subject matter, and a director with not only a proven affinity for but a love of fantasy and horror, Jordan is, in hindsight, the perfect choice to adapt Rice's book, with its polemic sexual overtones and horrific content. Ironically, Jordan had almost given up filmmaking altogether after *The Crying Game*, and it was only the fact that audiences worldwide embraced the film with such conviction that he decided to reevaluate his career.

Ever since *Company of Wolves*, Jordan's surreal, Grimms' fairy tales-inspired take on werewolf lore, he had been looking to make another film in a similar vein. When David Geffen, the record company mogul-cum–film producer who has spent the best part of a decade trying to get a film of Rice's novel made after having inherited the property from producer Julia Phillips, asked him to direct it, Jordan seized the opportunity. "The book is one of the most original pieces of Gothic horror fiction since Bram Stoker's *Dracula*," he raves. "It's a wonderful book and the themes are terrific; it's a vampire story written from the point of view of the vampire, which had never been done before. The minute I read it, I had to do it."

Although Rice had already written two screenplays, Jordan, who had had negative experiences making the big-budget supernatural comedy *High Spirits* and the Robert De Niro vehicle *We're No Angels*, demanded to adapt the book himself. "I had worked in Hollywood before," he admits, "and I had made a rule that I would only work on things I wrote myself." Over the years there had been numerous attempts to turn Rice's book into a script, none of them successful. At one stage, there were even plans to relocate the movie from its eighteenth-century beginnings in New Orleans and set it in Vietnam. Jordan's script cleaved close to the book, telling the story of an unholy Trinity of vampires, Louis (Brad Pitt), Lestat (Tom Cruise), and the child-woman Claudia (Kirsten Dunst), across two centuries.

"It is very faithful," Jordan says of his screenplay, "because the only reason I made the movie was that I liked the book. Anne's script wasn't successful. It wasn't cinematic. I don't think she had written many screenplays before, and it suffered from that. It was slightly theatrical. There was plenty of useful stuff in it, but it wasn't there. You couldn't have made it as a film."

Jordan, who believes that he and Rice should share screenplay credit (Rice was eventually granted sole credit), says that the author, in adapting her book, had left huge chunks of the story out and incorporated elements from some of her other novels.

"The thing about [her] screenplay was that it didn't get Louis's loss of soul, the moral dilemma of the central character, the way he has to adjust himself to the fact that he hasn't got a breath of humanity left in him," Jordan says. "I had to add a lot of stuff to bring out Louis's dilemma. In the book, after he kills the first few times and is disgusted by it, Lestat bites the head off a rat, puts it in a glass, and gives it to him to drink. That then becomes a whole theme; he lives off animals for a certain period and starves himself of human blood." Out, however, went Louis and Claudia's travels around Transylvania, which, says Jordan, "didn't go anywhere."

"I've tried to make a movie that deals with a sort of dysfunctional family," he explains, "with these three characters, two parents and a child—one is this kind of monstrous parent, the other is like a parent with a soul, and the child is Claudia—and to look at these characters like they were real people."

Throughout its five-month shoot, *Interview* was the subject of intense speculation by the tabloid press. Jordan denies, however, that he a) beefed up Cruise's part at the behest of the star, or b) that he toned down, as was also suggested, the film's homoerotic content at Cruise's request. Even the pedophilic issue raised by Louis and Claudia's relationship was essentially ignored by tackling it head-on and adapting the relationship as written. Indeed, the only major change in the script was introduced by Rice herself: When we first meet Louis in the novel, he is grieving over the death of his brother, while in the film it's over the death of his wife and child.

Throughout the film's seventeen-year gestation period, numerous names had been linked to the roles of Louis and Lestat, including Mel Gibson, Richard Gere, John

Travolta, and Cher. Rice's suggestions were Rutger Hauer and Tom Berenger, but both Geffen and Jordan wanted Pitt as Louis. "Brad is absolutely captivating," says Jordan. "He has an extraordinary quality and is a very instinctive actor, and when you have someone like that you can get a tremendous performance out of them. Louis suffers everything, and Brad really suffered this part."

Casting their Lestat proved more difficult and more contentious. Initially, they approached Daniel Day-Lewis. "He said he was anxious to read it, but he was making another movie," recalls Jordan, "and when he read it he said he didn't want to play a vampire. So we looked around at who to cast. We thought of Jeremy Irons for a while, and then we thought of Tom. It was my idea. His agent had called me up, and I thought about it and wasn't sure. It was a part everybody wanted to play, but Lestat and Louis had to be young men and Jeremy and Rutger are too old. It would have been a father-son relationship rather than equals.

"Also, it would have been very simple to cast in an obvious villain's way with Christopher Walken or Rutger," he continues. "But I wanted the audience to understand the logic of evil. I wanted them to understand Lestat's perspective; I didn't want a monstrous villain. Because the story is told from the point of view of vampires, I wanted the audience to understand their dilemmas, given that they live forever and they've made this Faustian pact with whomever. And I just thought Tom was the best person to do that, to make you empathize with evil. Tom is one of the most powerful young actors around, and he has a wonderful icy-cold quality which hasn't been seen before, and I thought he would go for this. David sent him the script and we met, and it became clear he would really commit himself."

The casting of Cruise, however, sparked a controversy which rivaled that following Michael Keaton's hiring as

Batman. Rice, in a less voluble moment, called the decision "bizarre" and her fans were duly horrified, but Jordan shrugs off the criticism. "People resent actors who are as successful as Tom Cruise," he states, "but they don't realize that their success is based on a whole range of things. The ability to carry a story and command an audience's absolute concentration—people don't understand how difficult that is."

Now that the fuss has died down somewhat and the film has been shot, Jordan is convinced that Rice's readers will be satisfied both with Cruise and that the film is a legitimate adaptation of the book. "Of course they will; think of the people who were going to play this role— John Travolta, at one stage Anne was going to have it as a Broadway musical with Cher in the lead," he points out. "I think they should be thrilled; the film's gotten to the screen intact. That's what I found bizarre about all that controversy with the casting. The kind of plans that were considered over the seventeen years were outlandish."

The director definitely believes that Rice should have kept her mouth shut until she saw the film. "Absolutely. I mean, I haven't spoken to her since all this happened, but I don't want to go on about it too much. It's just one of those things that happened and it's unfortunate. I think she's attached to the character of Lestat, and what happened was that she wrote that book and it came out and then she became obsessed with Lestat, and she made him into a totally different character in the other books. He's far more like Louis, and I think he's become her alter ego in some ways, her obsession. But I don't think she quite realizes the place that character has in the first book, the nature of the character, because in the second book he changed radically."

While Rice was certainly vocal in regard to the casting of Cruise, she also went on record to say she thoroughly approved of Jordan as director. "Well, she had seen my films, and I think she's from an Irish Catholic background in New Orleans," Jordan muses. "I'm from a similar background myself, so I know the world that she's coming out of, that world of plaster saints and bleeding hearts."

In addition to all the problems arising from the casting of Cruise, Jordan also had to contend with the death of River Phoenix. The young actor had been cast as the interviewer, a role eventually taken over by Christian Slater. "I had met River once and he was a lovely man," says Jordan, "absolutely lovely, and he said, 'I want to do your film,' and I said, 'Let's do it.' That was it, really. The next thing I heard, he was dead. I looked at a lot of people and thought about Christian. Now I've got three very good actors, all at different stages in their careers."

Given the film's $50-million-plus budget, its studio (Warner Bros.) backing, and the presence of a major-league Hollywood star in Cruise, Jordan says he was free to adapt the book as he saw fit, without studio interference. His track record presumably gave Warners the faith that he would treat the material with the sensitivity it required. "It was remarkable, really," says Jordan, "because it's a very large-budget movie, and I made it with people I've worked with before, almost like an independent movie within the Hollywood structure, which was great. I mean, the film is quite bloody and very disturbing, and I'm sure we will have problems. But we made it clear it would not be a PG-13."

Indeed, the novel's horrific and sensual aspects, Jordan says, are on-screen "the same way they are in the book. Sex does become horrific and horror becomes very sexual, which is probably not a very nice thing to do, but it's the nature of the book—their urge for blood and the taste of another's life has become the urge towards sexuality. But there's not a lot of sex in this film; the act of bloodletting and blood-taking becomes kind of sexual. Actually, it's quite a moral tale. That's one of the reasons I made it, because it is the story of one man's abandonment; he's abandoned by the light, he's abandoned by all possibility of redemption. In the end, the only way he'll find any kind of peace is to forget about ordinary human concepts such as guilt and compassion. The journey he makes is a black one, and he tells his own story because he wants a lesson to be learned from it. It's a bit like Lucifer saying, 'Look what happened to me. Don't go this way.'"

Yet even with all its intellectual undertones, Jordan shows no hesitation in pegging *Interview* as a genre piece. "Yeah, it is a horror film," he confirms, "a horror film told from the point of view of a monster, or monsters. So you don't get the situation you had in *Silence of the Lambs*, where you're identifying with Jodie Foster as a good, ordinary human being who's being threatened by Hannibal Lecter; you don't get the situation of the innocent under threat, because our central characters are not innocent. It's a horror film of a kind that hasn't been made before—it's as if you told Dracula's own story, really."

Providing *Interview's* special makeup FX and, through his company (formed with James Cameron) Digital Domain, the film's computer graphics is four-time Oscar-winner Stan Winston. According to Jordan, the FX wizard came to him and asked to work on the film. "He said, 'I really want to work on it,'" recalls the director with a grin, "'I *have* to work on this movie.' He's a brilliant man and I said OK; he was so enthusiastic."

Winston and Jordan worked together and came up with a look for the vampires that fitted the director's desire for the FX to be as subtle and unobtrusive as possible. "I wanted to make an effects film in which you were never aware of an effect," says Jordan, "where you would actually believe that these are vampires. These creatures have to live among ordinary people, so they can't look like Christopher Lee, they can't look like Dracula; we tried to treat them very subtly. My idea was that we would be able to see their veins underneath the skin, that their flesh would somehow be translucent because they've become creatures beyond nature.

"Then we went through the whole idea of the metabolism of the vampires," he continues. "What would happen to them when their throats were slashed, how would they weaken, how would they die, what would happen to their faces when they become vampires? We decided to use the whole range of special effects that are available now, mostly digital and computer-generated. There's one scene where Tom gets his face slashed and wounds appear, and the blood goes down and then vanishes, and people say, 'What did you do?' A lot of effects work does try to call attention to itself, but in this case they are so integrated into the fabric of this story that it's almost impossible to separate them."

And in keeping with the film's approach, the vampire transformations follow a similarly subtle path. "They're very simple," explains Jordan. "They grow teeth, the colors of their eyes change. We had to deal with the way people turn into vampires in Anne's book, which is that they drink all your blood and give you theirs. So we have to drain their faces of blood and see that happen on-screen. But it's still very subtle."

Despite the enormity of the production—the narrative spans two hundred years, and the shoot entailed five months of location work in San Francisco, New Orleans, and Paris, as well as interiors in London—Jordan says that the most difficult aspect was the fact that it all takes place at night. "One of the main things we had to do was solve the problem of night lighting, because a lot of it happens in swamps, in places where there's no available light, and when you point a camera at night there's no depth." The answer was more computer work. "I designed a whole series of shots, and into them will be added the sky, the moon, the river, all the stuff you can't light. It's very complicated."

It's all quite a long way indeed from Jordan's first fantasy/horror outing, *The Company of Wolves*, which was shot entirely on Anton (*Batman*) Furst-designed sets at England's Shepperton Studios, for a sum that was about a seventh of Cruise's reported $15-million fee for *Interview*. Jordan asserts that he is still very fond of the film and would love to see it rereleased, particularly in America, where he feels it was mismarketed as "a kind of gross-out horror movie."

"It was thrown in second-run theaters and not a lot of people got to see it who would have enjoyed it," he laments. "I like it. I mean, I would recut bits, make it shorter. But I think there is a more sophisticated audience now. *Company of Wolves* was a very complicated narrative structure-wise, one that general audiences wouldn't sympathize with; it's stories within stories within stories. It was an avant-garde movie, in a way."

Geffen, inevitably, already has an option on Rice's *The Vampire Lestat*. "We're discussing it," Jordan admits. "If *Interview* does well, we will do a sequel. I enjoyed working with Tom so much and enjoyed the character so much that if I could make sense of the second book, I would do it. That book is a bit like *Company of Wolves*; it's got stories within stories. I would have to think about it, and I would have to write it. So yes, we are talking about it—but let's see how this film does."

ANNE RICE:
Creating the *Vampire Chronicles*

MICHAEL CHARLES ROWE

"VAMPIRES," SAYS ANNE RICE, warming to a familiar subject, "have always been part of our culture. There have always been superstitions surrounding death and burial in western Europe, and the idea that the dead will come back. When you write a story about good and evil using a vampire, you are reaching back to the Renaissance for a figure as powerful as God and the devil. What I love about my readers is that they really understand what my books are about."

In the fall of 1992, Random House published the fourth volume of Rice's *Vampire Chronicles, The Tale of the Body Thief.* This installment in the narrative history of the vampire Lestat, recounts his search for his mortality.

"It's not the kind of book you'd want to give away the plot or the ending of," Rice insists. "To me, it represents a return to the intimacy with the vampires. It doesn't have the large cast and grand events of *The Queen of the Damned.* And the exciting thing is that it points to a new direction for the *Chronicles.*"

The series' first installment, *Interview with the Vampire,* features a smaller cast and more linear plot. Its main character is clearly the more somber Louis, with Lestat playing a supporting—and primarily destructive—role. In the subsequent novels, of course, Lestat becomes the star.

The progression of Lestat's character mirrors Rice's own growth as both an artist and as a person. She wrote *Interview with the Vampire* in 1973 in a white heat following the death of her daughter, Michele, from leukemia. Her grief for Michele manifests itself in the novel as Louis's sorrow over the loss of both his humanity and his chances for redemption.

"That was certainly my evolution," Rice says. "I was definitely Louis in the first book. There is a grieving for the loss of Catholicism and the loss of that worldview—a distrust of contemporary life and all its rewards outside those of the Catholic Church."

As she healed and became stronger, she began to identify more closely with the dazzling Lestat. "I became more interested in strong characters," she explains. "Lestat was a response to that. In the fourth novel, I'm totally Lestat. Louis is a major character in the book, and they have many arguments and quarrels. I had thought that when I started this novel, it would be the last book and that I had exhausted this material. But by the end, I became very excited about doing a fifth one [*Memnoch the Devil*]."

Body Thief brought back other old friends, including David Talbot and the child-vampire Claudia, who first turns up in *Interview* and makes a cameo appearance in *Queen of the Damned*.

"What readers like about the *Chronicles* is what I like: the real characters of Lestat and Louis," says Rice. "Claudia appears as a ghost in *Body Thief*, and part of that is Lestat coming to terms with the fact that he made Claudia a vampire. In fact, the novel comes to terms with everything. It's like a protracted comment on the entire

Chronicles, and a chance to get closer to the question of whether we would be vampires if we could."

Whether or not they would choose the eternal existence, readers across the world are reaching for Rice's dazzling vampires. In a time of wars, AIDS, and widespread economic hardship, the question of the vampire's appeal is worth noting. Is the public that reads about them identifying with the victims, or the bloodsuckers themselves?

"The vampire is always presented as someone who is living a heightened existence," says Rice, "and that is very seductive. He is also someone who is able to satisfy all of his cravings. I don't see this as a time of weakness at all." She points for comparison to the technological advances of the last ten years. "The vampire image reflects the enormous leap in visual perspective," she says. "This is the time of Federal Express, long-distance calls, and faxes. Someone can get up in the morning and call New York or Paris. All kinds of business transactions and close book deals can be made—it's like flying all over the world. Vampires are superhuman magnifications of us, of the way we feel in these powerful times."

In addition, Rice's vampires wear beautiful clothes and jewelry, live luxuriously, drive Harley-Davidson motorcycles, and worry, comparatively speaking, about very little. "The vampire is that glittering, dazzling rulebreaker and outsider who has gained ascendancy over time and place," she says. "And we are gaining that."

The Tale of the Body Thief is, in Rice's words, the most modern of all her vampire novels. In that spirit, she has set Lestat in Miami, America's hottest new fashion center. "My two favorite cities at the moment are New Orleans and Miami," Rice explains. "One of the reasons I love Miami is the weather; the other is the Cuban Catholic influence. It's a place where there's freedom of expression, glitter, and dash. I associate all that with Catholic countries." In *Body*

Thief, she has placed Lestat at the vortex of Miami's dazzling rebirth of the last five years. "It's really a lot of fun for me to take Lestat and put him in a place like Miami Beach, and explore his responses to it."

Florida is also where Rice completed the script for *Interview with the Vampire.* After a grueling dance of death with Hollywood over the filming of her work, which began in 1976 when Paramount optioned *Interview,* Rice was gently drawn back into the fray by producer David Geffen. But this time, she laid down the rules.

"It was a very strange moment," recalls the author, "because I had developed such a hatred of Hollywood that no one could have drawn me back except David, and he extended the invitation to me personally over the telephone."

Rice agreed to write the screenplay for *Interview,* the film she wished to see made. "The day I finished the script, I was at my house on the Gulf Coast," she remembers. "I called him and said, 'Whatever happens, I want to thank you for inviting me to do this, because I love this script.' And it was really a screenplay that was completely faithful to *Interview,* with very few elements from anywhere else. This Lestat is warmer, more like the Lestat of the later books. And the script revolves around the death of Claudia."

Rice, impressed by Richard E. Grant's performance in *Warlock,* believed that he would be a perfect choice to play Louis, although she admits to having no influence over the casting process. By complete coincidence, Random House engaged Grant to narrate the audiobook version of *Body Thief.* "I nearly fainted," laughs Rice. "Now Lestat, at the moment . . . I don't know who I'd want to play him. I don't really have any power in that department."

She has also relinquished control over the comic-book adaptations of her work, in spite of efforts to involve her.

"I don't really have time to have much to do with the comic books," she says. "The comic-book people [at Innovation] have offered me many opportunities to do so, but I am not a collaborative artist, and I'm not good at presiding over adaptations of my work." Her licensing deal gives Innovation a very liberal hand with her characters, a freedom which she seems to perceive with mixed feelings. Though she thinks the scripts are competent, Rice's praise is qualified. "I've been doing a lot of arguing of late," she reveals, "because I believe the drawings no longer reflect the books.

"In some instances," she continues, "they've had artists who didn't read the novels, and bragged about that. What I'm trying to do is return the comic books to the sensuality and beauty of the original, and stop making the characters look like low-grade English rock stars, or the bums in Greenwich Village."

She also feels that the comic books have dealt hamhandedly with Lestat's delicate, ambiguous sexuality. "There's too much overt homosexuality in the *Vampire Lestat* comics," she says flatly. "Lestat is not homosexual. He is transcendent, and loves both men and women. When you make him either a homosexual or a heterosexual in a comic book, that narrows things down. And that seems to be a mistake people make in Hollywood, as well as in comics."

Hollywood, at least, is finally listening to Rice. *Interview* made it to the screen in 1994. Though she at first attacked the casting of superstar hunk Tom Cruise as her beloved Lestat, the author eventually embraced the Neil Jordan film and it emerged as a box-office smash. The sequel—*The Vampire Lestat*—is promised for bigbudget cinematic treatment as well.

Although she has lived in Texas and California, Rice has returned to her birthplace of New Orleans in style, as a wealthy, famous, high-flying, and adored novelist.

Although her neighbors respect her privacy for the most part, Rice does fall prey to the public pressures which go with fame.

"Right now, I can't go out to get the mail," she sighs. "I step out of the front door, and somebody steps out from behind a tree and says, 'Will you sign a book?' I love my readers and don't want to be rude to them, but I can't do that all the time, or I wouldn't be able to work."

Then, she continues, almost apologetically, "It's wrong to complain, because when people read your books and make you rich, you should not whine about them.

"I'm still not that comfortable in public," she admits. "When I see a big line at a bookstore, there's an urge to run. But I'm changing all the time." She pauses reflectively, and there is a smile in her voice.

"Anyone who knew me in the sixties would have said that I'd never amount to anything," says the woman credited with reinventing modern vampire fiction. "That I was too disorganized and crazy.

"But I see people as full of change," she says. "And I hope that I'm changing all the time. The world looks very beautiful through my eyes."

BRAM STOKER'S DRACULA: James V. Hart, Screenwriter

BILL WARREN

EACH NEW GENERATION of moviegoers is offered either remakes of classic films or new movies based on famous stories. This applies, of course, to horror movies: Sooner or later, someone trots out a new *Dr. Jekyll and Mr. Hyde*, or another *Frankenstein*—or a revamped *Dracula*. And in 1992, the biggest horror movie was without question *Bram Stoker's Dracula*, directed by Francis Ford Coppola and written by James V. Hart.

There have been more movies featuring Dracula as a major character than any other horror figure; in fact, Dracula may turn up in movies more often than any other character at all, with his few rivals for the throne including Sherlock Holmes, Jesse James, and Tarzan. Dracula's been played straight, turning Christopher Lee and Bela Lugosi into stars in the process; he's been essayed in comedy and on stage—even in a musical; he's even been done kind of bent, as in *Andy Warhol's Dracula*. You'd think that after all this, the bloodsucking Count would have worn his welcome to a tattered rag. So why did Hart decide to script yet another adaptation of Bram Stoker's famous story?

"The response that I have given to that question, and will continue to give," he says, "is that it's never been done right. When I first read *Dracula* back in 1976, I was overwhelmed by what a brilliant novel it was, and could not understand why all the films had forgotten this great piece of literature."

Born in 1949, Hart is older than you might expect a writer to be in today's Hollywood, which has been accused (with justification) of worshiping youth and ignoring the experience, skill, and wisdom which come with age. After graduating from film school, Hart went into producing low-budget films, but became weary of the process and suggested that he and his wife move back to New York. "But what was I going to do for a living, I asked," Hart recalls, "and she said, 'You've been bitching about having to fix everybody else's screenplays while you've been out here; now you're going to write some of your own.' As it turned out, it was what I'd been doing all my life anyway: writing. This was in 1979–80, and I've been writing ever since. It was actually out of desperation. I'm a terrible employee; I couldn't hold a job, and I actually had to start writing to pay the rent."

It wasn't easy for Hart for the first ten years or so. He wrote a dozen or so scripts that never got produced, and only one (the 1985 teen comedy *Gimme an "F"*) that did. But he persevered; finally, lightning struck. His script for *Hook* was purchased and filmed on a huge scale by Steven Spielberg. Immediately afterward, on the same sound-stages, *Dracula* went into production under Coppola's direction. "As my kids say," Hart recounts, "the saddest day of their lives was seeing Neverland torn down on the sets at Culver City, at the end of August 1991. My children grew up with *Hook*. But the happy thought that followed was that they built Transylvania and London on the same stages.

"There was one great moment that I'll never forget. We were on the back lot—me and my wife, son and daughter. That day, two of the studio golf carts almost collided—and one said *Hook* and one said *Dracula*. The next day, there was a cart driving around that said *Hook* and *Dracula* on it together. It was quite a summer."

That season, which marked the start of production on his horror epic, was a long time coming. "I started working on *Dracula* in 1977," Hart recounts, "when I met Leonard Wolf, the author of *The Annotated Dracula*. After I read the novel, I was convinced that there was a movie here that had never been made. I spent time with Leonard working on a version of the script, and everybody thought we were nuts. The John Badham version, with Frank Langella as Dracula, went into production, which sort of killed the Dracula market for the next few years, 'cause it wasn't a very good film. It's a shame, because Langella was a great Dracula on stage.

"Then, every year after that, starting in about '84 or '85, I would go to my agents and say, 'I want to do *Dracula*.' They'd say, 'You're crazy. Why do another one?' The same question. Then in 1990, I finally convinced Bob O'Connor and Michael Apted to try to set it up as a television movie. It was Karen Moore at Wilshire Court Productions who jumped on it and said, 'I want to see this movie,' and gave me the opportunity to write it."

Hart was surprised at the support given him by Wilshire Court, a company that specializes in suspense thrillers made for the USA cable network. "Instead of getting in the way and starting to make the sort of cuts you'd need to make it affordable for television," he explains, "they gave the script back to us for a certain period of time, to give us a chance to set it up as a feature." When the executives finally saw the script, they were impressed that Hart had placed emphasis on the erotic side of the novel as well as its epic qualities, instead of keeping it at the level of just another horror movie. And they knew it might well work better as a theatrical film than as a made-for-TV effort.

"The other key for me was trying to write it as a woman's film as opposed to a man's film, from the point of view of Mina as opposed to that of Harker or Dracula," Hart says. "Anyway, we had six months, about the same time Spielberg pounced on *Hook*. It was an exciting ride there, because the scripts nobody wanted to do, which had taken years for me to get someone to finance, were now on the road to the screen.

"Whenever anybody asked me who I wanted to direct *Dracula*, I would always say David Lean, because I had always seen it as a sweeping epic," the writer continues. "One day I got a phone call. Winona Ryder had read the script and loved it; it was the kind of female part she was looking for, to step up from her teenage persona. Was it OK for her to give the script to Francis Coppola?"

This collaboration represented a coming round to full circle for Hart. In 1970, he had gone to Coppola's American Zoetrope company in San Francisco to show a film that he and his partner had made. "He was the rebel we always wanted to be like," Hart recalls. "We waited all day in the lobby for Francis, and finally, at the end of the day, he poked his head in and kind of went, 'Uh, oh yeah, saw your film. Keep making movies.' And he turned and went back down the hall. It took me a long time to get back in touch with him, but everything happens in its time."

As it turned out, Coppola was already a fan of Stoker's novel, which he'd read to his children as a scary bedtime story, and he also felt that the novel had never been given its due on screen. Now, as a result, Coppola wanted to make the movie which Hart had assumed would be a TV film. While talking with Coppola, Hart realized that he was perfectly suited for the material. "Here was the director I'd been looking for," raves Hart. "The script itself had found the right person to direct, who understood Stoker, who believed in Stoker, who was reverent to Stoker, and who understood the new relationship introduced in this screenplay."

That added element marks the script's only real break from Stoker's story, though the film is essentially very faithful to the novel. "The license we took," Hart explains, "was a relationship between Dracula and Mina." In the novel, she is simply Dracula's last victim, and there's no apparent relationship between them beyond that. "As written in the book," Hart maintains, "Mina's character is profoundly changed by her sort of blood wedding with Dracula, when he forces her to drink *his* blood. Her entire tone of voice changes, and she suddenly has sympathy for this creature that killed her best friend and who has brought all kinds of anguish into the lives of her and her husband. And at the end of the novel, it always intrigued me that there is this beautiful boy-child and that, seven years after the death of Dracula, the mother takes him to the very spot in Transylvania where the event happened. What mother in her right mind would do that unless she was also taking the child to the scene of his father's death?

"So my approach was to somehow bring out this compassion that Mina had for Dracula by portraying him in a new light—less that of a bloodsucking monster, and more that of a fallen angel, a bright, charismatic hero fallen from grace whose soul was redeemed by the love of a woman."

In *Bram Stoker's Dracula*, it's established that Mina (played by Ryder) is the reincarnation of Elisabetha, the lost love of Voivode Dracula (Gary Oldman). In a brief opening scene, we see Dracula battling the Turks. "I wanted to be sure that people understood that this man was a knight, sworn to defend the cross of Christ. [The real Vlad Dracula] was a great military strategist, and he saved Eastern Europe and Christianity from the invasion of the Turks. It's also an accurate historical event—his wife committed suicide." This is included in the film as well.

"I took this as motivation for him to turn his back on the Church and go to war against God, vowing to come back and avenge her death with all the powers of darkness. People are used to seeing Dracula in a tuxedo coming out of the fog in a coffin; I wanted people to see Dracula in a different light. This film is not what people are expecting from *Dracula.*"

At the same time, the film remains true to its source. "In the end, all of the characters are as Stoker wrote them, with the exception of what we had to do for budgetary reasons. I think all the Dracuphiles will appreciate the attention we've given Stoker. In fact, much of the dialogue is from the novel; the journal entries, which tie the narrative together the way Stoker intended it, have never been used before."

Indeed, the dialogue in the film is true to Stoker and to the Victorian period during which his novel was written. Making the flowery but authentic language accessible to modern audiences was another major challenge for Hart—as if turning a novel told entirely in diaries, letters, and journal entries into a script wasn't enough. "That was the real challenge," he says, "to be faithful to the language, but also make it feel contemporary and not camp it up. The nice thing about the entire cast—Gary Oldman, Winona Ryder, Anthony Hopkins, Keanu Reeves, Cary Elwes, Bill Campbell—was that they all embraced the language and insisted that it remain, that the language be as much a part of this experience as the special effects, the sex, the action, and the storytelling. They made it work."

When Coppola took on the project, he "dismantled"

the script, Hart says. "All directors do that when they're finding the way that they can make the material theirs. We must have done close to fifty rewrites. It was reassembled, much to my pleasure, with great visual transitions." The intense stylization of the film is going to come as a major surprise to many, as is the depiction of Dracula himself. "Coppola's problem was how to present this horrible bloodsucking monster we all have this image of, and yet completely change your mind by the end, where you have enormous compassion for Dracula and are very sad, but also grateful, to see his soul redeemed by his death."

In terms of faithfulness to both the novel and to Hart's vision, the scripter believes that Coppola was the right director for more than one reason. "Francis is a writer first, so there was great respect for what I had done in the screenplay," Hart says. "He understood that there was a lot of pain and suffering that went into cracking the novel and constructing the piece. He has obvious respect for the written word. Working with him was an experience I will not soon forget; I have continued to benefit from it."

On the postproduction level as well, Hart praises Coppola's intense dedication to the work. "Even in the editing stages," he points out, "Francis pulled Leonard Wolf back into the equation, again understanding Leonard's contribution to the whole view of Dracula, from Wolf's new approach in *The Annotated Dracula*." (An excellent book, it was reissued as *The Essential Dracula*.)

At the time of this interview, Hart had seen several rough cuts of the movie. "It's very theatrical," he notes, "not like any film we've seen in a long time. It's like a David O. Selznick production with lots of blood and sex and eroticism; with elegant sets, beautiful costumes, and incredible, dreamlike images." Hart also has high praise for Oldman's work in the title role. "His performance is electrifying," the writer raves. "Gary was Dracula twenty-four hours a day, seven days a week. He is not a matinee idol, but he is sexy. He is not a big, physical, imposing man, but he is threatening and overwhelming and powerful. It's an amazing performance, and people are going to come out saying, 'Wow! Yeah!'"

But the guiding genius behind the film remains not Oldman, or Hart, or even Bram Stoker—it is Coppola. "Francis is a wizard and a great artist and very much a Renaissance man. When they pull Francis's films out in fifty years," insists Hart, "everybody will understand the great risks he took and the wide variety of films and experience he brought to people."

BRAM STOKER'S DRACULA:
Gary Oldman

IAN SPELLING

ON HALLOWEEN EVE, 1992, Gary Oldman watched as a crew member on his film *Romeo Is Bleeding* sat stitching together one of the film's costumes. It brought forth a long-forgotten childhood memory, one that rings with irony in the context of his most visible recent role. "I entered a funny-dress competition when I was five years old, and I went as Dracula," he recalls in his soft British accent. "They painted in a widow's peak on my head, and my mother made this black cape costume out of crepe paper." He pauses. "I came in last."

Nearly a quarter of a century later, Oldman, thanks to his fine performance (and elaborate costumes) in *Bram Stoker's Dracula*, would win any such competition fangs down. He has taken a legendary character, one reinterpreted constantly on stage and in movies, one played alternately for laughs, chills, and romance, and made it his own. And yet, reviewing the count's previous incarnations was not part of his preparation.

"I didn't do much research," Oldman says, "I watched the Bela Lugosi movie, but I really just went from [James

V. Hart's] script. It's very different from what's been done before. As they say, 'If it ain't on the page, it ain't on the stage.'

"It was all there for me," the actor continues. "The journey is all there in the script. I also had a sense that the film would be slightly left afield, because I would be working with [Japanese costume designer] Eiko Ishioka and with Francis Coppola. I knew, in some way, that it would be unique."

The actor admits that he's not a fan of the horror genre, and that he expected *Bram Stoker's Dracula* to be a hefty cut above standard shocker fare. "I didn't see this as a horror movie; it's more of a love story," he explains. "I chose to do this because I wanted the opportunity to say those words. 'I've crossed oceans of time to find you.' 'I have committed unspeakable acts.' 'Many people have suffered because of what I am.' Don't you just long to say those words to someone?

"I was in my trailer during *JFK* when the script came," he continues, recalling how he came to be involved with the project. "There was a wait for lighting or something, and I read a good deal of it. I turned to my assistant and said, 'I understand this, and I'm going to get this part.'

"Then I met Francis and I screen-tested. But I knew from the moment I picked it up that I connected to it, to its passion and energy. It was *Beauty and the Beast*. All the prosthetics that would be involved, the makeup, didn't even cross my mind. That challenge I had to meet further down the road. It wasn't, 'Oh, Freddy Krueger! Here's my chance.' It goes beyond just being a horror movie. It has more than fangs and a cloak."

Another attraction to the role for Oldman was the endless appeal of his supernatural character. "People have been fascinated and intrigued with vampires for years and years, and they love this story," he observes. "He comes in the night. He completely feeds on and lives off feminine energy. Blood is a sacred thing. That was interesting to play. I don't know what it is about Dracula, but people are really attracted to him. That interest is eternal, as eternal as he is, in a way. In ten years' time, I'm sure they'll make another *Dracula*."

For comparative purposes, Oldman asks who the last actor to play the vampire was. He's informed that it was Frank Langella in John Badham's romanticized 1979 film, though some people first think of George Hamilton's comic Count in the same year's *Love at First Bite*. Oldman laughs upon hearing this.

"George Hamilton . . . well, that was the definitive Dracula," he jokes. "Maybe I should do the Wolf Man with Francis. I can become the Bela Lugosi of my generation."

In fact, Oldman tipped his hat to Lugosi by changing a line of dialogue that Hart had lifted directly from the Stoker novel. "Dracula says to Harker, 'You'll forgive me if I do not join you, but I have dined already and I do not sup,'" Oldman explains. "That's from the book and Jim had that in the script, but I wanted to change it. So, I did an alternate take, in which I used the line, 'I never drink . . . wine.' We shot the scene several times the way it was written, and only once with my change. That's the take Francis put in. It's my homage to Lugosi, who said it in the original movie," as did Langella in his *Dracula*.

Unlike Lugosi, Oldman appears in a number of Dracula incarnations in his film, among them a giant bat, a man-wolf, a deformed monster, a young man, and a white-haired, regally dressed older version. Of these various visages, Oldman preferred the aged look. "He was more fun to play," says the actor of the Dracula who appears in these opening scenes. "He toys with Harker [Keanu Reeves] like a cat does with a mouse.

"Dracula is not as vulnerable in Transylvania as he is in London," notes the actor. "Once he sees that picture of

Mina, all of those emotions are stirred in him. Before that, though, he's on his own turf, in his own home. He's four hundred years old and he has all of this power. It was fun playing that and giving him humor. He's witty, which I don't really get a chance to do after the film leaves Transylvania and I become young."

Since he's admittedly not a believer in the myths of vampirism, Oldman needed something to grab onto when attempting to create the character. One important source of information that helped him build upon the work of Dracula actors past was the popular Anne Rice vampire novels. "I don't know what it is to be a vampire and, clearly, Anne Rice does. You read those books and you say to yourself, 'I believe there are vampires in the world.'

"Don't quote me on that," jokes Oldman, realizing the potential for monumental misinterpretation. "If you wrote that, it would follow me for the rest of my life. But Rice really describes what it's like to be a vampire. I got ideas from that, particularly *Interview with the Vampire*. Francis told me his father had this saying: 'Steal from the best.' Actors and directors, any creative people, are terrible magpies. We are thieves. I was very inspired by that book."

Oldman's co-conspirators in bringing Dracula to life were, for the most part, actress Winona Ryder, who plays Mina, and director Coppola. "Working with Winona was lovely, just fine," he says of his on-screen love. "In fact, it was a jolly troop. That's what Francis strives for, to create a family. Unfortunately, I hadn't seen *Hearts of Darkness* before I did this," laughs Oldman, referring to the recent documentary about the crazed production of Coppola's *Apocalypse Now*, which casts the director as a man who thrives on chaos. "It was really the experience of a lifetime. Francis is up there with the greats.

"It's wonderful to have the opportunity to work with someone like that in your career." Oldman continues. "It was a collaborative process. He gives you tremendous freedom to do your thing. Here I am, this kid from a working-class family, and in this business you meet a lot of people who you've been a fan of, who you've seen on TV or on the movie screen.

"When I did *JFK*," he says by way of example. "Glenn Ford was going to be in it. He got ill and couldn't do it, but I did have a rehearsal with him and Jack Lemmon. That blew my mind. But when you work with these people, that sense of awe, of being a fan, just dissipates. You go, 'It's just Tony [Hopkins].' Tony's a nice guy, very funny and very witty. He does impersonations and keeps everyone rather jolly on the set. But with Francis, I never quite got over that sense of awe. *Godfather I* and *II* and *Apocalypse Now*—those are three masterpieces. To do just one masterpiece in your lifetime is an achievement."

As much as Oldman enjoyed working with Coppola, he wasn't thrilled with the pounds of costuming and layers of makeup the role required. "The costumes were fairly uncomfortable, but the makeup was the main mountain to be climbed," he says. "First, I had to sit there for five or six hours having it put on. Then I had to work a ten-hour day on top of that and get a performance through it, through plastic and rubber. For the old man alone, I spent about a hundred hours total in makeup.

"After a while, you have to go to another place," he continues. "You can't watch TV, you can't really listen to the radio or read because you're being pushed about. It got a little tiresome after a while. This was the most exhausting thing I've ever been involved with. Emotionally and physically, it was so demanding. I tried my best, and put everything I had into it."

Bram Stoker's Dracula is the latest in a long line of seriously dramatic roles for Oldman, in such films as *Sid and Nancy*, *Prick Up Your Ears*, *State of Grace*, and *Romeo Is Bleeding*. Now, Oldman wants nothing more than to topline a more humorous movie. "I'm desperate to do one," he says. "I'm fun-loving. I wish someone would send me a comedy, but they don't seem to see me like that. They don't read a romantic comedy and say, 'Gary Oldman, send it to him.' They say, 'Charles Manson. We know who should do that part.'

"I don't think you can engineer a career," he says. "You just have to go with the flow. People are so narrow-minded. They see you do something, or they see you do it well once, and they just imagine that is all you can do. So, if you do Sid Vicious or a film like *State of Grace*, they go, 'He's intense.' You become somewhat labeled. I enjoy playing these roles, but I would enjoy doing something a bit lighter."

BRAM STOKER'S DRACULA:
Anthony Hopkins

BILL WARREN

ANTHONY HOPKINS MAY have one of the key supporting roles in *Bram Stoker's Dracula*—that of Professor Van Helsing—but he still finds the film's style hard to pin down with words. "I don't know what it's going to be, exactly," he admits, "because it changed so much. It's kind of sensual, as well as baroque, almost like an Edgar Allan Poe piece more than Stoker, though they do follow his story. I read the book some time ago, and I do believe the film is going to be better."

It's surprising enough that anyone would tackle a new version of Stoker's novel at all, much less that it attracted an actor as important as Hopkins. But the Welsh-born Oscar-winner for 1991's *The Silence of the Lambs* claims that he's always looking for variety. "I want the roles I play to be different," he says. "I blank out everything I've done in the past. I don't compare them; otherwise, I'd get bogged down. I just take a part and do something with it. It's futile examining and comparing things. Why bother? I'm not interested in what I have and haven't done. When I played Van Helsing, I gave all my time to that. I couldn't waste time thinking about whether I had done this sort of part before."

Nor could Hopkins concern himself with others who had played this particular role before, such as the revered Sir Laurence Olivier in John Badham's 1979 film. In fact, the only version of *Dracula* he'd seen before taking the role of the Dutch vampire destroyer was Bela Lugosi's original. To Hopkins, the role of Van Helsing in the James V. Hart-scripted film represented an opportunity to work with one of the world's great directors.

"My agent phoned up and asked if I'd like to work with Francis Ford Coppola," Hopkins recalls. "He sent the script over, and I had about a day to skim through it. I'm not a fast reader, so I just got the general idea of it. Then I went to see Francis, and he asked, 'Would you like to play Van Helsing?' I said, 'Yes.' Who wouldn't want to work with him? He's a great director, a genius."

It was Coppola's very status that made *Bram Stoker's Dracula* seem so promising—not just to Hopkins, but to movie fans the world over. Never before in movie history had such a stellar director tackled such a traditional horror topic, and the results could only be fascinating. The cast he assembled is certainly interesting, demonstrating Coppola's excellent knack for casting. As the only long-established actor in *Bram Stoker's Dracula*, Hopkins found it "terrific" to work with the young performers, saying, "I really had a good time."

Gary Oldman, as Count Dracula himself, is Hopkins's chief screen nemesis—but since this version follows the original novel closely, Van Helsing and the vampire don't appear together often. "I just had two scenes with Gary—the confrontation in the abbey, then the one at the end," Hopkins reveals. "I worked primarily with Winona Ryder, Richard Grant, Cary Elwes, Bill Campbell, and Keanu Reeves, who plays Jonathan Harker."

Despite their lack of shared screen time, Hopkins

notes that an interesting relationship developed between the professor and the Count in this dramatization. "There's a very surprising opening to the film that I don't want to talk about," Hopkins says. "It shows that Van Helsing knows Dracula, and has known him for years."

Although Hopkins does not consider *The Silence of the Lambs* a horror film, he readily compares the filmmaking styles of Coppola and *Silence* director Jonathan Demme. "Demme just directs very straight on," Hopkins explains. "You have the script, and you come out to the set, you rehearse a little and you do it. With Coppola, it's a much more complicated process. You rehearse for three weeks, you improvise and the script changes all the time. There's constant rewriting, and then you have three weeks off.

"I don't know what Coppola does for those three weeks, but then you come back and start filming," the actor continues. "You do many takes, many versions of the scene, and you still improvise. It's very interesting. He's there on the set with you all the time, he doesn't sit in the Silver Fish," Hopkins says. (At the time this interview was conducted, some articles claimed that Coppola directed *Dracula* entirely from within his Silver Fish, a trailer always on the set, filled with electronic and video gear.)

Though Coppola was always supportive, working on the film was an adventure for Hopkins. "You never knew quite what was going to happen," he says. "Going to the set, I'd wonder, 'What's going to happen today?' And then the scene would evolve as it went, and out of you—he'd get a scene out of everyone. He'd create magical things, extraordinary things. I don't know how he does it."

Creating the character of Van Helsing was a true collaboration between actor and director. "We mutually agreed that there had been a kind of darker, hidden side to Van Helsing," Hopkins reveals. "In Stoker's book, one of the younger characters says he doesn't trust Van Helsing—he thinks he's as crazy as Dracula. They're as scared of him as they are of the Count, so I wanted to make him a much more . . . " Hopkins pauses, searching for the right word, "passionate figure, who'd been through all kinds of deep crevices in life, deep down into the pit, and comes out the other side as a man who's been cleansed by all that."

Van Helsing, the actor agrees, is one who knows evil because he's seen it. "When he comes out on the other side of this journey," Hopkins notes, "he understands Dracula. As Van Helsing, I have a great dueling scar down my face. I wanted to bring this deeper side to him, make him a man who understands the mysteries of life, and has dabbled in all kinds of disciplines, alchemy and black magic, who's drunk absinthe and smoked opium. He was experimental, like many creative people; he was self-destructive, yet managed to survive."

Hopkins is a thoughtful man who likes to assume the stance of someone who isn't thoughtful, someone who reacts to new ideas intuitively and impulsively. But anyone who's seen his performances down through the years since his feature film debut in 1968's *The Lion in Winter* knows that Hopkins does think through his work—the proof is there on the screen. He claims to approach acting in the same manner as Robert Mitchum, his favorite screen actor.

"It's better than working for a living, as Mitchum says," muses Hopkins. "He's my favorite because he just does it. I like that attitude. I think he's the greatest film actor around—he's always there, and doesn't make a fuss about it. He's like Jodie Foster—he looks like he's doing nothing. Donald Pleasence worked with Mitchum, and said that for a moment he didn't know what Mitchum was doing. He didn't seem to be doing anything, he could hardly even hear him speak. Then he watched the rushes, and there it was, large as life. I like that. You come in, do it, and go home."

Rather like Van Helsing, Hopkins has been through the fires of life; in recent interviews, he admits to having had—like, sadly, all too many great British actors—a serious drinking problem, which he's now overcome. He now has an aura of serenity, of willingness to accept life on its own terms and not ask more of it than it can deliver. And, more importantly, he doesn't make too many demands on himself. It's clear, reading between the lines of the interview, that Hopkins is a humble man, one who's flattered, yet puzzled, by the acclaim he's received.

"I'm mystified by the process of acting," he admits candidly. "I don't understand what I do. I don't rate myself in any way, I just do what's in front of me. I'm very pleased when it goes well and it's successful, of course. I'm enjoying this moment. But I'm very realistic. I've been around many years now, and I enjoy working more and more, but I don't understand the process. I just do it."

Born in Port Talbot, Wales, in 1937, Hopkins attended the Cardiff College of Music and Drama for two years, eventually being accepted at the Royal Academy of Dramatic Arts. Although the late Richard Burton also hailed from Port Talbot, Hopkins didn't necessarily consider him an inspiration. "I thought he was a very good actor, and it's sad he died so young, but I went my own way," Hopkins says. "I became an actor because I couldn't do anything else."

Since his *Lion in Winter* debut, Hopkins has been very active on both sides of the Atlantic, both in films and—surprisingly enough for an actor of his prestige—very often in made-for-TV movies. In fact, he probably made more fans for his telefilm *All Creatures Great and Small* (1974) than he did with starring roles in movies like *The Looking Glass War* and *When Eight Bells Toll*. Among his genre credits are Robert Wise's 1977 reincarnation tale

Audrey Rose, the following year's deadly-dummy thriller *Magic* and David Lynch's 1980 film version of *The Elephant Man*.

Although he's compiled a lengthy résumé of acclaimed stage performances, Hopkins prefers film acting and isn't troubled at all by the fragmented nature of moviemaking, wherein on Monday you can be playing the last scene in the film, and on Tuesday, the first. "It comes back to the fact that that's what you're expected to do," Hopkins explains. "If you set your mind to doing that, you come in, you do it, and it's easy, dead easy. You can make it difficult, you can complain, but I don't do that; I say, 'Where do you want me to stand?' and do it. If you make it easy for yourself, it becomes easy. If you make it difficult for yourself, then it'll be difficult, and if you make it difficult for other people, they'll make it difficult for you.

"I've been very lucky," Hopkins continues. "I've had a good, wide range of choices, like playing Bligh, Lecter, and my character in *Howards End*. When you get hold of a character, you find a way of getting into him. It's like driving a luxury car, you know. You get up in the morning, you start up the engine—that's exactly what it's like for me. You're inside a vast computer, or your own little space module, which is your mind. I don't cut off from the rest of the film company; I have coffee, I laugh, I joke around. But when they say, 'Stand by for the scene,' I close my eyes for a minute, and I go inside this space module, press a few buttons, and off I go."

To date, Hopkins's favorite role is the one that also won him the most fans: Hannibal (the Cannibal) Lecter in *Silence of the Lambs*. He claims that he had a good feeling about the movie even while it was being made. "I thought it was going to be a successful film, because it was such a successful book," he says. "Jonathan Demme was such a good director that all I had to do was show up and do it. I don't know how I do these things; I'm really very simple, you know."

The actor also professes a great deal of admiration for his *Lambs* costar and fellow Oscar-winner Jodie Foster. "She's a superb film actress," Hopkins praises. "I've been around her a great deal, and I'd seen her work before; I'm a great admirer of her. She always gives the impression, like any good actor, that she doesn't do anything. Very subtle; you don't have to 'act' on screen."

As for the possibility of a *Lambs* sequel, Hopkins confirms that he has been approached to play Lecter again. "They've talked to me about it, and of course, I'd do it, if it's a good script. I know Jonathan Demme would like to do the sequel, if it's a good story, but I don't know what shape the book's in; I don't know if it's completed yet, or even if Thomas Harris is writing it."

In the meantime, the busy star has aspirations beyond acting. "I'm going to direct a film [*August*]," he reveals. "Being an actor myself, I can see young actors struggling around, not knowing how to do a scene, and—I've done it in the past, so I know I can do it again—I can go up to them and say, 'Just try this. Do that. Keep it simple.' They do it, and it works. I love movies. It's the best way to work; I come alive when I'm working on a movie."

BRAM STOKER'S DRACULA:
Winona Ryder

IAN SPELLING

IN A MILLION YEARS, Winona Ryder never thought she'd have anything to do with a Dracula film. Then her agent handed her fifty screenplays, one of which was Jim Hart's *Dracula*, then subtitled *The Untold Story*. "When I first saw the script, I wasn't that excited," Ryder says. "I've never been a big horror movie or Dracula fan. I always pictured it as that campy 'I vant to suck your blood' kind of thing. I just thought it was corny. Then I read the script."

Ryder was especially taken by the fact that Hart remained unusually faithful to the source novel, and related the oft-told Gothic tale from Mina's point of view. "It was this incredibly emotional love story. I didn't have any idea it would be that way," she says. "I've never seen a *Dracula* film, except for the first *Nosferatu*. I really liked my role. It really hit me, her struggle and her independence in a time when it was freakish for a woman to be independent, to even type. I loved the romance, too. I thought it was very beautiful."

By now, of course, everyone who has cared to see Francis Coppola's big-budget, star-laden *Bram Stoker's*

Dracula has done so. Everyone knows its story, and most have heard of its behind-the-scenes origin, when Ryder gave Coppola the script after she had to drop out of his previous film, *The Godfather, Part III*. What remains is for Ryder to look back on the film and what it meant to her.

"It was really wonderful working with Francis—he was the perfect choice to direct this movie," says the twenty-six-year-old actress. "He's so theatrical and operatic and colorful. And he has so many ideas. He's really enthusiastic; a day didn't go by when he wasn't right there by the camera. He's very visual and great with the actors. He has a unique way of working that I don't think anybody else has."

Likewise, Ryder has great praise for Hart's script, which not only cuts straight to the heart of Dracula's eternal love for Mina, but also allowed the actress to tackle her first adult romance after a series of youthful roles in such films as *Lucas, Mermaids,* and *Welcome Home, Roxy Carmichael.* "It was the first time I ever played a woman, as opposed to a teenager in a high-school setting," she says. "There were a lot of different costumes, and it was a completely different era and setting. All of that was wonderful to explore.

"It was all there in Jim's script and in Francis's head," Ryder continues. "We had a very clear understanding of what we wanted to do. It's like when you read a really beautiful book, and you get very touched and moved and you feel passionate about it. That was how the script was for me."

Much of the story, as it relates to Mina and her best friend, the doomed Lucy Westenra (Sadie Frost), focuses on repression, the inability of women of the day to express themselves emotionally, physically, and sexually. "Mina is constricted," Ryder says. "Everything was about repression—the formal dialogue was repressed, even the corset I had to wear was restrictive. Women were prevented from saying what was on their minds. They were just expected to be dutiful, passive wives and never express passion.

"When Mina falls in love with Dracula, she blooms," the actress continues. "Eventually, as she becomes a vampire, she almost explodes with everything she's been holding in for so long. I really do let it all out during the campfire scene. We shot the film in sequence, which was very helpful, because I had to work up to that moment."

By the time Frost's Lucy finishes her transformation from would-be sexually aggressive aristocrat into a full-fledged, carnally voracious vampire, she has peeled away her clothing in a frantic attempt to free herself from any and all restraints. When Mina slips into vampirism, however, Ryder only pulls teasingly at her corset, remaining fully clothed throughout the sequence. In fact, the actress reveals, she ended up showing off far more than she planned.

"I won't do nudity," Ryder says. "The reason Mina's pulling at the dress is because, when you go through the whole process of becoming a vampire, you try to get everything off. You become very animalistic, and an animal wouldn't want to be in a corset. That's why I was pulling on my clothing. There was a lot of footage, which they didn't use, where I wasn't doing that. It looks now as if that was all I was doing, when there were maybe two moments that I did.

"Obviously, exposing yourself, just in general, is difficult," she says. "But when you're working with people like Francis and Michael Ballhaus, who is a great cinematographer, and our incredible camera crew, it's a lot easier than working with real strangers. Everybody was very protective; there was no gawking. It wasn't an atmosphere where you felt unsafe. It was very respectful."

By faithfully sticking to the story as written by Stoker, Hart and Coppola had to address the difficult issue of eternal love. Could Mina love her nineteenth-century fiancé, Jonathan Harker (Keanu Reeves), as much as her previous incarnation, Elisabeta, loved Vlad the Impaler four centuries earlier? "She loves Jonathan incredibly," Ryder says of her character. "She really, really does care for him, and then she falls in love with Dracula. But that is the Elisabeta in her. It's two completely different kinds of love. She and Jonathan have a real connection; they are madly in love with each other. The relationship with Dracula is very different. She's been reincarnated, and every time she sees him, she's almost hypnotized. I loved playing those scenes from four hundred years earlier. It was hypnotic, obsessive."

Bram Stoker's Dracula, with its $40-million budget and prestigious director, was able to secure not just stunning costumes, superior makeup, and monster FX and wildly ambitious sets, but also a who's-who list of stars ranging from Gary Oldman, Keanu Reeves, and Oscar-winner Anthony Hopkins to Bill Campbell, Cary Elwes, and Richard E. Grant. Early on in the production, Ryder spent a great deal of time with British actress Sadie Frost, making her American debut as Lucy after several English features, such as the thriller *Dark Obsession*.

However, it was with Oldman and Reeves that Ryder shares most of her screen time. "Actually, if you really watch the movie, I don't have that many scenes with Gary," Ryder points out. "He's a wonderful actor, really talented. He's also a very nice person; we got along really well. He's a very emotional actor with a lot of access to his feelings. He can just turn them on and off like a faucet, and I've rarely ever worked with an actor who could do that. He also had to go through a lot of makeup changes, so that must have been difficult for him. I felt sorry for him at times, but he came off great."

The actress has equally high praise for the rest of her costars. "Keanu is a special person, and he has one of the biggest hearts I know," she praises. "I knew him a little bit before we did the film; he's very talented and a wonderful person to be around. I really got along with everybody. I loved the guys and I loved Sadie. They were all exceptional."

Ryder has a reputation for being pretty exceptional herself, having stood out in such borderline genre films as *Heathers*, *Beetlejuice*, and *Edward Scissorhands*, the latter two directed by her close friend and mentor, Tim Burton. In fact, the actress's 1991-1993 films teamed her with Jim Jarmusch, Burton, Coppola, and Martin Scorsese, four of America's most distinctive directors. "It's been amazing; Jim is one of the coolest guys I know, and I really worship him," she says of Jarmusch, who guided her through a segment of the omnibus comedy *Night on Earth*. "Tim is someone I've known since I first started in the business. I met him when I was thirteen. He's very young, and we're very much alike in a number of ways. It's like working with someone your own age."

Apparently, this youthfulness is something all four filmmakers have in common. "They are all kind of boyish and very enthusiastic," Ryder says. "Tim is just crazy. It's amazing to work with a director who is also your friend. I'm really happy with both *Beetlejuice* and *Scissorhands*, and I'll do anything Tim asks me to, though I don't think [*Beetlejuice II*] will be it. Francis is very paternal and very operatic; he sings a lot. He's a very caring person, and he's really concerned that you're OK, that you have everything you need, and that the mood is right. He's very much a little boy."

Returning to *Bram Stoker's Dracula*, Ryder looks back on the filming affectionately and, having sat in on a packed screening shortly before its November 1992 opening, sounds pleased with the final result. "It's always hard to judge," she says, "but I'm really proud of the film and everyone in it. Everybody did an exceptional job. A film is always different from what you think you did, and I wasn't there for a lot of it—like the Castle Dracula scenes.

"We originally shot an ending with me running out of the castle and into Jonathan's arms," she continues, "and it wasn't used. The note that it ends on now is more powerful, because it concludes on me with Dracula. So, that was new to me when I saw it.

"I've worked since we finished," she concludes, "so I've separated myself from it. It's definitely a *movie*-movie. When I watched it I didn't think for a second of anything else, and I'm usually thinking about a million things when I'm at the movies. This was just very entertaining. I'm very happy with it."

CHRISTOPHER LEE:
The Enduring Count

BILL KELLEY

TIME HAS BEEN KIND TO Christopher Lee. The veteran British horror superstar turned seventy-four this year, but his age doesn't show. He continues to act as often as he chooses—most recently portraying an alien in the John Landis comedy *The Stupids*, Ramses II in TNT's *Moses*, and a mysterious character in the British chiller *Funny Man*. And he has triumphed over the worst typecasting an actor can endure—being so closely linked with a character that producers won't consider you for other roles.

In Lee's case, that character is of course Count Dracula. Over a fifteen-year span—starting with 1958's *Horror of Dracula*—he played cinema's most notorious vampire nine times, seven of them in England's Hammer Films productions, once in a Spanish remake by director Jess Franco, and, briefly, one final time in a European TV documentary called *In Search of Dracula*, which was released theatrically in the U.S.

In the 1970s, a myth sprang up in journalistic circles that Lee, struggling to leave his Dracula image behind him, refused to discuss the character in interviews. In truth, he simply asked the press to consider the Dracula movies as part of a vast body of work dating back to 1948, when he made his first screen appearance in the costume romance *Corridor of Mirrors.*

But the actor has declined to sit down with one interviewer and exclusively discuss his Dracula movies film by film—until now. Though the last of Hammer's sagas of the Count—*The Satanic Rites of Dracula*—was shot over twenty years ago, Lee still has a flourishing career both in and out of the horror genre. He is also in no danger of falling prey to the sort of typecasting that sadly doomed Bela Lugosi—the only other actor as closely identified with the Count—to a career of endlessly repeating himself.

In addition, the horror genre itself has changed. Lee, who views current trends in explicit gore less affectionately than many modern fans, now regards the later Dracula sequels by Hammer—of which he was sharply critical when they were made—with feelings often bordering on nostalgia.

"To try to put the whole thing in perspective," Lee begins, "this is probably the most successful type of movie ever made—I don't mean necessarily the horror film, but the genre of fantasy, the imaginative, the fantastic—going back to the 1920s in Germany, with *Nosferatu, Metropolis,* and the rest, and through to Karloff and Lugosi in America in the thirties.

"It had been dormant for a while by the mid-fifties, at least in the classic, Gothic sense," he continues, "so Hammer took a gamble and resuscitated it. In fact, they simply made *The Curse of Frankenstein*, with Peter Cushing as Baron Frankenstein and myself as the Monster, and the whole production shot in color for the first time. None of the Draculas would have followed if *Curse of Frankenstein* hadn't been such a big success.

"For Frankenstein's monster, Hammer wanted a big,

tall guy who could act without speaking," Lee recalls. "Frankly, I hadn't had much of a chance to do anything else in films up to then!"

After *Frankenstein*'s international success, the studio's next logical step was to tackle the creature's famous counterpart in the horror field: Count Dracula. But Lee says that, surprisingly, the Hammer management never met with him or Cushing to map out any particular strategy.

"No, they simply offered me the role of Count Dracula," he reveals. "They were shooting in the dark. They didn't know what they were onto. But they had the intelligence to see that the success of one of these films could lead to the success of others—and once they got going, they had a stockpile of Gothic literature from which to choose. It's virtually endless.

"When Hammer offered me *Horror of Dracula*—it was just called *Dracula* in Britain—they never said why. The part called for another big, tall guy; I looked darkly European and presentable enough," he says, chuckling, "and it was for a little more money than the Frankenstein picture: still small by Hollywood standards, but a raise for both me and Peter."

Apart from fairly prominent billing on the credits and the incredible discomfort of the makeup ("It was ghastly," the actor recalls), Lee says he got scant industry and fan response from playing Frankenstein's monster. Between *Curse of Frankenstein* and the start of production on *Horror of Dracula* in late '57, he continued to toil as a character actor in supporting roles.

"I don't remember getting very much fan mail with regard to *Curse of Frankenstein*," he recalls, "and no one in the industry knew it was me unless they read the credits or the reviews. I was unrecognizable. And the feminine population would hardly fall for a creature like that!

"Count Dracula is a different case. Dracula, no matter

who plays him, is at least *depicted* as irresistible—that's in the book, it's part of his appeal."

Lee's favorite film of all his *Dracula*s remains, not surprisingly, his first one. "I had read the Bram Stoker novel many times and loved it," he explains, "and reread it before we began shooting. Jimmy Sangster's script stuck within reason to the book—if you shot the whole book, it'd be four hours long!—and I determined how much of the character I could get across based on what was in the script. He doesn't have a lot of screen time.

"I don't think anyone on the film had a clear idea of where to go," Lee continues, "including dear Terence Fisher, the director. It was based on my instinct and imagination. Normally, I would not be so immodest as to take so much credit—and I'm not taking *full* credit. It was a collaborative thing, with dear Peter and Terry and the crew, and you'd accept a sound contribution from whoever offered it. But insofar as the character was played and interpreted—this came from me.

"I saw him as a very decisive, charming, heroic, erotic figure—irresistible to women, unstoppable by men—a sinister but aristocratic nobleman. He also had a tragic quality to him—the curse of being immortal by being undead. But I don't think very much of the sadness of Count Dracula came out in the first film, apart from brief glimpses, because he had relatively little screen time. He was more of a juggernaut, building to that ferocious confrontation with Peter's Van Helsing at the end."

Horror of Dracula, like *Curse of Frankenstein*, was shot on a six-week schedule at Hammer's modest Bray studios near Windsor, along the Thames River. Much of the movie's roughly $200,000 budget (some sources place the figure at closer to $150,000) went for the luxury of shooting in Technicolor. Like his Hammer colleagues, Lee is complimentary of the environment at Bray. "It was one big, happy family," he explains, "with the same crew and many of the same actors moving from one film to the next." This homespun atmosphere, along with *Horror of Dracula*'s economical budget, were belied by the film's sumptuous look—a tribute to art director Bernard Robinson and cinematographer Jack Asher.

Hammer's first *Dracula* opened in London in May 1958, and in New York later that same month. "I saw the first *Dracula* in a theater then called the Gaumont, in London's Haymarket district," Lee remembers. "It was a big theater, adorned with the most huge, lurid photographs of me outside and inside. I walked in, in an absolute paroxysm of embarrassment. I don't think anybody recognized me. Nobody came up to me, nobody spoke to me. The only thing I do remember, and I've never said this before, is that Michael Carreras—the executive producer—was sitting next to me, and he turned to me afterward and said, 'You know, you're one hell of an actor.'"

When *Horror of Dracula* arrived on American shores for its gala premiere, Universal-International Pictures (its U.S. distributor) accorded the film all the fanfare due a major production. Lee, Cushing, and Hammer cofounder Sir James Carreras flew to New York for the film's opening at Manhattan's Mayfair Theater. "I'd never been to America before," says Lee. "I was both nervous and excited. Universal had scheduled a midnight showing at the Mayfair, and Peter and I went. There was a gigantic painting on the side of a building of me holding the girl, God knows how many stories high. I hate attending these things; fortunately, again, nobody gave me a second glance. Peter and I sat right under the projection booth at the back of the theater, and the crowd came in. They were mostly professionals, who'd been to the theater or performed in it that night; they were shouting, they all knew each other, they were really in high spirits. Somebody fired a gun, a blank cartridge, and that got a few people's attention.

"Then the lights went down," he continues, "and there was this expectant bustle and hum. We heard the famous pounding musical score and a great cheer rang out when the blood dripped on the coffin at the end of the credits. The audience kept this noise up, a mixture of good-humored tolerance and enjoyment. Then there's the famous first shot of me at the top of the stairs in silhouette, and there was an absolute *roar* of laughter when that came on.

"At that point, I said to Peter, 'I'm leaving—I can't take any more of this. This is awful.' And Peter said, 'No—just stay.' And there was this great surge of applause as I came down the stairs, walked into the foreground, and opened my mouth to speak.

"I will never forget the instantaneous silence at that point. It was really quite extraordinary. Here was a reasonably normal-looking person speaking like a reasonably normal-looking person does: 'Mr. Harker, I'm glad that you've arrived safely.'

"And from then on," says Lee, "we had 'em. We had the audience's full attention."

Horror of Dracula was an overnight smash hit, even bigger than *Curse of Frankenstein*. However, Lee did not play the Count again until 1965's *Dracula—Prince of Darkness*, even though Hammer made other vampire movies in the interim. The actor asserts that, contrary to movie mythology, this wasn't due to his turning the part down for fear of being typecast.

"Hammer didn't offer it to me," Lee reveals. "Then, one day, [producer] Tony Nelson Keys asked me and my wife to have dinner with him at a restaurant in London, and he suddenly came out with this: 'How would you feel about doing another *Dracula* and a film about Rasputin, back to back?'"

The resulting *Dracula—Prince of Darkness* originated, in part, because of the success of a recent reissue of

Hammer's first *Frankenstein* and *Dracula* films. Lee counts *Prince of Darkness* as his favorite among the six Hammer sequels—but not without reservations.

"They pulled a couple more things out of Stoker's novel—the Renfield character, called Ludwig and played by Thorley Walters, for one," Lee recalls, "but my dialogue was abominable. At one point, Dracula is supposed to declare, 'I am the apocalypse!' I finally just decided, let's not have him speak at all if this is the best you can do.

"I don't know why Van Helsing's not in it," Lee continues, responding to a question frequently asked about the film, "except that they shifted the locale to the Carpathians—it all takes place fairly near Castle Dracula—and it might have been difficult to fit him into the story line. There is a surrogate for him, the character of the priest, Father Sandor, played by Andrew Keir—a very good actor, a very *strong* actor, and a very nice man offscreen—but I can see why the audience might miss Van Helsing's presence, since Peter was so good in the part."

From his own vantage point, Lee frankly missed the presence of another character: the Count himself! "I kept saying, 'Why don't you give him more to do?' And the reply would come back, 'Well, like what?' And I'd say, 'Look, if you're stuck, just go back and look through Stoker's book. It's all there.' However," he adds, "it quickly became a matter of inventing a story line and then saying, 'Now, where can we fit the character of Dracula in?'"

As an independent studio, Hammer had always been budget-conscious, but Lee asserts that the tandem productions of *Prince of Darkness* and *Rasputin, the Mad Monk* reflected Hammer's most glaring instances of corner-cutting up to that time. The shooting schedules were curtailed in midproduction; *Rasputin*, as the second film of the duo, suffered most noticeably. The actor also notes that the Hammer management winced at his reasonable salary demands—which were paid without question by other economy-minded producers throughout Europe, where his career as a "name" character actor was now expanding.

As a result, from 1969's *Dracula Has Risen from the Grave* onward, Lee's initial response to Hammer's paltry salary offers to reprise the Dracula role would be to reject them flatly. This prompted one of the more amazing incidents in his relationship with the studio.

"I got a call at home from Jimmy Carreras," he remembers, "saying, 'You must do this film, on my knees I beg you, I'm sixty-two years old and I cannot take this stress and strain. Do you know how many people you will keep from working at Hammer if you don't agree to do this film?' It really was a form of emotional blackmail. Plus, by then he'd had a deal with a major distributor, and there'd have been hell to pay if he didn't deliver the Dracula film he'd promised.

"Just to get them off my back, to not have to be bothered, I said, 'Oh, all right, I'll do it.' Plus, I admired Jim—he was a great showman, and I liked him."

Nonetheless, those good feelings don't always extend to the later Dracula films. *Dracula Has Risen from the Grave*, his third time out as the Count, contains what Lee feels is the most glaring degeneration of the character. "He pulls the stake out of himself because the boy who drove it in didn't pray afterward," says the actor, describing a scene that still causes his voice to ring with distaste. "I fought about that with [Hammer producer] Tony Hinds, who wrote the script under his pseudonym, John Elder. I said, 'You are destroying a legend here. You are totally turning the myth on its head—this is all wrong.' He said, 'It'll work, it'll look fine,' but it's ludicrous. I hated playing that scene."

Ironically, when it was released by Warner Bros. to American drive-ins as a summer 1969 event, *Dracula Has*

Risen from the Grave—ballyhooed by a campy ad campaign—made more money than any of the previous *Dracula*s.

Hammer then went to work on *Taste the Blood of Dracula*, a more horrific sequel (*Dracula Has Risen*, the first Hammer Dracula to go out under the new MPAA rating system, had been rated G!). The movie, which picks up with the Count's disintegration in the earlier film, had to be trimmed slightly from its original British version (a London brothel sequence was abbreviated by the censor's scissors) for a GP (now PG) rating.

"I didn't like the title—it was really corny—and Hammer gave me the same monotonous dirge about not having enough money for my salary," Lee says with a mild sigh. "But I liked certain elements of the story line, and apart from the absence of Peter Cushing—by now Van Helsing wasn't in the *Dracula* series at all—we had the best cast of any of the Dracula films. When actors like Geoffrey Keen, Roy Kinnear, Peter Sallis, and Gwen Watford are prepared to be in the movie, who am I to say no?

"But again, the character of Count Dracula had almost nothing to do. The special effects at the end, when Dracula is destroyed in the church, were very good, though."

Late in 1969, Lee strayed from the Hammer stable to recreate the role of Dracula for a competing producer for the first and only time. Harry Alan Towers, who collaborated with Lee on a revival of the evil Asian genius in 1965's *The Face of Fu Manchu*, had announced his intention to film Stoker's novel as it was written. "That one I only did because I was told I would have the opportunity to present the character *physically* as described by Stoker— as an old man getting younger as he consumes more blood," Lee explains. "[Prior to Gary Oldman], I'm the only actor who's done that."

Count Dracula was shot in Barcelona by the indefatigable

Jesus Franco, director of everything from hard-core porn to such innocuous fare as the last (and worst) of Lee's *Fu Manchu* series. "Jess is a much better director than he's given credit for," Lee says firmly. "He's *very* limited by what he is allowed to do financially, and by the actors and schedules at his disposal. I don't consider him to be a hack director—after all, he was Orson Welles's assistant on *Chimes at Midnight*—although he's been described as such."

Nevertheless, *Count Dracula* was a disappointment; Lee recalls sensing trouble from day one. "I saw the zoom lens on that camera and I thought, 'Uh-oh,'" he says. "And when I realized that I was doing nearly every one of Dracula's scenes by myself, without anybody to act with because they weren't there, it just made things worse. Klaus Kinski wasn't there, Herbert Lom wasn't there— Herbert and I are never in the same frame, although we're in the same scene; they cut back and forth while we are literally in different countries! And as I realized they were using zoom lenses and shooting day-for-night, and substituting German shepherds for wolves, I thought, 'Oh, dear, a great opportunity wasted.'"

It was back to Hammer after that for the first R-rated entry, 1971's *Scars of Dracula*. "That's the one with Patrick Troughton as my servant," Lee interjects warmly, invoking the name of the Hammer supporting player fondly remembered by *Dr. Who* fans as the second actor to portray the BBC's famed eccentric scientist. "And Dennis Waterman, who was a child actor in *Pirates of Blood River* [1962] at Hammer, grew up to be the *hero* in *Scars of Dracula*! I myself had more screen time for once— I actually had some dialogue to deliver. But it was rather excessively sadistic, and in some ways was the worst of the bunch for that reason."

Reminded that *Scars of Dracula* is one of the few latter-day Draculas to go back to the novel for inspiration—in the brief but eerie shot of Dracula scaling his castle's wall like a spider—Lee pauses for a moment's contemplation. "Yeah-h-h," he says slowly, "Roy Ward Baker and I kind of worked that out. But I can't take any credit for invention, 'cause it's in the book. But it works, hmm?"

Lee continued to make horror movies in the early seventies. "I've never turned my back on the genre," he says, "despite my reservations about what's been done with it on occasion." At the same time, his stature as a prominent player in major, nongenre features was also growing. Director Billy Wilder cast him as Mycroft Holmes in *The Private Life of Sherlock Holmes* (1970), and Raquel Welch, a big fan of Lee's Hammer vehicles, had him hired to portray the Mexican gunsmith who teaches her to shoot in the revenge Western *Hannie Caulder* (1972).

Meanwhile, the Hammer brass—what remained of them, with Anthony Hinds, Anthony Nelson Keys, and, temporarily, Michael Carreras now gone—had put their heads together and come up with a new approach to Dracula. In two features shot only months apart, *Dracula A.D. 1972* and *The Satanic Rites of Dracula*, Hammer brought the character into modern London.

"It was a terrible idea," says Lee, "but at least they also brought Van Helsing—or, more accurately, his grandson—back as well, so I got to work with Peter Cushing again in a *Dracula* film. The first one had all this 'swinging London'/Carnaby Street nonsense, which was anachronistic even in 1972. Dracula's appearances were restricted to a crumbling old church, so I was at least in a sort of Gothic setting."

In *Satanic Rites*, Dracula conceals himself as a business tycoon in a high-rise office complex as he prepares to unleash bubonic plague upon the world. When a suspicious Van Helsing pays him a visit, Dracula—hidden in shadows behind a massive desk—speaks to his nemesis . . . in a Bela Lugosi-like accent!

"That was something I threw in," says Lee, remembering the vignette, if not the movie, with fondness. "Not just to have fun with it, but to put off the moment of revelation a little longer . . . to give the audience something to puzzle over. 'Gee, maybe this isn't Dracula just yet—who is this mysterious figure behind the desk?' I always said that my character, D.D. Denham—honest to God, can you believe that?—was a cross between Howard Hughes and Dr. No. I thought if I gave this great business tycoon a foreign accent, it *might* work; people might not catch on in the first five seconds."

Lee pauses for a few moments and then remarks, "Yeah, well, that was it for me. That was the end of it. I said never again."

Soon thereafter, a one-hour TV special called *In Search of Dracula* was shot on Romanian locations. The Swedish production traced the historic roots of the fiendish nobleman who was the inspiration for Dracula: Prince Vlad, a.k.a. Vlad the Impaler. By narrating the documentary (padded with unrelated footage to bring it up to feature length for U.S. release), Lee was able to visit actual locales and, appearing in costume as Vlad Tepes, connect the dots between the fictional Count and his real-life, bloodthirsty alter ego.

"It was a fascinating footnote, having portrayed Dracula so many times, to be able to host this documentary and visit the actual homeland of Vlad Tepes," says Lee of the film. "But it's not a Dracula movie per se."

Also not part of his authentic *Dracula* filmography is a curio made in France in 1975, *Dracula Père et Fils*—released in the U.S. in 1979 as *Dracula and Son*. Lee recalls, "It's based on a very well-known novel called *Paris Vampire*, and isn't about Dracula at all. I did it in French for Edouard Molinaro—who later directed *La Cage aux Folles*—because he wanted to adapt this famous story as a comedy. We shot in daylight and everything; he's not supposed to be Dracula. I naturally had no control over the title change in America, or the redubbing of my voice." The credited culprit for this appalling domestic version, its mangled "camp" script, and Lee's altered voice, is Bob Dorian—who went on to be host and "trivia expert" of the American Movie Classics cable channel.

"I also do not portray Dracula," Lee continues, "in *Uncle Was a Vampire* [1959], an Italian comedy I did with Renato Rascel, or in *The Magic Christian* [1970]—though I play a generic vampire in each. I made a decision, early on, not to parody Dracula, to always play the character himself completely straight."

Many actors have portrayed Count Dracula in the two decades since Christopher Lee retired his cloak—and he has viewed some of their interpretations with interest and enjoyment. "There've been about twenty actors since I stopped," he ventures. "Even Peter played him in a French film in the seventies that I didn't see, *Tender Dracula*. I thought Jack Palance was very impressive in that television special he did in America. Denholm Elliott was good, in different ways, in a British TV production— there was more of the animal in what he did. Louis Jourdan, again on TV, had moments, particularly because they used pieces of the book that were quite correct. But I never saw John Carradine in *House of Frankenstein* or *House of Dracula*, and I never saw Frank Langella."

In the early 1980s, Lee startled a female journalist who asked if he'd ever consider playing Count Dracula again by telling her he'd be happy to—for a million dollars! Reminded of that, he laughs, then explains, "My point was that it would start the typecasting all over again, years after leaving the character, and I would need to be compensated financially. In view of the current star salaries in this industry, the fee would be somewhat larger today!" he adds good-naturedly.

It's true that Lee has had a few disappointments and

frustrations, trying to portray Count Dracula under what were often less than optimum circumstances. But what was most *satisfying* about it?

"That I made him believable; it's as simple as that," he responds. "When you're taking a character who is comprised of myth and legend, a little fact, and everything else, if you're able to convince an audience for ninety minutes that maybe it could happen, that's the best victory an actor can have."

FRIGHT NIGHT:
On-set Diary

ABBIE BERNSTEIN

IN THE SUMMER OF 1984, Columbia Pictures gave the go-ahead to *Fright Night*, a present-day vampire movie concerning average teenager Charley Brewster, who discovers that his suave next-door neighbor Jerry Dandrige is really one of the undead. Herb Jaffe was the producer; Richard Edlund's Boss Film Company facility handled the effects, and screenwriter Tom (*Psycho II*) Holland made his directorial debut with the project.

When I initially interviewed Holland during *Fright Night*'s preproduction, he generously invited me to come visit the set as frequently as I wished. This resulted in the set diary you're about to read.

WEDNESDAY, DECEMBER 19, 1984

My first trip to the set. It's the monsoon season in Los Angeles, and a fierce rainstorm batters the downtown lot where the *Fright Night* company vehicles are parked. The lot is conveniently right behind today's location, a former hardware store converted for use as a soundstage. A sequence for *Body Double* was shot here, and the nightclub set has been left semi-intact. The ground floor is filled with tables and chairs; more tables and chairs dot the upstairs balcony that runs along the upper floor.

At least a hundred extras are on hand today, dressed in studded leather and Day-Glo New Wave chic to lend colorful background as the vampire kills a pair of disco bouncers who get in the way of his pursuit of Charley and Amy, Charley's girlfriend, played respectively by William Ragsdale and Amanda Bearse.

First assistant director Jerry Sobul megaphones instructions to the mob of extras: "Everybody take a position on the runway, except the blood people." This refers to the lucky souls soon to be splashed with a mixture of Karo Syrup and food coloring.

Chris Sarandon enters the set, in costume as Jerry Dandrige. Earlier, Sarandon had admitted to me his hesitance in taking this part; after his Oscar-nominated performance as a nervous transsexual in *Dog Day Afternoon* was followed by a turn as a vicious rapist in *Lipstick*, he found it hard to persuade the film community he could play characters other than oddballs and villains. After shaking the mold, he wasn't anxious to risk more typecasting, but says he was won over by Holland's vision of the vampire as "a very attractive, sexy guy. The thing Tom wanted most from this character was not the evil awfulness of him, but the fact that he was tremendously charming. Tom wanted him to have a sense of humor and also a sense of the price he has to pay for being who he is and what he is. Eternal life is not necessarily a great gift; there's a kind of mythic, tragic proportion to that."

Right now, Sarandon looks like just another handsome leading man—until you notice the two-inch fingernail extensions secured to his right hand by latex false fingertips. Someone yells for the makeup artists to get the "baby fangs"—slightly exaggerated canines our vampire sports when mildly annoyed. (When Jerry's really upset, he grows Doberman pinscher-sized chompers.)

In another area of the set, Rick Stratton, John Goodwin, and Ken Diaz (the head of the on-set makeup unit) are applying baldcaps to the bouncers' stunt doubles: strips of Kleenex are affixed to the edges of the caps then sprayed down with the surgical sealant Aeroplast.

Stratton spends a lot of time in the lab, where he and frequent partner Steve Neill sculpted some of the appliances used in this shoot. However, he also enjoys working on the set: "In the lab, you're an unsung hero; on the set, you're representing yourself. Also, I like working with actors."

Special FX worker Darrell Pritchett walks through the set, fanning smoke around out of a film can containing a burning compound of nontoxic oils. The smoke's purpose is to give visual definition to the shafts of light streaming down from the ceiling.

Michael Lantieri, the supervisor of on-set special FX (as opposed to the creatures and makeup prepared at Boss Films), readies a fire-extinguisher-type contraption that will spray "movie blood" onto the extras, just before the stuntman's body is thrown off the stairway landing and into the crowd below by the vampire (actually, he propels himself off the landing, but on film it will *look* like the vampire does it). The body crashes down on a table full of partiers, knocking a stuntwoman backward into the breakaway table behind her. At this point, the whole disco crowd freaks out and stampedes. Dangerous though it appears, the stunt comes off without a hitch.

The next shot calls for Charley and Amy to push past the other bouncer, played by Ernie Holmes. Before the bouncer can get to the kids, Jerry gets to *him*, squeezing the life out of the poor guy's throat, then tossing the body off the landing onto the dance floor.

Within an hour, carpenters erect a platform that

extends out from the landing. To create the illusion that Holmes is really being lifted up and held high over the dance floor, the actor stands on a wheel-mounted box, manipulated below camera range by Lantieri and Pritchett. When he's supposed to be standing on his own, Holmes crouches on the box so that he's eye level with Sarandon. As Sarandon uses his long-nailed hand to "lift" the bouncer, Holmes (who winds up doing his own stunt) straightens his knees. The added height of the box puts his head high above Sarandon, so that he really seems to be held in midair. Then Lantieri and Pritchett wheel the box from the landing onto the platform—on-screen, it will look as though Holmes is being dangled over the landing's edge. As Holmes flails at his attacker, Holland reminds him, "His claws are two inches into your neck! You're slowly dying!" Holmes dives sideways off the box onto a massive airbag, concluding his "death scene."

At 9:10 P.M. they're done for the night. Sarandon, "blood" on his hands, breaks off his false fingertips and flings them one by one at the makeup people: "Take that! And that!"

FRIDAY, JANUARY 4, 1985

On Soundstage 8 at Laird Studios in Culver City, a large sheet of fake grass separates sets for both Charley's and Jerry's houses. A Champman camera crane sits on the grass, waiting to peer in the second-story window of Charley's room, mounted on wooden scaffolding.

Ragsdale says, "I always liked horror as a kid—I lived in sort of a small town, El Dorado, Arkansas, so I guess believing in witches and vampires and things like that sort of zested it up a little."

How would he feel, faced with his character's predicament? "If I found out there was a real vampire living next door to me, my response to that would just be shock. It's like the stages of death: denial, resignation, anger—those are stages Charley goes through. It's interesting to try and touch on those in performance, never having been that close to death."

He's been close to minor disaster, though; a few weeks back, during a shot in which Charley runs down a stairway, Ragsdale broke his foot. Thanks to some inventive rescheduling and reblocking, the show and Ragsdale are both going on, but the actor's foot is still in a cast, which sometimes poses problems even when he's sitting down.

Like now, for instance: The upcoming shot has Ragsdale scrambling around on his back, having been thrown into Charley's closet by the vampire, and his feet are going to show. No shoes big enough to fit over his cast can be found, but costumers Bettylee Balsam and Mort Schwartz hit upon a solution: They slit Ragsdale's shoe in several places, slip it on, then cover the portions of cast gleaming whitely through the slits with black cloth.

Charley's mood in this scene is, according to director Holland, "stark balls-out terror" as the vampire reaches down, seizing his intended victim by the neck and belt. The first take seems all right, but Sarandon grabs Ragsdale's shirt instead of his neck. On the second take, Ragsdale reacts with proper fear, but when "cut" is called, Sarandon is the one looking startled and pained; Ragsdale accidentally stepped on his foot. On the third take, Sarandon grabs his prey so violently that he slams his own shoulder into the camera lens.

When they get a good take, they move on to the next shot. The camera takes over Ragsdale's position in the closet, assuming Charley's point of view. The lack of a body where he's reaching for Charley throws Sarandon off a little, so Holland obligingly sits in the closet next to the camera. He asks if Sarandon would like him to offer resistance to being pulled up. "Yes, please," the actor says.

"Scare me to death," Holland instructs. Sarandon duly gets scary; Holland is pleased. "Really good, Chris."

It's 6:15 A.M. Diaz and Stratton, along with Jeff Kennemore, have already been working on Sarandon for over an hour in the makeup trailer. Today sees the actor in the third-stage vampire makeup, which is the most extreme; Jerry is at the height of fury, and thus at his most inhuman, because Charley's just stabbed him through the hand with a pencil.

A baldcap with a long fringe of hair attached is on Sarandon's head; Stratton has applied latex thumb tips to Sarandon's hands. Now Stratton painstakingly starts gluing down all the latex fingertips on Sarandon's left hand, keeping the fingers separated with little foam wedges; Kennemore begins work on the hand.

Diaz puts adhesive on the actor's nose, then stretches a one-piece foam latex appliance over Sarandon's entire face and begins applying adhesive under the unattached portions of the piece.

Kennemore holds up a weird-looking appliance, resembling a latex glove with the fingers cut off, and asks what it's for. This is the "pencil-stab" piece (sculpted by Neill); Kennemore powders Sarandon's right hand, then with Stratton's help, stretches the appliance onto it.

"What a stupid way to make a living," Sarandon says. "Well, not stupid—silly."

Stratton: "Who, you or us?"

Sarandon: "Me. You guys are having all the fun."

Pritchett comes in with the plate that goes under the hand appliance, consisting of the pointed half of a pencil attached to a nickel-sized base. Kennemore makes an incision in the appliance's palm with scissors, then fits the base into the slit, along with a plastic tube that goes between Sarandon's forefinger and thumb, disappears into the hole, and emerges again at the actor's wrist. The tube will pump smoke out of the hand as Jerry is stabbed.

Diaz uses his own left hand as a palette on which he mixes colors of makeup, alternating between a paintbrush and a sponge as he adds hues to the facial appliance. Talonlike fingernails have been attached to the latex fingertips; Stratton applies liquid latex around the back of the nails to build up simulated cuticles.

Randy Cook, who with Steve Johnson designed and sculpted most of the *Fright Night* appliances and strange creatures, pitches in to help by attaching eyebrow pieces—real hair woven into very fine mesh—to the appliance brow. The fake eyebrows tangle in Sarandon's real eyelashes; Cook disentangles them and cautions Sarandon to close his eyes. Sarandon, who's being a very good sport about all this, seems just a bit uneasy at all the strange things poking and prodding near his closed eyes. Cook reassures him, "This is just my finger, not some implement of death."

Diaz and Cook adhere a hairpiece to the top of Sarandon's baldcap; the lace on one side buckles. They peel it back with infinite care, but a tiny patch of makeup comes up with the lace. They readjust and reglue the hairpiece, then repaint the patch of makeup.

Hairdresser Marina Pedraza joins the group, trimming and shaping the hairpiece so that the contours of Sarandon's head won't be obscured, taking special care around the pointed ear appliances.

Diaz steps back for a look at the whole ensemble: face, hair, ears, hands, "It looks great," he says.

Stratton quips: "Let's go home. Chris, the contact lenses are over there, the teeth are over there, if anything comes loose, they can fix it in the cutting."

At 12:55 P.M., almost eight hours after they started, the makeup crew is done. Johnson puts in the finishing touches—fangs and contact lenses—when they arrive on the set. A crew member who hasn't been near the makeup trailer this morning walks up, takes a good look at Sarandon, mutters "Jeez," and walks away again.

THURSDAY, JANUARY 24

I arrive on Soundstage 9 at 3:30 P.M. Holland promptly grabs me by the arm and drags me over to today's set, the bedroom of Charley's mother, where Stephen Geoffreys is in full makeup as "Evil Ed" Thompson. The character starts out as a weird high-school kid and winds up as an even weirder vampire. He looks really ghastly: Ed has just had a cross burnt into his forehead and some of his flesh is melting off (thanks to a full-face latex appliance), his eyes are vacant pools of darkness (via opaque contact lenses), his fangs are huge and, because of Ed's sense of humor, he's wearing a Raggedy Ann wig.

Geoffreys wishes he had more scenes in the heavy makeup: "It's great, great fun. At first, I was worried how to make it look real. 'Should I be a human monster, should I be real sympathetic?' But I figured you've got to just go all the way for it, open your mouth as wide as you can and be as terrifying as possible. And Evil Ed loves putting on a show like that, this is his big chance. And he does a good job."

TUESDAY, FEBRUARY 18

"On a scale of one to ten, isn't that a terrific bat?" Holland is proudly showing me the latest wonder from Boss Films, a special FX bat with a body the size of a greyhound, an eight-foot wingspan and a remarkably mobile cable-controlled face.

We're on Soundstage 15, which houses the ornate set for the main entrance to Jerry's house, complete with a staircase from the original *Gone with the Wind* set, leading up to a balcony topped by a breakaway stained-glass window.

The bat and its handlers—Cook, Johnson, John

Axford, Kevin Brennan, Craig Caton, Screaming Mad George, and the bat's personal makeup person, Theresa Burkett—occupy one corner of the floor at the foot of the stairs. In the other corner, cinematographer Jan Kiesser's camera crew set up a shot of the bat attacking Roddy McDowall as Peter Vincent, an aging ham horror actor who reluctantly becomes Charley's ally. "He's such a terrible actor," McDowall says of his character. "He's got such a sad life, he's sort of cowardly and then he finds his strength as a human being."

Right now, he's fighting for his life as the bat swoops in for the kill, knocking McDowall backwards (a stuntman lies below camera range to catch the actor as he falls). Brennan and Wilson use poles to manipulate the bat's right and left wings, respectively; Cook crouches under its body, holding it aloft as he runs from tall box to small box to floor, so that the bat appears to swoop swiftly down at McDowall in a graceful, smooth arc.

"I'm seeing Randy," camera operator Craig Denault reports as he peers through his camera's viewfinder.

"Do you have any more material the bat's made of to put on Randy's shirt?" assistant director Sobul asks, hoping to camouflage Cook. Unfortunately, no one does, but the scene is reblocked so that Cook no longer shows up beneath his creation.

For the next shot, the last few steps of the stairway are replaced with a wooden platform on which McDowall lies for the continuation of the bat attack. Denault yells: "Effects! We're gonna need some bones on the stairs!" Lantieri and Pritchett inspect the "human bones" they've concocted in the special FX truck, selecting the most photogenic ones to scatter above McDowall's head.

During rehearsal, McDowall grapples with the bat, defending himself by grabbing a bone from the stairs and thrusting it between the creature's jaws. At least, that's what's supposed to happen. First the bone slides under the bat's chin, then bops it on the nose, but keeps missing its mouth. Holland tells McDowall to let the bat come to the bone instead of trying to put the bone in the bat's mouth. This works much better.

On the last take, there is a mishap: McDowall pulls too hard on the bone while it's in the bat's mouth, causing a separation in the beastie's skull. The shape of the bat's head changes weirdly as its right eye sinks down into its throat.

Holland is understandably dismayed. "I *love* that bat. I want the fucker to work."

The bat crew strives frantically to salvage their creature. Cook says the smile control is broken, but the bat can be made to work well enough for some shots over its shoulder while it's on McDowall's chest. The bat's close-ups will have to wait for two days, when Cook and company will have had sufficient time to do more thorough repairs.

Finally, they're as ready as they'll be tonight. Ragsdale kneels at the edge of the platform to lean into the shot more easily with his stake and crucifix as the bat exposes McDowall's neck. Sunlight hits the bat and it "screams" (that is, it lifts its head into the air and shakes—the sound of the scream will be added in postproduction), then drops back out of the frame.

"Is the bat in sunlight yet?" Cook asks.

"No," says Holland, "can't you tell?" From his position under the bat, Cook can barely see *anything*, so Holland talks him through the action: "OK, go in . . . sunlight . . . bat out! Bat out!"

Shooting on *Fright Night* is officially completed at 3 A.M. Saturday, February 23. Of course, there will be pickup shots—retakes of bits and pieces that didn't turn out right the first time—and work will continue at Boss for weeks on the opticals and FX, but for most cast and crew, this is it.

Two weeks later, there is a wrap party, giving everyone a chance to say good-bye (or, in some cases, "see you later"), in a relaxed, congenial atmosphere. It's fun and pleasant, but it lacks the intense camaraderie of the set. In other words, it's a good party, but it's not the same as making a movie. Then again, what is?

CHRIS SARANDON, VAMPIRE

ED GROSS

IN THE PAST, cinematic vampires have been portrayed as pale-skinned ghouls wandering around cemeteries, draped in cumbersome black capes, and threatening to suck the blood out of any victims who happen by. Then in the late 1970s, Frank Langella romanticized Bram Stoker's *Dracula* in the play and film of the same name, proving that vampires could be, above all else, charming.

In 1985, Chris Sarandon contemporized this incarnation of evil to great effect in Tom Holland's *Fright Night*, a film which has more in common with the Universal horror classics of the thirties and forties than the current crop of slice-and-dice productions which have proliferated in the genre.

In this updating of "The Boy Who Cried Wolf," Sarandon plays Jerry Dandridge, a vampire who will go to any means to make sure that his secret remains safe, including killing Charley Brewster, his teenage next-door neighbor, who has learned the truth.

"The thing that appeals to me about Jerry," explains Sarandon, "is that he's totally contemporary. That was something we all strived for, and something I found very interesting about the character because he wasn't the

Count of legend or Bram Stoker, but a guy who everybody knew and couldn't believe was being accused of being a vampire. He isn't the personification of pure evil that vampires are known to be."

What impressed the actor most about the character was his multidimensional facets.

"Just think about this guy's problems," he says sincerely. "On the one hand you've got somebody who's got something which everybody would probably love to have, which is eternal life. Also, he's tremendously powerful physically, and attractive sexually. What he does, people are attracted to for some reason. But at the same time, how would you like to know that if people found out about you, nobody would really want to hang around you? That is, to spend eternity—but to spend eternity shunned by any normal kind of society; not being able to form any kind of normal human relationship. To be, in a way, damned to eternity. There's a sense of this guy's tragedy as well as his attractiveness."

This obvious enthusiasm is surprising, especially when one considers that the actor nearly turned the role down.

"I was sent the script by my agent and immediately sort of got sucked in by the plot because it's wonderfully constructed and plotted," explains Sarandon. "After I read it, I said, 'Gee, this is going to make a great movie. It's a shame that I'm not really interested in playing this part.' The reasons for that are that over the past couple of years I've played a few villains and didn't want to get locked into playing another one. I thought the character was an interesting one, though I didn't think it was quite fleshed out. Despite my reservations, I had some conversations with Tom, we came up with some ideas, and I ended up doing it."

"I made a promise to Chris," adds Holland, "that I would make Jerry sensual and into a leading man; to show that side of him. He didn't want to do another wild and crazy character role."

Sarandon felt that what was missing was the character's haunted quality, part of which would come across in the playing, and that there were a few things needed in the script which would express this.

"The character's not so much the personification of pure evil as he is a person who became a vampire by circumstance," he says. "We did all that groundwork for ourselves in terms of who this guy was and what happened; how it happened. Tom was very encouraging about that. To come up with that kind of life for the character so that he ultimately ends up more interesting for the audience."

Coming up with identifiable characters has been an objective of the actor's since graduating from the University of West Virginia, and, besides numerous stage roles, he's tried to achieve this goal via his various screen personas, from Al Pacino's gay lover in *Dog Day Afternoon* (which won him an Oscar nomination) and the rapist of *Lipstick*, to a tool of the devil in *The Sentinel* and, finally, a leading role with Goldie Hawn in *Protocol*.

Bearing this in mind, one wonders if he had any aversions to the idea of playing a vampire, certainly one of the most bizarre roles he's been offered.

"It wasn't so much that," he counters, "but that the guy was such a bad guy. In a way he was, but in a way he wasn't. I think that I carried in some of my prejudices when I first read the script. Rather than reading it in a very objective way, I read it in a much more 'What's it going to do for me?' way. Having played a couple of villains in the past, I was a little worried about it.

"I don't want to get locked into playing anything," he elaborates. "I don't want to be known as a heavy, or as anything in particular but just a good actor who can handle anything that comes along. Wishful thinking, but that's the image I would hope to have in the industry. That's something you cultivate over time by the choice of roles you take. Also, I think I underestimated the fact that in the movie I did just before *Fright Night*, *Protocol*, I was playing Mr. Total Straight Arrow. As nice a guy and as totally uncontroversial a character as you'll find anywhere. Considering that that's the one I did just before this, I think I needn't have worried so much. I came to realize that after a while."

One thing which came close to being a problem was the marathon makeup sessions which enabled Sarandon to go from being the suave and good-looking Dandridge to the snarling, batlike "spawn of Satan" during choice moments.

"We had certain stages of change," he says, "which had a lot to do with just how pissed off Jerry is at any particular moment . . . how provoked he is.

"I was stuck in makeup so damned much of the time," he sighs. "I had two weeks of eight-hour makeup calls, every day. I'd go in at 4:00 in the morning and the makeup people would have to be in at three-something. They'd start on me at 4:00 and I'd go to work at noon or 1:00. Quite a remarkable experience. You either learn how to hypnotize yourself and meditate, or you become stark raving mad.

"I tried to do the former," the actor laughs.

A big question on everybody's mind throughout production was whether or not *Fright Night* could find a niche for itself in this age of the slasher or splatter film.

"That's a good question," he says. "The feeling I had, and I have reasonably good instincts as an audience, is that it would work. When I first read the script, I couldn't put it down. I don't mean that as a cliché, I mean that for real. When I read that script, I remember sitting in the very chair I'm sitting in as we speak, my wife sitting in bed knitting and I said, 'Sorry, honey, I know it's time to

INTERVIEW WITH THE VAMPIRE
Tom Cruise
1994
Copyright © 1994 Geffen Pictures

BRAM STOKER'S DRACULA
Gary Oldman
1992
Photo: Ralph Nelson
Copyright © 1992 Columbia Pictures Industries, Inc.

DRACULA HAS RISEN FROM THE GRAVE
Christopher Lee
Veronica Carlson
1968
Copyright © 1968 Warner Bros. Inc

DARK SHADOWS
Ben Cross
1991
Copyright © 1991 NBC

CHILDREN OF THE NIGHT
1992
Copyright © Columbia Pictures Industries, Inc./TriStar

THE LOST BOYS
1987
Copyright © 1987 Warner Bros. Inc.

FRIGHT NIGHT
Chris Sarandon
1985
Copyright © Columbia Pictures Industries, Inc.

INNOCENT BLOOD
Anne Parillaud
1992
Copyright © 1992 Warner Bros. Inc.

go in and start dinner, but I can't yet. I have to finish this.'
I put it down like an hour and ten minutes later and I figured that it was going to be a terrific movie. My original
instincts were correct."

The horror genre is one that has intrigued him over
the years, though he isn't really a fan of splatter films.
Friends of his love those really shocking horror movies,
but he is much more of an aficionado of the older ones,
such as the original *Dracula* and *Frankenstein*.

"And of practicioners like Hitchcock," he adds, "who
really understood an audience. People who are much
more interested in creating work which leaves a lasting
impression. I'm much more interested in the resonance or
haunting quality of the really good ones, and it'll be interesting to see if we've got one of those.

"There are a couple of things towards the end of the
film where there's your requisite sort of special effects,
bodies flying around and falling apart, and things like
that," he continues. "But that specifically comes about due
to what's going on in the script.

"When I first read the script, there was, interestingly,
very little real physical violence in it. What's so startling
about it is you are in constant anticipation of a violent act,
and that comes from good scriptwriting. The film also has
a lot of humor, but it's intentional. It is a humor of irony
in situation. Any humor comes out of the fact that the
audience has invested a certain amount of emotional bag-
gage with the characters, and if something funny happens,
they're going to laugh at that. We're having fun with it,
but we're not making fun of it.

"Also, I think you'll find in this movie that in the first
forty minutes or so there's only one violent act, and that's
somebody sticking a pencil through somebody's hand.
The rest of that time is spent leading up to something
happening. You know something's got to happen, but
nothing does. To me, that's much more effective, a kind

of Hitchcockian approach to that sort of material. What's much more important is how you lead up to the act rather than the act itself. It's not what you see, but what you've dreaded seeing," he explains.

Could he see himself returning as Jerry Dandridge?

"I might, but who knows?" concludes Sarandon, who was not part of the ill-conceived *Fright Night II*. "Let's see what happens with this one first. It's an interesting character for me. I could perceive bringing him back, but it would depend on the circumstances. It's a little premature to talk about that now."

MAKING *THE LOST BOYS*

WILLIAM RABKIN

YOU CAN HEAR the screams all the way down the beach.
You can hear the old man shout and hear the crash of
bodies smashing into walls.

It's just another typical argument in Santa Cruz,
California. In this city built on bean sprouts and granola,
you have to expect fights over lifestyle between an aging
hippie and a middle-aged establishment guy. But there's
one difference between today's battle and the ones that
get played out here every day of the week: This conservative is a vampire with blazing cat-eyes and two-inch fangs.
And the old hippie is doing his arguing with a six-foot
wooden stake.

Welcome to the Burbank Studios version of Santa Carla
(an ersatz Santa Cruz), home of the Richard (*The Omen*)
Donner/Warner Bros. production, *The Lost Boys*.

The story begins with the arrival of divorcee Lucy
Emerson (Dianne Wiest) and her two sons, Michael
(Jason Patric) and Sam (Corey Haim). After moving in
with Grandpa (Barnard Hughes), the boys take to the
local amusement park. While hanging out, Michael is ini-
tiated into a teen vampire gang (led by Kiefer Sutherland)
and Sam meets up with two junior monster hunters

(Corey Feldman and Jamison Newlander). The battle lines are drawn . . .

In the middle of this cross-cultural conflict, no one is thinking about what a hit *Lost Boys* may be. They're thinking about how long they've been on the endless production. And how they can't wait to finish.

"I should write a composition on what I did on my summer vacation," says "aging hippie" Hughes. "I feel like I've been on this picture forever."

Actor Edward Herrmann, who plays Wiest's suitor and a vampire suspect, expresses similar complaints. But at least the actor got the opportunity to wear some trendy, flashy duds, unlike past highbrow Herrmann characters.

"That's one of the reasons I chose to do the part: I wanted to get out of suits," laughs Herrmann, who has made a career of playing Franklin Delano Roosevelt and millionaires who dress like him. "Or at least get out of three-piece suits and get into hip ones."

Also looking for the opportunity to star in "less serious" fare, the distinguished Herrmann dove into *The Lost Boys* project with total abandon. "*Lost Boys* is fun," notes the Tony Award-winning actor. "And at least this one isn't gratuitously ugly. There are some very attractive people here."

Right now, most of those attractive people are being used to mop up the floor. Bam! There goes Corey Feldman flying across the room. Boom! Watch Jason Patric smash into a wall. Ouch! Jami Gertz slides into a pile of furniture.

"It's been tough, physically," admits Gertz, who plays the teen vampire chick who seduces innocent Michael into the world of the Lost Boys. "It's been a long haul. I did stunts yesterday, and my whole neck hurts, my arm hurts. One big character is going crazy and he's throwing everybody all over the room. This is a tough life. I deserve to go to Hawaii."

But being thrown to the ground by kindly Ed Herrmann is hardly the worst Gertz has suffered on this production, as noted in her collection of shooting anecdotes: "Running through real caves without shoes. Riding on the back of a motorcycle with Kiefer Sutherland driving. I love Kiefer, but he's an animal. When he's driving, be careful. 'Don't worry, don't worry,' he says, then he pops a wheelie and breaks his hand. If I had been on back, I would have been dead.

"We've been doing some scary stuff," she continues. "We had to descend these stairs down a cliff with water running down them. Those stairs weren't very sturdy, and the water made them slippery. We were running up and down them all night."

And then there was the cave, the atmospheric Lost Boys hideout. "The cave was absolutely incredible," Gertz gushes. "It's this old hotel that has fallen into the ground, and it looks great. But when designers design sets, they put a ramp here and a staircase there, and they never consider anyone having to walk on this ramp or up those stairs. It can get difficult. They had to carry half of us up the stairs. But I'm in a great mood. I haven't worked all day. I've been in makeup since 7 A.M. I'm happy."

She's not as happy as the man with the ponytail who keeps shouting for more smoke. Director Joel (*St. Elmo's Fire*) Schumacher looks downright delighted to be helming this picture. And there's no reason he shouldn't be. It seems practically a matter of luck that he ended up with the project.

Certainly, he wasn't anyone's first choice to direct *The Lost Boys*. Richard (*Psycho II*) Franklin was, back in the days when the picture was still considered "Peter Pan with vampires" (which explains why they never grew up). But after some conceptual reshuffling and a rewrite by Jeffrey (*The Dead Zone*) Boam, Franklin was replaced by Donner.

And then Donner discovered Shane Black's *Lethal Weapon* script and decided to direct that instead.

Donner stayed attached to *The Lost Boys* as producer and went looking for another director. He approached Schumacher, best known for comedies, who was bogged down in studio bureaucracy over a proposed film of Jay McInerney's yuppie best-seller *Bright Lights, Big City*. Seeing that project going nowhere, Schumacher signed on with *The Lost Boys*.

Schumacher might seem like a strange choice to helm a big-budget horror film. His only previous genre offering was the Lily Tomlin vehicle *The Incredible Shrinking Woman*, and Schumacher prefers to forget about that one. But if you ask Donner's longtime producing partner Harvey (*The Omen*) Bernhard about the choice, he merely smiles enigmatically and says, "Joel thinks in color."

Right now, the color Schumacher is thinking in is *more*. More smoke. More snarling. More death. This is, after all, the end of the picture. It has to be big, and it has to be exciting.

"Vampires are sexy, as opposed to other great monsters," offers Schumacher. "They're beautifully dressed, they come into your bedroom. I actually think that in Victorian times, vampires were created so people could express oral sex. Think of those Victorian ladies who used to swoon all the time in their musty old houses: They dreamed of old men sucking the life out of them, and of themselves being so totally under their spell that they were unable to resist.

"We're not going for a very classic vampire, not as you've seen them so many times," he adds. "They don't sleep in coffins, there's no neck-biting, they're not dressed in white tie and tails or capes. But they're beautiful. Vampire legends are etched so indelibly in everybody's mind that you don't have to retread ground that has been covered before."

That's appropriate for Schumacher, who is essentially breaking new career territory all through *The Lost Boys*, especially in terms of the FX. Greg (*Vamp*) Cannom handles the vampire stuff, while Dream Quest, who did *The Fly*'s opticals, supply *Lost Boys*' flying magic. "There were effects in *The Incredible Shrinking Woman*, but nothing like we have here," the director insists. "The effects in *Shrinking Woman* were to show the ordinariness of life turned into madness for the heroine by her turning small. Here we're using effects to make people fly, kill, and maim. Fun things.

"This has been the hardest job I've ever had in my life, but it has also been the most fun and rewarding at the same time. I think sometimes, now that we're finally finishing the movie, that if I had known at the start how hard this was going to be, I wouldn't have done it. It's like having your first baby; by the time you know how hard it is, it's too late. Between the special effects, the flying, the kids, the motorcycles on the beach, the dogs, and the cave set, everything's been quite a challenge."

Schumacher turns back to his physical FX crew. "More smoke," he bellows, and once again the vampire starts writhing.

Meanwhile, in a trailer across the lot, the vampire's killer is reclining comfortably with a book. "I keep wondering why they keep giving me these old duffers to play," Hughes complains. "I suppose there's a good reason for it."

Like so many of his "old duffers," Hughes's *Lost Boys* character is strong-willed and good-natured. "Although there's not much seen in the picture, the history of the family is that he was a rather uptight, conservative man with a daughter who was a hippie type," the veteran actor explains. "Because of the difference in values, she left home. She got married and had two children and divorced and went back. Now she's a rather conservative wage earner, and the old man has become something of a hippie. It's really not exploited in the film, but at least that's the spine of our relationship. There's enough going on in the picture without introducing a subplot that can hardly be explored, but it's comforting to me to know where I came from and where I'm going.

"We're finally about to shut down and move on," Hughes grins. "I'm going back to New York. I kept coming and going, but this time it's for good. I left the set almost six weeks ago and came back to find they've almost totally destroyed my house. And I finish up destroying what's left of it this afternoon."

Back on the stage, Schumacher has finally got the right amount of smoke, and now he's calling, "No more!" But smoke keeps pouring into the living room. Bernhard, dressed completely in black, stands to one side and watches patiently. After the difficulties on *Ladyhawke* and *The Goonies*, the problems of *Lost Boys* haven't seemed so bad.

"I've made three tech films in a row, and now I'm looking for something simple," Bernhard laughs. "Something about people sitting around the table talking. This has been very smooth, but it's a very tough picture. You can only do a little bit at a time. There are no clumps of dialogue where you can shoot three pages. It's an eighth of a page and an eighth of a page and an eighth of a page. It takes a long time."

And taking longer all the time. Sometimes it seems like it will never end. And no one will ever get to go home.

On the set, Schumacher throws up his hands. The smoke has gotten completely out of control.

"No more! No more!" an assistant director screams through a megaphone as the smoke continues to pour in. "Which word didn't you understand?"

BEHIND THE SCREAMS:
Innocent Blood

BILL WARREN

A GRANULAR SNOW is falling on downtown Pittsburgh, covering cinematographer Mac Ahlberg's unoccupied chair. The crew of *Innocent Blood* stands around watching—which is what most movie crews do much of the time, just because of the way movies are made—as John Landis, standing behind the camera, waves his arms and yells. Landis does both of these a lot.

In the street lies the wreckage of a bus and a taxicab that have smashed into one another. They sit there quietly, blackened and smoky, until Landis gives the order for the fire to be switched on. Bright orange flames roar upward from the bus and cab, and soon a blazing figure walks—*walks*, mind you—from the inferno and stops in front of the camera. Still covered from head to foot with fire, he gestures, as if giving a speech. Suddenly he falls to his knees—a cue to the FX assistants, who rush in with fire extinguishers. All the onlookers applaud Rick Avery's stunt, as well they should.

Innocent Blood writer Michael Wolk is enthusiastic about the downtown Pittsburgh location, jazzed up with lots of flashy neon by the movie crew. "This is all ours," he explains, "all this stuff." He points up at the gaudiest of the signs, some of which had gone unused since 1959 before being restored for the film. "There's a giant neon figure of a girl taking her bra off, revealing tassels on her nipples. It's lovely."

Smiling hugely, director Landis walks over to the *FANGORIA* reporter, greeting him warmly. This, he says, is "a *horror movie* horror movie!" (Landis talks with a lot of italics and exclamation points.) "There are chases, there are demonstrations of supernatural powers, there are explosions, there are car chases, there's a great deal of action—leaps and jumps and falls! There's a *lot* of stuff! Also, I don't know if you'd call it *action*, but there are interesting displays of superstrength and invulnerability on the part of the vampires."

Landis is friendly and outgoing; a true movie buff, stuffed with great anecdotes, he's the kind of guy who also assembles his own experiences into wonderful little stories to illustrate his points. On the set, he's relaxed, thoroughly in charge of the situation, comfortable with his position as director. He can be chatting amiably with a visitor to the set about mutual friends, movie history, social issues, anything but the movie at hand—yet he's also totally aware of what's happening on the set. He even jokes about this ability to effectively divide his attention. When the crew reminds him they're about to shoot, Landis will shout "Action!" without even looking at the setup. Whirling about to face the actors, he says in tones of mock disappointment, "You didn't *do* anything!"

Makeup maestro Steve Johnson admits that he was originally a bit put off by Landis's brashness. "The fact is," admits Johnson, "John has a very intimidating personality until you get to know him. He's larger than life, he's a cartoon character. I'm sensitive about my work and about other people's opinions of my work; I want to please so badly that anything that's not praise makes me very, very paranoid. But now, when there's been a long string of John *not* being 'mean' to me, I feel like he's not paying enough attention to me. Now that I know what he's like, he gives me a lot of energy on the set, and you never have to guess how he's feeling about something, which makes for open communication that can only help the final product. The next movie I do, I'm going to be spoiled. Out of all the directors I've worked with, I've never enjoyed working with anyone as much as John."

Actor Robert Loggia also enjoys his relationship with Landis, grinning and throwing an arm around the bearded director almost every time they meet between scenes. "I think John was born an *enfant terrible*," Loggia says, "and he'll be an *enfant terrible* when he's ninety years old. He is an incredible energy source; he goes full-scale into the storm, taking things head-on. He's got so much energy in this picture, even though it's a sorry way to shoot it. In Pittsburgh? The dead of winter? At night? He's indefatigable; he has a marching band and his own pom-pom girls cheering him on. He is an amazing cauldron of energy."

Innocent Blood is Landis's first genre film since his groundbreaking *An American Werewolf in London* back in 1981, and he's apparently having a great time filming this urban cop thriller/horror movie with occasional laughs. He's a little apprehensive about any possible differences between what Warner Bros. *thinks* he's making vs. what he really *is* making, so when he sends the assembled footage (Landis cuts his films as he goes) back to Burbank, he sometimes shoots little scenes of himself explaining to Warner Bros. executives that this is, by gosh, a horror movie—even though a lot of it is pretty damned funny.

Landis came to this project in a fairly roundabout way; he had been getting an unrelated vampire movie called *Red Sleep* ready for filming for Warner Bros. and Joel

Silver when the project collapsed. "Warners came to me and offered me this," Landis explains, "and gave me the script. I was very taken with some of the characters, and Michael Wolk's dialogue is wonderful. I said to Warner Bros., [producer] Lee Rich and Michael, 'If this guy lets me make changes with him, I'd be interested.'"

Wolk was perfectly agreeable. He and Landis worked together to produce a script packed with action, interesting characters, humor, horror, romance—and opportunities for cameos. Among others, Sam Raimi, Dario Argento, Tom Savini, Forrest J. Ackerman, and comic art archive publisher Russ Cochran all have their little moments of glory in *Innocent Blood*. So does Johnson's then-wife Linnea Quigley, who appears as a nurse.

"There's this nice girl, you'd like her," Wolk begins as he outlines the plot. "Marie, she's a vampire. She doesn't always feel good about this; sometimes she's full of self-loathing, as a matter of fact. When the movie starts, she's a very hungry girl; she hasn't found anybody *bad* enough to eat. Then she reads that a crime war has started in Pittsburgh, of all places, and the capo of the local Mafia, Sal 'The Shark' Macelli, is battling with rival groups, with people getting killed all over the place. She figures she can take a few Mafia victims; nobody will miss them, and nobody will be suspicious about their demises. She goes out looking for food, and the problem arises when she puts the chomp on Macelli."

When she chows down on a victim, as we see in a scene at the beginning, Marie (played by Anne Parillaud) always takes care to "finish the food." As Landis explains, "Every film, every book, every play, you have to create the rules. Once you create the rules, you follow your mythology. This story follows most of the traditional vampire lore, such as once you've been bitten and killed by a vampire, you can become a vampire but first you have to die. In Michael's mythology, you have to perform a central nervous system disconnect, which essentially means either severing the head, or shooting them in the brain. That guarantees the dead will remain dead.

"Like a werewolf, vampires are victims," Landis continues. "They're cursed, they have a disease. When you see Marie's love scene, she explains how she became a vampire. The movie intimates that there is a code of ethics among these people; you try not to pass it on."

Marie feels partially responsible for revealing, in the course of her actions, that Joe (Anthony LaPaglia), who's been part of Macelli's mob for three years, is actually an undercover cop, and goes to take care of Sal the Shark. Unfortunately, Sal's about to eat a dish of mussels and garlic, and Marie becomes faint. "Whatsamatter," Sal sneers. "Are you a *vegetarian*?" Well, hardly, as he learns a few minutes later when her teeth rip out his throat.

With a dying burst of strength, Sal shoots Marie, and she has to flee before she can kill him dead. So later, a very surprised and frightened Macelli wakes up in a morgue, steals a car (from Forry Ackerman), and flees to Manny, his lawyer, played with great relish by Don Rickles. Manny tries to calm Sal down. "Manny, you smell," says the gangster. Manny nervously offers to douse himself in cologne. "No, you smell *good*." Whoops.

The script is full of this kind of dialogue, horrifying/funny lines that are also precisely in character. It's a difficult feat to accomplish, and yet this is Wolk's first screenplay. "I did a couple of mystery novels," he explains, "one called *The Big Picture* before everything was called *The Big Picture*, and one called *The Beast on Broadway*. Did a couple of plays, one called *Femme Fatale* and one called *Heart Stopper*."

The writer professes to have always had an interest in drama. "I was an English major in college for a couple of months, then I was trying to be a theater major, but they wouldn't let me into the department," he says. "This is my revenge! Nyah hah hah!" He began writing a straight gangster novel, but then remembered a previous rejection, when an editor had said Wolk's submitted novel seemed "very familiar to us."

Wolk decided to try a different approach. "One day, I just thought, 'What if the girl was a vampire?' Suddenly, the character started talking to me: I heard her voice. She became more real as a vampire than just as a person, and it just went off from there. The whole idea of the gangster as vampire, bloodsuckers in society, seemed to fit so well. It really rolled when I made that decision to juxtapose the supernatural with current mobster reality. It became easy to write, and I enjoyed it." Enough so that he realized its filmic possibilities, and took the chance of writing it as a screenplay.

When the script was purchased by Lee Rich Productions, Jack (*The Hidden*) Sholder was originally intended to direct. But he moved on to another project and Landis stepped in, bringing his own casting ideas to the film. "While I thought the lead they had chosen was pretty and capable, I needed someone *extraordinary*," Landis explains. "I was surprised by how many actresses wanted the role, because I told them this has explicit sex"—there is an amazingly hot, but not exploitative, love scene between Marie and Joe—"and it's very violent. I needed someone who could really be horrific, who could make you believe in her supernatural powers and ferocity, but who could then be terribly vulnerable and sympathetic. There have been performances like that throughout film history, the most famous, obviously, being Karloff's Frankenstein Monster. I needed someone who could do that *and* be sexy.

"I mentioned *La Femme Nikita* to the casting director," Landis continues, "where Anne Parillaud's character starts off as this lowlife junkie, shooting a cop in the face—she's hateful. But somewhere in the middle of the picture, your sympathy goes to work. So I thought, what about her? I flew her to LA, and she was enthusiastic.

"I knew if I found a girl sexy enough and beautiful enough, I could make the movie work," the director adds. "I'm very lucky to find a woman who's beautiful and a great actress. She can convey so much information with her face; it's like it's printed across her forehead—you can *read* her thoughts, read her brain." Landis's enthusiasm for Parillaud's performance is genuine: During dailies, and during the screening of the partially complete rough cut for *FANGORIA*, he exclaims over and over, more to himself than to his guests, "Isn't she *great?*"

While Landis was doing his Sylvester Stallone comedy *Oscar*, he'd met with Anthony LaPaglia, who turned down a role in the movie. "The little shit," Landis jokes. "I like him on the screen, I think he has a nice quality." The director cast LaPaglia as Joe, the film's only non-undead lead.

Macelli was the hardest role to fill. Landis made a "short list" of possibilities, including Al Pacino, Armand Assante, and others, including Loggia. "If you're a smart actor," he explains, "you see at once that Macelli is a great part." Being a smart actor, Loggia seized the chance to play a role that could turn out to be one of the great screen villains. Macelli is scary, funny, elegant, crude, vital, and absolutely in your face in every scene. He's slightly based on reality, too. "It was very coincidental and fortunate that the John Gotti trial was going on while we were shooting," Landis points out. "A lot of Macelli's lines are based on things Gotti really said, from the trial transcripts. Bob was uncomfortable at first, though, when I said I wanted him to wear a toupee."

Loggia confirms this, recounting his initial reaction to the wig when Deborah Nadoolman Landis, the film's cos-tumer, first came up with it. "I said, 'Oh, shit! I never wear makeup,'" the actor recalls. "John said, 'We don't want you to look like Bob Loggia, we want you to become the character.' I went with it, reluctantly, and now I'm in their debt. I'm so delighted that they had that concept of this guy's look, because he's so vain! It's a terrific character to attack, a wonderful character."

Once the casting was complete, other production concerns had to be addressed. The script had originally been set in New York, but after scouting some locations, Landis decided to use Pittsburgh. "I needed a town that would have a believable Mafia presence, which turns out to be most northeastern cities. When I came to Pittsburgh, I was unprepared for how cinematic the town is. Did you see when you came out of that tunnel [coming in from the airport]? WHAM!" Landis shouts, spreading his arms.

There is a downside, of course, to shooting in the Northeast in the winter. "Logistically, this has been a very tough movie," producer Leslie Belzberg admits. "We've been in a different location every night, and the weather has been very bad. It's nine and one-half weeks, all nights, shooting from 6 P.M. to 6 A.M., or from 7:00 to 7:00, six days a week. It's very hard on the crew. The schedule changes a lot due to the weather. It's been a very difficult movie to make." Even during the two nights that *FANGORIA* visits the location, the weather ranges from clear to snowy or rainy.

To help put the movie he wanted on-screen, Landis turned once again to cinematographer Mac Ahlberg. The director had "rescued" Ahlberg from the legion of low-budget films he'd been working on since coming to the U.S. (such as *Re-Animator* and numerous other Charles Band productions) with *Oscar*, and their collaboration has continued on *Innocent Blood*. "A good cinematographer should not give his look, but the director's look," Ahlberg says. "Every story finds its own form, its own style; you must have a look that fits the subject. In *Oscar*, it was a certain kind of story, and so had a certain kind of photography: rich, a little dark, but still a comedy. This one is more Gothic, more urban. It's a fantasy, a city that does not really exist."

Bundled up, watching Landis work, Belzberg muses, "One of the nice things about John's movies is that they get shown a lot for a long time. He's interesting and creative and brings a real cachet to all of the stuff he does. He just has a certain kind of insight that he gets to show off. He's incredibly talented at it. But *Innocent Blood*," she says, "is a *very* weird movie."

DIRECTING
CHILDREN OF THE NIGHT

BILL WARREN

"A MOVIE DIRECTOR IS, in many ways, like an orchestra conductor," says director Tony Randel. At the time of this interview, Randel is just putting the finishing touches on his second "symphony" as director. *Children of the Night*, a tale of bloodsuckers overrunning a small American town, is the second project for *FANGORIA*'s production company, and also the director's sophomore effort, his first being *Hellbound: Hellraiser II*.

Randel is taking a break in his apartment in the San Fernando Valley, with a European Godzilla poster on the wall and a hospitable black cat strolling along the back of the couch. Randel is a friendly, average-looking guy, not much given to jokes, but very clear and articulate as he chats about *Children of the Night* and other projects.

He goes along with the sage wisdom of his former boss, Roger Corman, who has often said that if there's a good director of photography, a good production manager, and a good assistant director on board, anyone can direct a movie. "That's absolutely true," Randel agrees. "In many ways, the director is not essential on the set, as strange as that may sound. If you have an experienced DP, he'll see to it that the scenes are covered. The DP has to understand editing, has to understand screen direction—there are all sorts of things he has to know more than anybody. And if you have good actors, they can direct themselves."

So then what, other than having first choice of the donuts at the craft service table and calling "action" and "cut," does a director do? "The director is the person who has to keep sight of everything," Randel explains. "If the director doesn't know what he's doing, you're not going to get a lot of preplanning and preproduction, which means the film's only going to be so-so. Little things you see in movies that work really well are there because they're planned. I do a lot of work on the way scenes go together, flow together—that's all preplanning. A good director also keeps the performances in line and true to what's going on. That makes the difference between a merely watchable film and a good film."

On *Children of the Night*, there was plenty to keep sight of. Working from a script by William Hopkins, revised by producer Christopher Webster. Nicolas Falacci, and Randel himself, in twenty-six days Randel and his crew had to shoot car chases, explosions, vampire monsters, underwater scenes, a truck smashing into a building, gory deaths, FX sequences, and other colorful bits that make up this energetic thriller.

The story takes place in two towns, Allburg and River Junction, about fifty miles apart. "We begin the story with two girls, Lucy [Ami Dolenz] and Cindy [Maya McLaughlin], who are best friends. Cindy used to live in Allburg, but moved away; Lucy has now decided to move away as well, to go to college. Whenever anyone moves away from Allburg, they have to perform a rite of passage, a swim in a submerged crypt below an abandoned church.

"Unbeknownst to them, down in the depths is a vampire"—Czakyr (pronounced "Za-keer"), who came over from Europe many years before—"who has been hiding out underwater with children he captured around fifty years ago. Lucy loses a crucifix off her neck; it lands on Czakyr's head and wakes him up. He bites Cindy, but Lucy escapes and hides out in her grandmother's house, while Cindy becomes a sort of vampire—a young vampire."

A few days later in River Junction, Mark Gardner (Peter DeLuise), a teacher, is approached by an old friend, Father Frank Aldin (Evan MacKenzie), who needs his help. He takes Mark to the home of Cindy and her mother (Karen Black), who are now both vampires—but not the usual sort of coffin-sleeping bloodsuckers. These vampires sleep underwater, and extrude their lungs inside out through their mouths; the balloonlike lungs float on top of the water, enabling the bodies beneath to breathe. (With a grin, Randel admits this is something of a science-fiction-type solution to a fantasy problem.) Mark goes to Allburg, and teams with Lucy and town drunk Matty (Garrett Morris), who quickly sobers up to help combat the results of Czakyr's activities: an entire town of vampires. This involves reel upon reel of action.

"When I look at it now, I can't *believe* how much action there is," marvels Randel. "Where did we *shoot* all this? You have things going on down in the crypt with Czakyr and Lucy and Cindy and the children, and then you have Mark fighting upstairs, and Matty fighting vampires on the street. It's very, very busy, but the pacing worked quite well. In fact, it's one of the easiest productions I've ever been involved with in that respect, how things fit together the way they were supposed to."

Children of the Night is a relatively low-budget film, which precluded a great deal of storyboarding. "On *Hellbound*," Randel notes, "I storyboarded a lot, but I had a storyboard artist with me for several weeks. On this film, only certain effects sequences were storyboarded, because they had to be." Randel feels that it's not necessary to storyboard dramatic scenes. "I come on the set with a shot list. We'll start the scene with a low angle, and push in, etc. As we block the scene, I'll have the DP standing behind me, and as the actors are performing, I'll look back to give him hand signals, so he'll know what shot I'm talking about. Push into close-up here, move it over here for this shot; all this pretty closely follows my shot list. After it's blocked, we shoot it."

"We" in this case includes cinematographer Richard Michalak, who hails from Australia. Randel met him in Yugoslavia in 1989, on a movie then called *Dead-Fall* (now known as *Fatal Skies*); Randel was a consultant, and Michalak was shooting the film. "We got to know each other, and became friends. He showed me a film he had done called *Encounter at Raven's Gate*. I told him the next time I did a film, I'd hire him. Within two weeks. I got this job, and I made good on my promise.

"I'm very happy with him—he'll shoot everything I do. What a lot of people don't realize about the cameraman is that in many ways, he's the most important person on the set. It's not just photographing the image, getting the right exposure and the lighting—it's also the style of the picture, the way the film is covered, the way the camera moves. That is a product of the relationship between a director and a cameraman; the better the relationship is, the better the work will be."

Children of the Night, says Randel, is different from other vampire movies. "I like to consider it a sort of social satire. There are plenty of very creepy horror elements to it, but a lot of it is very satirical—which I guess other vampire films have been as well. But probably because of the stylistic approach, it does differ from any other vampire film I've seen. It's something of a dark comedy, though the humor is *very* dark; you could actually look at the film and not see it at all. I tend to think some of it is pretty funny, but others wouldn't see that." He grins wryly. "I'm not very good at evaluating my own work, especially when I'm right in the middle of it."

The vampires are somewhat more monstrous than in the old Hammer film days, more in keeping with today's *Fright Night* look. The KNB EFX Group did the prosthetics for the standard vampires, as well as the more elaborate makeup on head ghoul Czakyr (played by David Sawyer). KNB also did the floating lungs, and a scene in which Black's character cocoons herself.

The most difficult scenes to shoot were those in the flooded crypt. "The camera was in the water a lot," explains Randel, "a $200,000 camera floating on a plank of wood. We were in a pool in the studio; it was very hot, never got below one hundred degrees in there, with one hundred percent humidity, I'm sure. The other difficult thing is that a vampire movie will, of course, take place mostly at night. We shot in the summer during the shortest nights of the year, in the northern part of the country, so we had only six and one-half hours of darkness. You start seeing the sun coming up at 3:30 in the morning," which always sends vampires scurrying for their coffins.

Randel is very happy with his cast, whom he considers likable and warm. "That's where the quality of the film comes from, really; there's a warmth about the people that really comes across." With the help of Robin Monroe, his casting director, Randel cast the film in two weeks, but "in three or four cases, the very first people I saw were the people I cast," such as Dolenz and DeLuise. "With Garrett Morris, somebody suggested him, and I said perfect, cast him. Karen Black was the same way. I never read anybody else for those two parts."

As with *Mindwarp* and *Severed Ties*, the other two *FANGORIA* flicks, *Children of the Night* was shot at Windsor

Lake Studios in Eagle River, Wisconsin. "It was very nice working up there," says Randel. "I really enjoyed it. Great locations, and I had a very good crew. Windsor Lake was built as a studio, very warehouselike; it's not sound-proofed perfectly, the walls are white when they should be darker, and there are other little problems, but it func-tioned very well. They have actually made six movies there in a year and a half, not bad at all."

Randel worked his way up in the movie business the way many people have: by starting with Roger Corman. He began as an assistant editor on the FX for *Battle Beyond the Stars*, then worked on a variety of films for Corman and others, primarily dealing with the editing of the FX sequences. He coedited a feature, *Space Raiders*— largely because the movie included many clips from other Corman science-fiction adventures, and Randel knew more about the various sequences than anyone.

After Corman sold the company, Randel wound up doing "a lot of film doctoring" at New World, "on *Godzilla 1985*, *Def-Con 4*, *C.H.U.D.*—I took a number of pictures that were marginally releasable and made them really releasable. I was the studio supervisor on *Hellraiser*, and decided I wanted to direct. I asked to do *Hellraiser II*, and they let me do it."

Which naturally raises a question: What did Randel think of the severe cuts made in the gore sequences for the release of *Hellraiser II* in the U.S.?

"I don't like the cuts, not at all," he grumbles. "The mattress scene, which is still one of the best things I've done, doesn't play at all in the rated version. The unrated video version I like very much. I was definitely targeted by the MPAA; it was very difficult to get the movie through. It would be an easy NC-17 now, but even that rating is going to get into trouble."

After *Hellbound*, Randel worked on a couple of projects as a director for hire—*In the Mountains of Madness* and

Alcatraz 2000—which never made it to principal photography. More recently, he did several short films for the Playboy Channel show *Inside Out*. "It's a ten-week series. They hired a different director to come in each week and do a few short films. I shot one eight-minute and two twelve-minute shorts."

Having always wanted to make a science-fiction movie, he's pleased that one of the shorts is set in space, "with miniature work by Bret Mixon. The effects look terrific. It was written by Peter Atkins, too. One of the other shorts is a suspense piece, and one is a dramatic piece. As they are for Playboy, they have little erotic vignettes. But from my standpoint, none of them being horror was very good for me, career-wise. People will see that I'm capable of doing other things, as these turned out very well. I like doing horror, but I want to do other types of films, too."

But in all his future projects, be they horror, science fiction, or anything else, Randel is determined to be the director. As he says, "It's the only job to do on the set."

TO SLEEP WITH A VAMPIRE:
Bloodsuckers on a Budget

MARC SHAPIRO

NINA THE STRIPPER stands apprehensively, her black leather outfit showing off her ample cleavage, in the tumbledown house that serves as a vampire's lair. Unbeknownst to her, the vampire himself—fangs and taloned hands at the ready—crawls on his belly like a snake toward her leg. He rises, hand massaging her thigh as his taloned finger tears a jagged hole in her nylons.

Or at least attempts to.

"Damn it! Cut!" yells director Adam Friedman as he steps out from behind the camera and onto the set. Actor Scott Valentine sits there sheepishly, his finger dangling from a small tear in Charlie Spradling's stocking. *To Sleep with a Vampire* has quite literally run into a snag.

"What's the problem?" laughs Friedman. Valentine indicates a difficulty in getting his nail through the super-strength hose. "Let's try it again," Friedman says. They do. The results are the same, except this time, the nail manages to cut Spradling's leg. Pressured by the film's eighteen-day shooting schedule, the director gets both impatient and ingenious.

"Let's cheat the hole a little bit [director's lingo for opening a tear in the nylon prior to shooting the scene]," he instructs. "If he doesn't get it this time, we'll just film the scene until he starts to go up her leg and then shoot an insert later. Let's not discuss it! Let's just do it!"

To Sleep with a Vampire certainly sounds like a Roger Corman movie. From the looks of the proceedings at Concorde Pictures' Venice, California, studios (with everybody from the assistant director to the grips throwing their two cents in), the film's coming together in typical Corman frat-party fashion. Despite this familiar atmosphere, Corman claims to have received interesting responses when he's described this low-budget entry in the early-90's vampire boom.

"When I mention *To Sleep with a Vampire*, people say it does not sound like the movies we normally do," says Corman, whose announced reentry into horror after a spate of erotic thrillers featured the dinosaur flick *Carnosaur* and *Dracula Rising*, the flip side of *Frankenstein Unbound*. "And they're right. This is a different take on the whole vampire movie cycle. It's definitely not predictable."

According to Corman, *To Sleep with a Vampire* is "a reworking" of Katt Shea Ruben's 1989 horror drama *Dance of the Damned*. The script by Carolyn Gail, based on Ruben and her partner Andy's *Dance* screenplay, focuses on a vampire who's frustrated with his nocturnal lifestyle. Wandering into a strip club, he meets an exotic dancer named Nina, who is contemplating suicide. The vampire convinces Nina to accompany him to his lair, and between the hours of midnight and 6:00 A.M., they have what director Friedman describes as "a strange and wonderful relationship" that mixes the quirkiness of a David Lynch film with elements of Anne Rice's *The Vampire Lestat* and the movie *My Dinner with Andre*. Angst is the order of the day in *To Sleep with a Vampire*. And yes, somebody dies at the end—but it's not quite who you expect.

"This is not a horror film in the classic sense," admits Corman, who concedes that the sudden popularity of vampire films was a consideration in producing *To Sleep with a Vampire*. "It's a love story, a character study, a relationship movie. It contains erotic elements and a take on the fantastic that hasn't been seen often."

Back on the set, Friedman has gotten his "leg shot" in the can and is continuing with the scene's dialogue. At the director's signal, Valentine's bloodsucker continues his odyssey up Spradling's body.

"What are you?" asks the frightened Nina.

"I think you know," replies the vampire as he works his way up and wraps one hand around her throat.

"Let me go. I won't tell."

The vampire backs off and gives Nina a drop-dead look. "Tonight, I have to feed."

So does the cast and crew, and it is during a lunch break that Friedman explains how he and this small-scale bloodsucker epic crossed paths. "I got a call from [Concorde producer] Mike Elliott, who wanted to know if they could send me a script," recalls Friedman, whose writing and directing credits include four segments of the anthology video *Inside Out*. "They needed to speak with me the next day. Well, that night, I played with my band and partied afterward and didn't get home until 2 A.M. I was too beat to read the script, but I set my alarm for 6 A.M. and picked it up then. The first thing I saw was *To Sleep with a Vampire*, a Roger Corman picture, and I thought, 'Oh boy! It's going to be blood and breasts.' Then I started reading, and when the first scene had the vampire walking into a strip club, I thought, 'Oh my God! It's going to be blood, breasts, and strippers!' But I kept reading, and all of a sudden this story took on an aura of something magical and wonderful—a very nontraditional vampire story."

Friedman echoes Corman's assertion that the film is

not in keeping with accepted bloodsucker lore. "The typical vampire stuff with the mirrors and the crosses is not what this film is all about," the director explains. "Nina and the vampire have strong personal and interpersonal arcs, and both go through distinct transformations in their outlooks on life."

A different kind of Corman movie? Perhaps. But it is being made in typical Corman fashion (a week of preparation, eighteen days of shooting, and a budget somewhere between nonexistent and the cost of a six-pack). The lack of time, according to the director, has been the biggest challenge.

"But that was no surprise," he reasons. "I knew going in that I would be faced with having to shoot a lot in a little time. But, working with those restrictions, we've been able to come up with some nifty, subtle camera effects. There are a few neat point-of-view tricks and, in a scene where the vampire sees Nina in the club, we've managed this great image of Nina and the vampire's eyes in the same shot.

"I've also been real lucky to have actors who are used to working quickly and who could play living, feeling people and/or creatures," the director continues. "From an actor's point of view, we've been able to do some rather experimental things. In the scenes where the vampire is angry, I've been directing Scott to play him sad. Not because I wanted people to feel sorry for him, but rather so the audience could understand his frustration and his pain."

Friedman describes his short time with Corman to be "interesting. Roger has his very own set of ideas about how he wants to do things," he points out. "But, within the parameters of what Roger is after, you are left alone to do what you want."

Well, not necessarily, as Valentine reveals during a break in filming. "We are getting some flak from the powers that be around here," the actor confides. "Some people are a little nervous about the direction this film is going, and would like it to be much more of a traditional vampire film."

But Valentine, fresh from another change-of-pace film (at least for him) called *Killer Instinct*, is quite happy with the ambitious nature of this small movie. "My initial reaction was, 'Oh shit, another vampire movie,'" he relates. "But it's more of a love story than anything else, a romance between two characters existing on the outskirts of society. My character is not living in a castle on a hill. He's a creature of the night who wants to finally live a life vicariously through Nina."

Always on the lookout for a challenging role, Valentine found this facet of his character particularly enticing. "There's a certain vulnerability to him," he explains. "I'm playing him more like a fish out of water. He's lived for more than a thousand years, but has never really had the conversation with a real person that he craves now. This is all new for him. In order to get this woman to share her life with him, he has to come across as somewhat endearing rather than frightening. I feel this film will go a long way toward getting the blue-collar-boyfriend-from-*Family Ties* image off my back."

Costar Spradling feels the same way. The actress, known for appearing in various stages of undress in such films as *Meridian* and *Mirror Mirror*, claims footage from *To Sleep with a Vampire* "will definitely be my show tape for casting directors.

"This will change the perception people have of me," she continues. "I've done a lot of films, but this is really the first time I've had a chance to show people I can act. There are only two characters and over seventy minutes of screen time. That's a lot of dialogue and a lot of opportunities to perform."

Spradling has remained a trouper despite the sixteen-hour days and a day-to-night turnaround that has left her nearly sleepless for the past two weeks. But her reward has been a free hand to play Nina her way. "She's a pretty straightforward person," judges Spradling of her character. "Her being a stripper and having a Hollywood attitude was not that hard to act. It's pretty much me. Adam senses that, and has let me do what I think is right for the character."

The actress also shares the convictions of those who feel *To Sleep with a Vampire* will rise above its low-budget pedigree. "It's not the usual B-movie," she affirms. "It's an art film; it's not cheesy. And I know it's going to help me turn the corner and get away from that scream queen tag."

Lunch over, the cast and crew return to a living room set where Nina, seated on a couch, will listen and talk to the vampire as he bemoans his fate.

"OK," calls Friedman. "Let's try a rehearsal."

Valentine, posed near a back wall, turns to face the couch where Spradling sits.

"Six," he hisses in an almost reptilian manner.

"What?" she questions.

"The dawn comes at six," he says, crossing to the couch, eyes ablaze with passion. "What is it like out there?"

"I don't know," Nina stammers.

"Yes you do!" he screams. "Tell me what it's like outside!"

The rehearsals continue. Valentine and Spradling appear to be on top of their material, but the lengthy block of dialogue ultimately begins messing up the timing. Friedman grows increasingly impatient and, at one point, gets into a screaming, profanity-laden argument with Spradling. As they insult each other's ancestry, Friedman picks up a table and slams it to the floor, splintering it. Spradling tells Friedman to perform an impossible sex act upon himself and storms off the set.

Everyone chills out, but when the actress does not return, the director does what anybody on a difficult schedule would do. "Let's shoot the scene and keep the camera on Scott for reaction shots," he says.

A script girl is recruited to feed Valentine his lines, and some of the vampire's memorable acting moments are knocked out while his costar fumes in her dressing room. The script girl's performance, for that matter, is also quite good, and she receives a well-deserved round of applause from the crew.

Spradling eventually returns to the set. But, two minutes later, she and the director are at it again. Good-bye Charlie storms off once more. Paul Faaland, FX coordinator on this picture and a number of previous Concorde films, shrugs his shoulders. "I don't know what to tell you," he laughs. "We've never had any problems until tonight. They must have known you were coming."

Faaland then takes the opportunity to describe his contributions to *To Sleep with a Vampire*, which are subtle and minimal.

"The vampire fangs are clip-ons taken from a mold of Scott's teeth," he explains. "His nails are shaped metal that are glued onto his fingers. There's also some light makeup and prosthetics. This isn't a really gory film, so what we're doing isn't very over-the-top or spectacular. But it does serve the purpose of helping the story along, which is the important thing."

Spradling eventually returns to the set. She and the director iron out their troubles and the scene runs to a satisfactory conclusion.

Later, Friedman concedes that *To Sleep with a Vampire* is the dark horse in the 1992 vampire movie sweepstakes. "We obviously can't compete with the Francis Coppola and John Landis films in terms of scope," he says. "That's why I'm not spending all our money on effects. What I'm attempting to do is take the time to come up with some really wonderful moments: a vampire contemplating his own death; a love story involving a vampire and a human. If this movie comes together the way we're attempting to realize it, we may just surprise a lot of people."

SEX & BLOOD:
Embrace of the Vampire

ANNE MOORE

EMBRACE OF THE VAMPIRE: What would you give for eternal life? This phrase from the movie's promotional material captures the basic fascination of the myth of the vampire. The legends of these undead have been around for thousands of years in almost every culture of the world, and have touched our imagination in the realms of both horror and sensuality. Many recent movies have delved into the provocative and potentially lucrative area of vampire erotica, and *The Nosferatu Diaries: Embrace of the Vampire* is the latest to exploit the sexual fascination with these undying creatures.

Embrace of the Vampire, a New Line Home Video release, has a classic story line: A young man (Martin Kemp) falls for Charlotte (Alyssa Milano), a beautiful young woman who reminds him of his first love, his one true passion ... before he became a vampire. To save his own existence, he must take Charlotte and her pure virgin blood before she gives herself to her boyfriend, Chris (Harrison Pruett); he knows that the two young lovers have made special plans to celebrate Charlotte's upcoming eighteenth birthday. Soon the vampire begins to haunt the girl's dreams and draw her into his world of physical pleasures and unfettered sexuality, setting up a triangle of love and desire where only one of Charlotte's suitors can win.

Scripted by Halle Eaton, Nicole Coady, and Rick Bitzelberger, *Embrace of the Vampire* costars Charlotte Lewis and Oscar-nominee Jennifer Tilly, and marks the feature directorial debut of Anne Goursaud. A French woman who speaks with a lilting accent, Goursaud is primarily known as a top international film editor. Her past experience includes work on such major features as Jack Nicholson's *The Two Jakes*, Bruce Beresford's *Crimes of the Heart*, and Francis Ford Coppola's *One from the Heart*, but her most pertinent credit is as coeditor on Coppola's hit *Bram Stoker's Dracula*.

"I am very fortunate to have worked with such inspired people, and quite wonderful guys," Goursaud says, "but I have always wanted to be a director. I studied art history at the Sorbonne, and then went to film school at Columbia University in New York and got a Master of Fine Arts degree. I went to film school to be a director, but while there I decided to go into editing first. I was broke and in a foreign country and editing seemed to come easily to me, so I thought I'd use that to help make my dream come true. It took a little longer than I thought; I was an editor from 1980 to *Dracula* [in 1992], which was the last film I did."

Goursaud, in fact, had already begun taking the helm before working on Coppola's film. "I was really committed to becoming a director after I edited *The Two Jakes*," she recalls. "After that, I directed a short for Playboy and a few little things. But I went back to editing when Coppola called me. He assured me that *Dracula* would only take a month, and of course it took six or seven. But I don't regret it, because it was my best work and my most successful film. After that, however, I was really intent on directing and just refused editing jobs. I did a *Red Shoe Diaries* with Charlotte Lewis called 'Midnight Bells' for Showtime, and that led to *Embrace of the Vampire.*"

Goursaud was taken by the script's focus on the erotic aspects of vampirism as opposed to the usual blood and gore. She credits her new attitude and outlook to her old friend and boss, Coppola. "It is from him that I understood what a vampire story really is," she reveals. "Personally, I never had any interest in vampire stories. Maybe because I grew up in France, and it's not a country which is big on vampires. It's more German or English—long winters—a Gothic sort of setting for vampire tales. When Coppola asked me to come on *Dracula*, I was very surprised that he would think of me for it. Until, of course, I read the book and then the script, and I saw I was completely perfect for it. I realized that the vampire story is really about female sexuality.

"I was fascinated by the story and I had the greatest time doing it," Goursaud continues. "Vampire stories are about female passion, which is something that society has condemned and has to control. Female sexuality has never been celebrated to this degree in this type of movie.

"In Bram Stoker's book, he talks about it, but in the end he has the hunters bring Mina back to the fold. I interpret it as conventional bourgeois mentality winning and a woman's sexuality becoming trapped in the process. She goes back to the traditional role of mother and wife. In Coppola's *Dracula* we didn't finish it like that. Mina stays with Dracula, and we never see her go back. They actually shot the same [ending] as in the book, but we changed it in the editing. We left Mina with Dracula, which I think is essential."

What is also necessary in this kind of love story is the overt attraction and sexual tension between the two lovers—in this case the vampire and his innocent victim.

The audience must believe in the fantasy world of the undead and the power of the vampire, or the entire concept is lost. The story's erotic elements only make it more intriguing and fascinating, but often more difficult to fulfill. Goursaud, however, believes *Embrace* delivers all of these elements. "I am very proud of it," she says. "We shot it in fourteen days for $800,000, and that was very hard. It's a very visual film, and I think we all did a great job in terms of pulling off an intelligent movie that really works without compromising too much. The film has sold worldwide and gotten a very good response.

"New Line picked it up before it was even finished," she reveals. "When I went in for an interview for *Lily* [the sequel to *Poison Ivy* she was directing at the time of this interview], they wanted to see the feature, which I was in the process of editing. So I had to show them an unfinished film, and they bought it right then. The response has been quite good. Alyssa Milano is getting some flak [for her explicitly sexual scenes], but I believe it will be good for her. Her acting shows a great deal of range, and it took a lot of courage. She made it completely believable."

Goursaud laughs in appreciation as she continues. "I'm very fortunate; I love my job," she says. "I try to create a crew and a cast of people who really have a kinship and work to keep the team going. Alyssa is in both movies [*Embrace* and *Lily*], and she is a dream come true for a director. She is a complete professional; she's technically superior as an actress and getting better all the time. She is going to be a big star, I am sure of that."

Milano had to make a tough decision when she agreed to do *Embrace of the Vampire*. The sexually explicit scenes could have backfired on her, but she was determined to change her wholesome TV image as the star of the sitcom *Who's the Boss?* She knew she had to take a chance, and with the right project, Milano was willing to experiment with almost anything. "That is why she did the film," the director says. "*Embrace of the Vampire* is very erotic and daring, and she really wanted to change her image. She is immensely talented, and I really believe in her."

Milano isn't the only one for whom Goursaud has such high praise. She also credits her hardworking crew and cast, especially British actor Kemp as the lead blood-sucker. "He was just so perfect, so professional," she praises. "You know how those Brits are. They come to work and they just do it.

"Kemp was cast from London, so I had very little time to work with him," she continues. "He arrived on the set Tuesday from England and he was working on Wednesday. We were already working nights, so he was in makeup at about midnight and he finally came to work at about 6 A.M. The scene called for him to lick blood off of a door while Charlotte was on the other side; it was the remains of another girl he had just killed. Kemp and I didn't know each other, and we had barely spoken for an hour at that point. It was 6 A.M. and I explained the scene to him, how he had to lick the blood off of the door and that it had to be very erotic. And he just did it—brilliantly. Then he went to bed and didn't work for another two days. You love those kinds of people, so professional."

Kemp and Milano weren't the only ones who trusted the soft-spoken director and were talked into doing unusual things. Goursaud ended up working with over fifty college-age extras for a very unusual "party" scene. "In *Embrace* we have a big orgy scene," she explains, "where I used fifty local young people who had never been in a movie and got them all to do what was required of them. It was fun and very easy. It was kind of a high point for me, as a director, to work with fifty people in various stages of undress; they were partially disrobed in all sorts of situations, but not naked. I didn't want it to be pornographic, just erotic.

"I gave them a speech, which I really believed, that the scene was like a Renaissance painting where we were trying to create beautiful pictures," she continues. "And we did. They all went with it, all of these erotic tableaux that we invented. It was astonishing, all of the trust they had and all of the fun they were having. All beautiful and sensual. That was quite an accomplishment."

A good deal of the fourteen-day shoot was spent in Faribault, Minnesota, at a former military school called Shattucks. (The institution's main claim to fame, before *Embrace* was filmed there, was that Marlon Brando is a former student.) Working under such adverse circumstances in strange situations with a limited budget and schedule doesn't always make for a good movie, but *Embrace of the Vampire* has proven to be an exception, with Goursaud's background as an art student evident in the strong visuals.

The director notes that working on an inexpensive movie led her to strive to accomplish more for her money. "With any low-budget film, you have to add things and try to elevate them," she says. "*Embrace* has an element of being a thriller and it is erotic, but it is a lot more than that. It's not pornography. It is quite beautiful, not graphic but reaching an erotic mood without going overboard. The important thing is to find and develop interesting characters in a world where you can create fascinating visuals."

Goursaud continued this approach with *Lily*, which, like *Embrace*, is less oriented towards visceral thrills than sexuality. The film focuses on the title character (Milano), who finds the diary of Ivy (played by Drew Barrymore in the original *Poison Ivy*) and goes on a journey of sexual awakening. "It's about coming of age as an artist and as a woman, so it has an erotic content as well," Goursaud says. "The producers [Marilyn Vance and Alan Mruvka of The Ministry of Film] wanted to do an erotic thriller and

I had other things in mind, but they proposed this one to me. It's about sexual exploration, and I could find enough themes in it to connect with."

It is those themes that she hopes she has successfully brought out in her 1995 release. "Vampire stories are great to direct, because they are not real and so you have a lot of leeway to create interesting concepts," she concludes. "I am a very visual director, and it is important to me to use images to tell the story and create a whole visual world. I don't see myself directing something that is word-driven. I would not do well in television. I want to create a world of imagination, which I like to live in while I'm making the movie. It's a lot of fun. It beats editing and just paying the bills."

FANGS OVER FRANCE:
The Two Vampire Orphans

PETER BLUMENSTOCK

WHAT A BIZARRE and beautiful place this is!" murmurs the man with the worn-out, dirty coat, preparing for his cameo appearance as a gravedigger while wandering dreamily amongst the old, moss-covered gravestones and rusty iron crosses of the little cemetery of Epigny Champlatreux outside of Paris. One would think that after making such films as *The Nude Vampire*, *Requiem for a Vampire*, and *Living Dead Girl*, famed French director Jean Rollin has spent enough of his lifetime in places like this to get used to their haunting otherworldliness.

Yet this enigmatic atmosphere is obviously as fascinating for him as for anybody else on the set of *Les Deux Orphelines Vampires* (*The Two Vampire Orphans*), Rollin's eagerly awaited return to filmmaking in general and vampire cinema in particular.

Based on his best-selling five-book series, published in France by Fleuve Noir (the titles are *Les Deux Orphelines Vampires*, *Anissa*, *Les Voyageuses*, *Les Pillardes* and *Les Incendiaires*) with an American edition of the first published by Redemption USA, Rollin's latest effort combines the most beautiful elements of all five novels, centering on the tragic adventures of the two blind orphans Henriette and Louise, who regain their vision at night and become vampires, prowling around and meeting other strange creatures of the darkness who share their solitude. "It's a new, logical approach to vampirism," Rollin explains. "The two vampire girls are not asleep and hiding during daylight, they are just blind and therefore helpless.

"The success of the books and the forthcoming English edition helped us a lot with financing this film," continues the director, who also wrote the screenplay and is producing the $1-million project for his own company, Les Films ABC. "The budget may sound like peanuts in comparison to what films usually cost nowadays, but for my type of cinema it is more than decent. This film is completely independent—no money from big companies or television involved, which means we're taking a lot of risks, but it also guarantees the creative freedom I need."

And risks are something Rollin has surely gotten used to over the years. For every one of his films that proved to be successful at the box office, the next one usually failed miserably because it was too personal and ambitious to please a large audience. Often mistreated by French critics and foreign distributors, who gave his films the most awkward new titles to attract the raincoat crowd and ruined the dialogue with substandard dubbing, Rollin's work was misunderstood and often written off as unimportant exploitation fare with pretentious art-house overtones. When his first film, the surreal *Le Viol du Vampire* (*The Rape of the Vampire*), was first screened in Paris during the student riots in 1968, the unprepared audience went berserk and threw garbage at the screen, and Rollin was seriously afraid they would lynch him afterward.

Yet there is hardly any other director who has developed such a strong, dedicated following over the years.

His reputation has steadily grown, and now more than ever, magazines and video companies all over the world are interested. Even the French Cinematheque dedicated an evening to the director and his debut feature, and while for many years most of his movies had only been available on bootleg tapes in the U.S., Thomas Weisser's Video Search of Miami recognized their potential and recently bought the American rights to many of them.

It is Rollin's unique style, blending the joys of delicious eroticism with artful, surreal images, poetic dialogue and pulp storytelling, that has left audiences either entranced or annoyed. "It's curious, but people are starting to get tired of the common formulas," he says. "They're looking for something unconventional. I am glad about this deal with Video Search, because it opens the American market for French horror cinema. They will probably release 12 of my films in all. A couple of years ago, nobody cared one bit and I seriously thought about abandoning cinema forever and focusing solely on writing my novels." Times were hard, and rumors even had it that Rollin was forced to make a living as a taxi driver, a notion he dismisses with a laugh.

While his 1991 made-for-TV film *Perdues dans New York* (*Lost in New York*) was rejected by every French TV station and eventually distributed on video by Rollin himself, *Killing Car*, a sinister tale about a woman who violently avenges her lover, shot by Rollin three years ago, is still in limbo. "*Perdues dans New York* is a film which I basically made just for myself," he says. "I got very sick and it was supposed to be some sort of testament. A producer asked me if I could shoot some stock footage of New York for him. I agreed, and while I was there, I met some film people I knew, and we thought we could turn it into a little movie. It's very much improvised and very personal, full of homages and quotations from my other films. *Killing Car* was just a joke! It cost next to nothing. I made it just for fun, in order to be behind a camera again and to keep the spirit alive.

"This project is something completely different," Rollin says of *The Two Vampire Orphans*. He then steps in front of the camera to dig a grave for a "dead" dog with a horrible neck wound, caused by the two orphans during one of their nightly trips. The dog has been anesthetized by a veterinarian under the worried eyes of its owner, Philippe d'Aram, the composer of the film's soundtrack, who previously worked with Rollin on *Fascination, Living Dead Girl,* and *Perdues dans New York.*

"I know that Jean wants a lot of music for this film, about twenty-three tracks running almost an hour," he says while watching his narcotized "best friend" making his screen debut without even knowing it. "The whole film will be full of music underlining the images. It'll be a strange mixture of strings and synthesizer, classical but also very modern and powerful, just like Jean's screenplay."

"I know that I am an outsider, even within the boundaries of the genre," Rollin continues after his acting job is done, "but it's a deliberate choice. It's a pity that there are hardly any directors left who see the low-budget genre film as an opportunity to make something of interest and not just exploitation. I make my films like that because they represent myself, my love for a certain type of cinema. And the people I work with share the same kind of love, the same enthusiasm. We all grew up with this affection for movies and have been carrying it with us all our lives. That's what makes us tick. It's like a family. I know them and have been working with them for decades."

And they need this enthusiasm badly. With one week of shooting in New York behind them, they are still in for three more weeks of hard work in Paris, dealing with rain, mud, cold nights, and the obstacle of shooting with direct sound. The crew consists of only thirty-seven people, including the cast, and the family atmosphere is quite obvious on the set.

Some of the performers are also active behind the camera, such as Natalie Perrey, who previously worked with Rollin on *Levres de Sang (Lips of Blood)* and *Perdues dans New York*. Aside from playing the Mother Superior of the film's orphanage, which is run by restrictive nuns who are more than shocked to find out about the mysterious goings-on in the old building, she is also responsible for the film's continuity. Jean-Noël Delamarre, Rollin's first assistant, had a brief appearance as a bank robber in the opening scenes of *Requiem for a Vampire* (a.k.a. *Caged Virgins*, among other inappropriate retitlings). There's also Sam Selsky, the legendary producer, who gave Rollin his very first shot in 1968 when he produced *Le Viol du Vampire*, and Lionel Wallmann, who has been working with Rollin on the production side since the early seventies.

Night has fallen over the little cemetery, and Rollin is back behind the camera checking the setup in front of a huge iron gate, where the film's two leading ladies are about to shoot their first scene of the night. Dressed in transparent nightgowns, their pale faces marked by little rivers of blood dripping from their lips, Isabelle Teboul and Alexandra Pic appear on the scene. One blonde, one dark-haired, both young women are a feast for the eyes, and their remarkable acting talent and modest nature suggest major careers that have only just begun; *The Two Vampire Orphans* marks the feature debuts of both actresses after appearances in short films and on stage.

"It all started with an ad in a newspaper," Pic mumbles, obviously having a hard time speaking with the fangs in her mouth. "A film production was looking for two young actresses for a vampire film. I answered and it turned out to be Jean. I'm glad they chose me." Teboul wholeheartedly agrees with her fellow bloodsucker. "I really enjoy being here." She smiles, exposing her deadly teeth to her interviewer. "It's not always easy, as we have lots of difficult lines, full of passion and emotional impact, but the friendly atmosphere on the set really helps. It gives me a lot of confidence and allows me to concentrate on my role." The girls don't have much time for further conversation; they'll be busy all night, dancing among the gravestones and delivering long dialogue passages again and again, until the perfectionist director is finally pleased with the interpretation of his text.

Their costars include Brigitte Lahaie, with whom Rollin has worked on *Fascination*, *La Nuit des Traquees* and *Les Raisins de la Mort*, playing a woman looking for a taxi who eventually falls prey to the two bloodthirsty orphans. Also in the cast are American model Martin Snaric and Tina Aumont, the famous *enfant terrible* of European cinema in the seventies.

One new face on the set is director of photography Norbert Marfaing-Sintès. "I met Jean on *Perdues dans New York* in 1990," explains Marfaing-Sintès. "When principal shooting had been finished, he realized that some dialogue scenes with Natalie Perrey were still missing, but the regular director of photography, Max Monteillet, was already busy somewhere else. I'd done several short films with Natalie before, so she remembered me and gave me a call. I was a nobody at that time, but Jean gave me a chance. Now it's my turn to say thank you. He called and I came." Today, after five years and with more than twenty-two feature films, several television series, and countless commercials to his credit, Marfaing-Sintès is one of the hottest French cameramen around, and he saw the opportunity to work with Rollin on this project as a true challenge to his talent and abilities.

"I know that we're operating with a shoestring budget here," he says, "but that can be made into an advantage. We have to be inventive; it's real craftsmanship that is required. It's work at the core of the medium in a very positive sense, a very human, emotional process. I am sure we will be able to overcome our financial obstacles. Everybody here is so dedicated. Nobody really works for the money; they work for Jean and for the film."

Watching Marfaing-Sintès at work with the little Arriflex camera is a real treat, as he is lighting his compositions like a painter uses a brush, evoking the wildest emotions. Soon the little cemetery shines with an otherworldly appearance, its many crosses and statues illuminated for the strange and macabre ballet that is about to take place. "For me, this job basically means a lot of hard work," he sighs. "I am not only the director of photography, but also the camera operator, so I have twice as many things to take care of. And that's a lot! Jean is a very visual artist. His films are like poems; the images and the decor are the tools with which he tries to haunt the audience.

"It's important to understand the nature of Jean's filmmaking, his attitude," Marfaing-Sintès continues. "One has to open one's eyes and learn to see again. He has a very strong vision and a unique style which he has developed over the past twenty years, and that has to be maintained. On the other hand, I try to include some new, fresh things. This is one of the most beautiful scripts I have ever read, wild and romantic, with dialogue very much reminiscent of classical French literature. Jean has had a very hard time in recent years, and I want this film to be his triumph—I want him to finally get the recognition he deserves. No matter how hard I have to work on it."

With locations ranging from an old, abandoned church, a huge quarry and a circus to the famous Père LaChaise cemetery, where hundreds of tourists visit Jim Morrison's grave every week (and in which Rollin got permission to film for the very first time), there is no doubt that the film will be visually striking. The most impressive site, however, is a gigantic French castle which Rollin's production company has rented from its owners to transform into the Orphanage of Glycines. In more than 150 rooms—a large number of them empty because the owners can't afford to keep the building and the interiors in shape, while others are stuffed with sculptures, old paintings, and ancient furniture—the dreams of every lover of Gothic atmosphere come true. The walls are breathing with history and tradition.

It is within this building on another day that the deaths of two of Henriette and Louise's fellow inmates are being shot in a small chamber under the attic that's been dressed up as the laundry room. The two vampires discover the girls smoking a forbidden cigarette there. The end of the scene is mayhem; with their necks bitten through, the two girls are lying on the knees of their killers, whose mouths are dripping blood, and the room is virtually covered with the precious life liquid. One of the victims is Sandrine Toquet, who appeared in Rollin's ultragory *Living Dead Girl*, the director's most popular film to date (it even earned him the Audience Prize at the Italian Fantafestival). "There will be some nice special effects in this movie, created by Maryvonne Harrouet," Rollin says. "We have a winged vampire lady, who guides the two orphans into a catacomb where she has her resting place in a coffin, some neck wounds, and a wolf woman with badly wounded breasts. However, this is not a gore film. If you have seen some of my other movies, you know that I am not really interested in that.

"*The Two Vampire Orphans* is something of an alternative to today's horror cinema," he continues. "It's really serious, and people who are fed up with childish monsters and stupid stories trying to cash in on a successful film will hopefully recognize its qualities and the effort we're investing in every single detail. My partner, Lionel

Wallmann, is currently trying to make some arrangements with American distributors, so I have high hopes that it will get a proper release in the U.S."

What is probably best described as a postromantic horror fairy tale for adults could also become a new starting point for Rollin's career. "I really think we have a chance to make a good, timeless film here, one that will not just attract admirers of Jean's previous work," says Wallmann, who usually resides in Miami with his production company Nordia Film. "There is also another project for Jean which I am working on right now in America," he continues enthusiastically. "It's called *Miami Vampire*, based on a treatment I wrote, and a lot of people are really interested in putting some money into it. What can I say? The future looks bright, and we can only trust that the audience is willing to give small, independent films a chance again. We have done everything possible to turn *The Two Vampire Orphans* into a great movie everybody involved can be proud of, be sure of that. Now it's up to the audience to make their decision. Jean and I, we count on you people."

STEPHEN KING'S *SALEM'S LOT*— The Miniseries

SUSAN CASEY

"VAMPIRES DON'T EXIST. It's a wholly unbelievable concept," admits *Salem's Lot* producer Richard Kobritz, "but what if you have an insulated and secure eastern hamlet, and things start to happen . . . two children die, then two men. And a young writer senses that something evil is behind it all."

In a nutshell, that is the plot of the four-hour television adaptation of Stephen King's best-selling novel, produced by Kobritz with director Tobe Hooper, best known for his sensational work on his first feature film, *The Texas Chainsaw Massacre*. Set in a small town in Maine, the vampire tale is all the more chilling because of its setting—not in some faraway Transylvanian castle, but in a neighborhood that might just as easily be the one that you or I live in.

David Soul, Hutch of *Starsky and Hutch*, plays the part of Ben Mears, a writer who grew up in the sleepy town of Jerusalem's Lot. In the opening scenes of the teleplay, Mears returns to the town of his birth in order to clear his mind of his chilling childhood memories of the ancient Marsten House.

When Soul first arrived in Ferndale, California—the town chosen for location shooting because of its "New England" look—the first thing he did was drive to the hill that is the site of the three-story set construction of the Marsten House, overlooking the entire town of Ferndale.

"Small towns have haunted houses—and they're considered a joke," muses Soul in his dressing room outside the imposing Marsten House set. "Jerusalem's Lot should not be different from any other town. When things start to happen and you've got this crazy writer running around saying, 'It's an evil house, it's an evil house!'—the townspeople won't explain things in terms of the house. They'll think, maybe this guy has something to do with the missing people."

The focal point of the evil doings in both the novel and the TV miniseries is the Marsten House, a crumbling Gothic structure that's been empty for years since owner Hubie Marsten murdered his wife, then took his own life, long ago. It's the place that young Susan (Bonnie Bedelia) and Mark (Lance Kerwin) investigate in order to solve the riddle of the mysterious deaths. And it is the den of Barlow, the vampire.

Though over twenty locations in Ferndale were used practically "as is" in duplicating scenes from the King novel, no house was found that captured the mood or appearance of the Marsten House. So art director Mort Rabinowitz tackled the job of constructing a three-story Gothic facade over an already-existing two-story house that overlooks Ferndale just as the Marsten House overlooks the town of Salem's Lot.

More than $80,000 was spent on set construction for the Marsten House. Atmosphere was created by shingled sideboard, a roof painted to look shingled, turrets, pillars, promenade steps and synthetic rocklike sheets for the outside of the cellar area. Weeds from around the existing house were replanted at the base of the facade. Paint that immediately aged when applied over wet lacquer, gave the house the appearance of permanence. (So convincing was it that one Ferndale resident slammed on his brakes when driving by and said in amazement to one of the construction workers, "I can't believe this. I've lived here for twenty-five years and I've never noticed this house before.")

While the effect of the facade set against a grove of pine trees is weathered, it is not as disheveled as the house in the novel. But it is imposing, as imposing as its resident, R.T. Straker (James Mason), who in the miniseries is always meticulously dressed in a black or gray suit and is often seen stepping out of his shiny black Cadillac. Kobritz explains the change in the appearance of the house in terms of Straker: "Straker is the human go-between. The shark doesn't choose its own direction, there is a fish that leads it. Straker leads the way; Barlow does the thinking. Straker is his liaison to the world.

"Straker is pristine like the outside of the house. Inside is a chamber of horrors, representing Straker's inner self. The house is beyond your wildest nightmare; everything rotten, no furniture. Everything falling apart.

"How could a man live in absolute decay?" Kobritz asks dramatically as we sit on the Warner Bros. lot.

And absolute decay is a good way to describe the inside of the house, which is even more horrid than the one in the book. Thick, spongy, slimy greenish walls line dark corridors of the sets constructed on the soundstage at Warner Bros. A mantlepiece is almost unrecognizable for the slimy mass that envelops it.

"For the inside of the house," says Rabinowitz enthusiastically, "we were reaching for something so bizarre and disgusting that it's like nothing anyone could imagine. Moss and lichen and algae grow from the walls. Creating it was like creating a painting underground. We kept adding glazes and tremendous amounts of plaster—eight or nine layers—for the texture. Before shooting I wet down the entire set so it was dripping damp and dank. The green fungus seems to fester and ooze, which gives it a sense of evil itself. The root cellar, where Barlow makes his home, is like one large grave."

Further enhancing the mood are the techniques of director of photography Jules Brenner, whose other credits include *Helter Skelter* and *The Glass House*. He chose to light interior scenes in a low-key manner with more black areas than light. "It's a movie," he points out while setting up the lighting for the scene at the mortuary, "where anything can crawl out of the shadows at any time. The more shadows, the more the presence of evil. Tobe Hooper and I worked together to develop that image."

One scene calling for a particularly surreal atmosphere involved the use of a special effect that proved quite effective despite its basic simplicity. In the film, one of the supporting vampires (a townsperson victimized by Barlow) appears at a window, and then disappears in a mist when one of the human characters raises a cross to the glass. In filming the scene, the vampire, in a body harness suspended from a crane, was moved toward the window as smoke spurted from plastic tubing concealed in his clothing. In the finished film, the footage runs backwards, giving the impression that the vampire slowly drifts away to be mysteriously enveloped by the mists.

In creating the look for Barlow, Kobritz first considered the recent proliferation of vampire "types." "We didn't want a sensual vampire, or one like Lugosi or George Hamilton's," says the producer. "We wanted something like the Nosferatu of Murnau's 1922 film where the vampire was walking death, ugliness incarnate, a skull that moved and was alive."

"Creating the image of the vampire was a little like a fishing expedition," admits makeup man Jack Young, who in his many years as a makeup artist has worked on films from *The Wizard of Oz* to *Apocalypse Now*. "I changed the model at least six times," he says, displaying a small card with Polaroid shots of each of the six renditions in his lab on the Warner lot. "We tried him with light pink on his face, but he looked phony, burlesque. We finally came up with the light gray, which is dead and bloodless.

"Reggie Nalder [who plays Barlow] has such a wonderful face; he always plays some pretty grim parts, so we just put ears on him, made him bald, put gray horrible makeup on him, and used his own lips," Young continues. "For the teeth I made impressions of his, created a false set, and then aged them by airbrushing shadows on them. They look yellow and like they have cavities."

Barlow's eerie eyes are created by contact lenses almost like half a Ping-Pong ball—light green in color with red veins—that fit over the eye and can only be worn for fifteen minutes at a time. The pupils reflect, as do the eyes of the other vampire characters in the film, an effect created by yellow screenlike contact lenses. "They spark when the light hits them," says Young deviously. "It looks awful, like they have searchlights coming out of their eyes."

In the scene near the movie's end, when Mears is driving the stake through Barlow's heart, Barlow's clawlike hand flies up and grabs Ben's wrist. "For the claws," says Young, "I made a composite you can form with your hands. It's like a clay you can bake, but it has flex. It wasn't originally made for nails, but that's what I used it for. It's all part of the attempt to get away from the stereotype Dracula."

As Ben continues to drive the stake in, Barlow's head starts to rise from the coffin to meet Ben's. Then suddenly the flesh seems to fall from the head, revealing a ghostlike skull. "I had to make the head about four or five times to get it to come out right," the makeup man admits. The final one is hand-carved out of plaster, then covered with a composition of wax that would sag, not drip. "I got the skin to appear to fall away by turning a heat gun on the completed portrait head," Young adds. "When I was testing it I thought I had it just about right, so I called in the producer and a few others. As I turned the heat on one of the heads, the wax was sagging just like I wanted it to; then the heat activated the fire alarm sprinkler system and we all got drenched."

In terms of suspense, makeup, FX, and camera movement are all secondary to the basic story of *Salem's Lot*, yet transferring the internal fear of the novel to the screen was no small task. "Stephen King is the master of American horror," says Kobritz. "Too many people rip the genre off cheaply. That degrades it. Only with him do you realize how manipulative it can be on an emotional level. Yet how do you externalize the story and create the sense that the walls are closing in? A lot of writers tried. We had four versions of the teleplay before we went with the one by Paul [*Carrie*] Monash.

"Barlow is seen only three times in the movie; a big change [from the book], but we don't want people guessing at makeup techniques," Robritz continues. "Also unlike the book, he's found at the Marsten House. We felt that was imperative, that he not be found in someone else's cellar. And he has only one line: 'Let me go.' That's a big change, but since I don't know what a vampire sounds like, it would destroy some of his credibility to have him speak any more."

The real tension and fear of *Salem's Lot* is in the confrontation of characters—particularly the scene between Mears and the vampire. To many, Mears is the hero—or so it seems. He is the one who exposes Straker; he drives the stake through Barlow's heart. But in his effort to assume and understand the character of Ben Mears, Soul sees it differently. "He is a hero in the sense that he's the protagonist. He may be a hero in terms of his vulnerability, but what I see is a man who goes out of his mind, who becomes a total neurotic mess. He knows what's happening and couldn't leave town like the others did. He's hooked, and the last bit of sanity he has is to maintain some semblance of order. I could play it straight when he's gathering the hawthorn and the crucifixes, but it's not like that at all; he's half-mad. He's a victim already, and he hasn't even looked in the vampire's eyes. This man's life falls apart as he drives the stake through the vampire's heart."

With the efforts of the entire crew and cast directed at creating terrifying scenes, one might wonder if some of the atmosphere of fear and evil affects them. Soul confesses that the sense of evil reminds him of faith-healing experiences of his youth. Female lead Bedelia admits to chilling feelings about getting bit. Several crew members confess to nightmarish dreams. But, after all, things are relative. Makeup man Young gets a glint in his eyes while talking about the ominous yellow eyes and the weathered teeth. "They're wonderful," he claims. And producer Kobritz concludes, "My attitude towards this kind of entertainment is that it's fun. The audience likes to scream."

ILLUMINATING *DARK SHADOWS*

R O B E R T   P E G G

MOVIE AND TV HORROR FANS always like to compare favorites: Who was the scarier Dracula—Bela Lugosi or Christopher Lee? Which was funnier—*The Addams Family* or *The Munsters*? Who was the best Scrooge—Alastair Sim or Mr. Magoo? Now, *Dark Shadows* fans have their own dilemma: Who do they prefer as that charming vampire Barnabas Collins—the original, Jonathan Frid, or the more recent Ben Cross?

In all fairness, that's a question for minds greater than ours. Let's just say that both actors brought their own unique interpretations to the role, and both managed to humanize the concept of the vampire on television. They also both made their own indelible marks on pop culture in the process—the middle-aged Frid became a teen idol and appeared on bubble-gum cards and lunch boxes; the forty-four-year-old Cross's Barnabas was also hyped as a sex symbol and graces Innovation's lushly romantic *Dark Shadows* comic book. For what greater celebrity could either man ask?

In 1991, when *Dark Shadows* creator/producer Dan Curtis announced plans to resurrect his original creation with an all-new cast for NBC prime time, fans wondered if Curtis would tamper with Frid's original concept of the character and if the show would resemble the _Dark Shadows_ they ran home from school to watch twenty-five years before. Not to worry: When fans tuned in to the two-hour pilot movie, they were reassured to see that Curtis hadn't tampered with anything. Indeed, he had lifted entire scenes and whole chunks of dialogue from the original soap and the _House of Dark Shadows_ film.

But what _was_ different was Cross's contribution to the new series. To his credit, he brought a fresh and original interpretation to the Barnabas role, keeping the show from becoming a mere remake. And like Frid, he alone _carried_ the entire series.

Whereas Frid's Barnabas was tragic and sympathetic, Cross's creation was intense and arrogant; where Frid's vampire was repressed, looking as guilty and secretive as a closet junkie or alcoholic, Cross's was sensuous and animalistic, taking a savage delight in the act of sucking blood.

Today, Cross says he deliberately took a different approach to the character simply because that was his job as an actor. "I'm an interpreter," he claims. "Someone else writes the script, someone else costumes me, and I interpret that role. I'm like a conductor or a musician who is playing someone else's notes. I don't think it makes me a pure artist. It's a job, it's a skill—it's more artifice than art."

He adds that he deliberately chose not to watch any of the old episodes to see how Frid played Barnabas. "Some people have asked why I didn't just carry on with Jonathan's interpretation, and I have to laugh because, of course, I'm _not_ Jonathan," Cross explains. "I understand what he did with the part, and that's all fine and good, but if you put us together, and we both played Hamlet, we'd give completely different interpretations.

"But no, I didn't look at any of the old episodes," he

continues. "I decided it would be counterproductive, in a sense. After all, it was a daytime half-hour black-and-white soap, and the new project was a one-hour show in color with plenty of production values. It was a much more high-gloss sort of thing. It was to be a Gothic *romance*. We were making a supernatural drama, not a soap.

"A lot of people who were avid fans of the original were possibly disappointed that I had perhaps not been faithful to the original—I've no idea, and really, that's not my concern. But Dan Curtis certainly had definite ideas about the character. For instance, he insisted that Barnabas not have a sense of humor. Now, I understand that he can't be cute or flip, and I definitely wouldn't have camped him up. But I would have liked to see some scenes of Barnabas coming to grips with the twentieth century—maybe learning how to drive. You know, there's a difference between observing him in a humorous situation and actually seeing him smile or wink into the camera."

Had Curtis acquiesced to Cross's desires, it wouldn't have been the actor's first time playing a vampire in a funny vein. His introduction to bloodsucker roles was in the 1989 made-for-cable comedy *Nightlife*. "Now *that* was camp," recalls Cross. "It was pure, high camp, and I really liked it—plus the fact that it took me to Mexico for the first time, which I really enjoyed."

His only previous venture into the world of the supernatural was in 1988's *The Unholy*. When the film is mentioned, Cross laughs in an ironic and self-deprecating way, although there was nothing intentionally funny about the movie. "I'll tell you about that film: The director, Camilo Vila, is a very good friend of mine," he states. "What happened was that the film was taken away from him and there were two different endings shot by two special effects companies, neither of which actually served the film. I think everyone involved would agree on that.

"In hindsight, Camilo later realized that the ultimate temptation would actually have been to give me, as the priest, the chance to liberate the tortured souls in hell if I would give myself over. If you remember, the floors of the church open up and you can see into hell, so the ultimate temptation would have simply been for me to give in and release those people from hell to go to heaven. That should have been the climax of the movie, but no one knew it at the time, and that's why we had little dwarves in rubber suits crucifying me to the altar, and so forth."

For better or worse, Cross's part in *The Unholy* is consistent with the pattern of roles he has played over the years. Superficially, they may seem like a diverse group—an Olympic runner in the Oscar-winning *Chariots of Fire*, a jewel thief in the caper film *Diamond Fleece*, and the TV-movie *Steal the Sky*, where he played an Iraqi pilot opposite Mariel Hemingway as a femme-fatale Israeli spy.

But one thing his characters have in common is that they are obsessives with a tendency toward moral ambiguity. In *The Unholy*, he's a priest fighting fleshly and other temptations; in *Chariots*, he's driven to win a gold medal for running, yet admits he's unsure of what he's actually pursuing; and in *Dark Shadows*, he's a vampire who loathes what he has become and yet knows he has no choice but to kill in order to live.

This duality is what Cross claims he looks for in a character. "The basis of all good drama is some kind of conflict. All good stories have a dilemma, whether it's moral or sexual or whatever," he allows. "And I find that I'm attracted to a script because the story and the character will have all that, and then you say, 'OK, there are choices to be made.'"

Cross found all sorts of conflicts—moral and sexual— to work on in *Dark Shadows*. "I tried to make Barnabas as interesting and complex as I could on every level," he says. "But the way a woman sees a vampire is different from the way a man does. So I tried to play it for as much sensuality and eroticism as I could.

"But then, there's Barnabas the vampire and Barnabas the man," he continues. "When you first see him in the series, he's kind of arrogant and distant—but then, too, you might be a bit insolent and angry if you had been buried alive for two hundred years. And in order to make him more interesting, we jump back in time to the 1700s before any of this happened, and he's just a really nice guy with a very happy family.

"What happened to him then is a cautionary tale for all married men: He has a fling with the wrong woman and soon regrets it. Ironically, in becoming a vampire, he's as much a victim of his own condition as the people he finds himself biting."

That victimization aspect is the one thing Cross has in common with Frid's interpretation of the guilt-ridden vampire. During the new series's run, Frid talked about *Dark Shadows* old and new and how he approached the role.

"I always knew that I had a cadaverous, evil-looking face," Frid begins, "so I can afford to be as sympathetic in a villain's role as I want—that's what gives you depth and makes you believable. But I never thought of myself as being terribly *scary* when I played Barnabas. After all, I was playing him as sort of a pathetic man, not a scary monster.

"Barnabas was a full role, you know," he continues. "The only time I had to play the vampire was when I had to do the silly gnashing of the teeth, which was about once every six weeks. The rest of the time I was playing off other things.

"With the new show, you know where I think they were almost right on track? And it's ironic for me of all people to say this, but in the first episode of the new series, they show him biting a girl and then her boyfriend in a parking lot, and he plays it like an animal. And I thought, 'Now, there's the *clue*—there's nothing sexual about all this; he's just a predator, an animal, and that's the way he should be.' Well, of course, I did the very opposite of all that. But if they're going to go that way, they should *go* that way and *stay* with it.

"But I think all this sexuality about it really has nothing to do with it—for him to exist, he needs blood. Now, if you were to cut your hand, I'd probably faint, but blood on television has no effect on me. To me, the new show is too numbingly violent and just so much blood dripping down chins, and that's *so* boring."

Although Frid is clearly dissatisfied with the updated series, he finds no fault with the actor who succeeded him in the vampire lead role. "The problem isn't Ben Cross; I think he's a marvelous actor," Frid praises. "I was very impressed with him in *Chariots of Fire*, and he's very good in this, too. But the show itself should have been more than just a reworking of the old *House of Dark Shadows* movie.

"I myself never expected to be asked to do Barnabas again for the new show," he points out. "After all, it's twenty years later, and although vampires aren't supposed to age, actors do."

Although Frid has plenty of previously documented complaints about the old series, he admits that as bizarre and inconsistent as it was, it had its moments. "The show really did have something," the actor says. "It strived and reached for the stars quite a bit—and fell flat on its face a lot of times. But every once in a while it coalesced into something really quite beautiful. It was almost like *Brigadoon*, very Never-Neverland."

As Frid knows from his own experience, being too closely identified with one role is a double-edged sword when it comes to an acting career. Cross admits that he, too, had concerns of being typecast as the vampire—particularly since he had signed a five-year contract to play one.

"I did worry, frankly," Cross confirms. "I was concerned that if the show did go for five years, I would be in that pigeonhole. But in fact it didn't last, it was only the one season, and since then I've done three or four very different things, so being typecast as a vampire just didn't happen."

Cross doesn't like to speculate on what went wrong with the series, but he does acknowledge that having the last half of the season set in the 1700s probably didn't help hold the interest of a fickle, channel-hopping TV audience. He sums up the show's failure with succinct diplomacy: "Why was the show canceled? I suppose not enough people watched."

Cross reveals that he originally took the job on *Dark Shadows* as an opportunity to do American episodic television. "It was one of the things that I'd never done, and that I wanted to experience."

But what about the future of *Dark Shadows*? The original series, you may recall, ended with an epilogue on the final episode that read, "There was no vampire loose on the great estate that night . . . and the dark shadows at Collinwood were but a memory of the distant past." Yet twenty years later, it was resurrected; once again, crazy Willie let Barnabas out of his box. Face it, you can't keep a good vampire down. Rumors persist of a *Dark Shadows* feature film, although Curtis's office continues to deny it. Would Cross be willing to reprise his role as Barnabas?

"I would certainly consider it," he says. "But I've heard nothing. It's in the hands of the gods and Dan Curtis, really. It's something that we'll have to wait and see, but I certainly would consider it. If they were going to make a decent movie out of it and the script was good, sure."

Still, don't *ever* count the TV version out. As Cross's Barnabas told his beloved Josette near the end of the short-lived series, "One day in another time, another world, you will glance across a room and see a stranger you have known forever—and it will be me."

So who knows? Maybe in a few years, Curtis will have another of his infamous dreams and bring us *Collinwood 2000*.

NICK KNIGHT, VAMPIRE COP

MICHAEL CHARLES ROWE

TORONTO IS A canyon city at night, a warren of sky-scrapers and dark alleys; it's definitely safer than some urban centers after dark, but it's still a place where vampires might make themselves a comfortable home. Production trucks and trailers clustered around a gritty block of buildings in the city's warehouse district do not lessen the forbidding atmosphere—in fact, a fog machine that sends clouds of dry ice into the alley only serves to enhance it.

Tonight, on the set of Paragon Entertainment's TV series *Forever Knight*, there is a giddy sense of barely contained euphoria. Filming for the season ends tomorrow night, after a long seven and a half months of night shoots to produce thirteen episodes in the unlife of Nick Knight. This unlikely hero is a seven-hundred-year-old vampire, whose quest for redemption and absolution from the evil of his existence has led him to the Toronto police force, where he is a homicide detective. Naturally, he works the night shift. His car (a 1962 Cadillac, the vehicle with more trunk space than any other in history) doubles as a coffin when he can't get to his downtown loft. Each week, Knight uses his dark gifts to solve crimes, all the while tormented by vampires from his past, and attempts to resolve his future.

If the plot sounds oddly familiar, it should. Viewers might recall the character's debut in the 1989 TV movie *Nick Knight*, starring early-eighties rock star Rick Springfield. The film was intended as a pilot for a series starring Springfield, but didn't fly. When Toronto's Paragon Entertainment picked up the series in 1991, the locale was switched to Toronto; Knight's role was reassigned to Geraint Wyn Davies, a handsome, classically trained stage actor whom the producers felt could deliver the depth required by the role.

The show revolves around three creatures of the night: Knight himself; Lacroix (Nigel Bennett), the evil vampire who inducted him into the undead fold in Paris in 1228; and Janette (Deborah Duchene), Nick's lover of many centuries who—somewhat improbably—runs a Toronto nightclub for bloodsuckers called Raven.

"Ultimately, most vampires have forsaken their humanity out of the belief that they will become better than mere mortals," explains Naomi Janzen, the series's supervising producer. "What Nick has discovered is that mortals are actually something rather exalted, and vampires and evil are on a lower plane. He wants his humanity back. In the last hundred years, he hasn't killed anyone."

Forever Knight is an atmospheric walk on the dark side of the city's heartbeat, a world where the undead exist unnoticed by criminals and cops alike. At its best, it's not only tremendous fun but a metaphor for cycles of the predatory: Criminals feed off the innocent, vampires feed off everyone, and the police try to clean it up. In *Forever Knight*, the boundaries between predator and prey become indistinct.

The challenge facing the series's cast and crew, of course, is to keep the show from lapsing into sloppily handled, timeworn themes of unhappy vampires miserably bewailing their immortality and (yawn) questing for peace. As a motif, it's been done, so to speak, to death. *Forever Knight* is not exempt from this danger: There's even a kindly female pathologist working to find a way to cure Knight of his vampirism.

Perhaps it is the Canadian, non-Hollywood element that gives the show its otherworldly look; perhaps it's the use of stage actors (all of whom have worked on the screen) to portray the vampires. But there is every reason to suspect that *Forever Knight* will continue to be unlike anything previously aired.

Davies (whose previous credits include *Dracula: The Series*) plays Knight with a degree of humor, and with admirably less melodrama than he might. Communicating a seven-hundred-year-old perspective, he says, depends upon subtlety. "The idea of wisdom, weight, and gravity demands also that you can't suddenly 'lose it,'" he says in a Welsh accent (born in Wales, the actor moved to Canada as a child). "If you've seen it all for seven hundred years, there is more than a petulant response demanded."

"It's a sense of alienation," Janzen concurs. "There is a great sacrifice for immortality. You're invincible, but you're always alone. Geraint has a really wonderful ability to portray that resonant aloneness."

Davies politely dismisses the Springfield pilot as someone else's headache. "When they created that movie, it didn't have any of the history that this show does. It certainly didn't require as much from the actor." In fact, Davies admits, he didn't even watch the pilot until two months into shooting. Coming to *Forever Knight* directly from a theater run as Hamlet, he doesn't see himself as following in the footsteps of any former rock star, thank you very much. "Playing Hamlet after Laurence Olivier . . . now that might be a problem," he says dryly.

Every Knight has his nemesis, and Nick's is the evil bloodsucker Lacroix. As Knight's undead foe, actor

Bennett embodies the vampire's dark sexuality. Who would want to give up immortality to work as a cop? Who would give up an endless number of nights in the quest for absolution? Not Lacroix. He loves the darkness, the blood, the freedom to abandon completely the constraints of conventional morality. And he makes it all appear so *cool.* By comparison, Nick Knight looks like Ward Cleaver.

Lacroix embodies the pansexual, all-powerful appeal of the undead, with black leather, platinum hair, and glittering yellow eyes. The sensual allure of a character like Lacroix is not lost on Bennett. "Sucking blood from someone is a very erotic thing," he says. "And the fact is that a true vampire doesn't care if his victim is male or female." The actor has read Anne Rice ("an amazing writer") and is a devotee of the Hammer films which featured Christopher Lee as Dracula. Bennett himself played Dracula in England during a fifteen-year stage career before he moved to Canada in 1986.

Throughout the series, Knight and Lacroix's differing views on the vampire life bring them into constant conflict. "Lacroix goes through eternity just enjoying what he does," explains Bennett, "and that's his major problem with Nick Knight. He doesn't understand why Knight, who asked to be 'brought over' seven hundred years ago, has such a problem with being a vampire."

Janette, Knight's ex-lover, is played by a stunning Renaissance beauty: Canadian stage actress Duchene. Her character seems far more like Miriam Blaylock in *The Hunger* than Dracula's daughter. The show's viewers would probably have an easier time imagining the aristocratic and sophisticated Janette making the ultrachic late-late-night party circuit (or running a vampire nightclub, for that matter) than drifting around graveyards, dressed in white.

Duchene, the daughter of a Baptist minister, is acutely

aware of the moral conflicts embodied in the vampire character. "Vampires bring together religion and sexuality," she says during a break in filming. "Religion represses sexuality; vampires repress nothing. I tend to bring the character of Janette inwards a great deal. She hasn't had many moments of flash and dash so far, but when she does, I try to show the orgasmic rush of the feeding."

No stranger to playing such spiritual roles, Duchene essayed the lead part in *Agnes of God* on stage, and is sensitive to the potentially conflicted feelings Janette would have for Nick Knight. "She's a little envious of his strength," muses Duchene. "She finds something almost endearing about his attempts to become human, but she enjoys what she is and wouldn't want to be like him."

Forever Knight is (of course) being filmed almost exclusively at night, stretching actors and crew alike to their professional limits. The demands on the crew are manifold: provide a dark, sensual backdrop for the show; convince viewers that vampires do indeed walk among us; frighten, exhilarate, and entertain us. And all of this in a one-hour (with commercials) weekly program that can't be too gruesome for Mr. and Mrs. America, yet has to keep both vampire and cop fans riveted.

The FX demanded of a show with limited time and format pose special challenges for the team of stunt coordinator Rick Forsythe and special FX coordinator Michael Kavanagh. The latter is no stranger to the genre, having worked for David Cronenberg on films like *Videodrome*, *The Dead Zone*, and *The Fly*. "We had to sit down and establish a set of rules," explains Kavanagh, "things that vampires could or could not do. Can they fly? Can they get AIDS?" Constrained by comparatively few of the traditional rules of vampire lore, Kavanagh and his team set about bringing their powers into view.

The show's bloodsuckers fly, but do not transform.

"We've used classic techniques for the flying sequences, like wire cables," Kavanagh says. "We also used a lot of counterweights so that we could just let them go and get that momentum. Even if it's just used to take them out of frame, it's so fast it looks good." Spliced with point-of-view flying, the trick works quite well.

Feeding frenzy and rage are communicated through the use of opaque contact lenses ("quite miserable," jokes Duchene) and a yellow eyelight that makes them glow. "These contact lenses come from Italy," says Kavanagh, "and they're worth about two thousand bucks a pair." The actors found that the expensive eyewear is irritating and produces tunnel vision, but they're stunningly effective on film. The fangs are traditional porcelain dentures, cast for each actor who wears them. "We have to make sure the vampires don't lisp while wearing them," chuckles Kavanagh, who freely admits that he wishes there was more vampire action in the show. "I'm an effects man," he says. "Of course, they have limitations. They have a story to tell."

Whether that story is more oriented toward the vampire or cop element, however, has been a matter of some debate. "It's a vampire show, but [then-broadcaster] CBS's main focus is that it's 'Crime Time after Prime Time,' so it's a police detective who's a vampire," says the show's production supervisor, Noella Nesdoly. "We have a fifty–fifty split, I think. We love the vampire end of it. We know that's hot right now, but we still have the police side as well."

What the producers see as an equal division of genre, the actors uniformly view as a vampire show—illustrating, perhaps, the timeless triumph of supernatural drama over cops and robbers. "Oh, I see Nick Knight much more as a vampire. Not like a cop at all," laughs Davies. "In fact, that's one of the things I'm trying to avoid. He's chosen this function to atone for his past. Nick Knight is not a do-gooder. He functions as a cop because he can work the night shift."

Flying, fanging, moral conflicts: What better way to fill an hour, for a vampire or an actor? Even if it *does* mean seven months of sleeping all day and working all night. And so, as the production prepares to take its hiatus and the actors return to the daylight, leaving their respective characters in their respective coffins, the question of whether vampire fans will take this production to heart remains to be answered. Will *Forever Knight* go the way of *Dark Shadows*, or will its stint in syndication (via USA Network and the Sci-Fi Channel) ensure a long series of dark knights? Is America ready for an invasion of vampires from north of the border? Will the sheer possibilities of the show's premise produce a loyal, if cultish following?

"The people who are inviting you into their homes have to get to know you," reasons Davies. "Yes, you can surprise them a bit. But essentially, they want to know who's coming through the front door."

TOP TEN VAMPIRE BOOKS

L I N D A   M A R O T T A

Sleep all day. Party all night. Never grow old.
Never die. It's fun to be a vampire.
—AD FOR *THE LOST BOYS*

IS THERE ANYONE out there who hasn't ever wanted to be a vampire? *Dracula* was originally published almost a hundred years ago and hasn't been out of print since. Today there are vampire newsletters, societies, comic books, films, TV shows, songs, cereals, and puppets, with no dying dawn in sight.

In literature, we use monsters to say something about ourselves. Dark and dangerous, vampires are attractive symbols for our own concerns of alienation, immortality, and transformation. Sexually, they can represent everything from general perversion to blood fetishism, necrophilia, cannibalism, rape fantasies, and incest. Novels in the subgenre run the gamut from tales of sophisticated psychic vampires who prey on the soul to gory exploitations of the popular (and marketable) motifs. The following books feature different takes on the mythos, and have each become legends of their own in the growing body of vampire lore. They reflect the changing culture, even as their basic antihero remains the same. This is my own biased list of the ten all-time best novels of vampirism, in chronological order:

1. *DRACULA*
(BRAM STOKER, 1897)

In what is arguably the finest horror novel ever written, Bram Stoker brilliantly combines Romanian superstition, Victorian morality, and the historical Vlad Tepes with nineteenth-century fears of Jack the Ripper and premature burial to produce the masterful standard against which all other works of vampirism are usually judged. It is at once personal in its epistolary style of letters and journal entries and universal in its Gothic atmosphere, suggestive of dark, forbidden forces at work.

Heavy with suggestions of sexual repression, *Dracula* has been analyzed in terms of psychosexuality (one long rape fantasy with the passive Lucy symbolically penetrated by the evil older man and all those transfusions from her suitors), religious allegory (Dracula as an infernal Christ figure), social commentary (transition between old-fashioned and modern times) and feminism (fear of the female's "voluptuous wantonness"). In his book *Hollywood Gothic*, which explores the Dracula mythos, David J. Skal concludes that Stoker "managed to tap a well of archetypal motifs so deep and persistent that they can assume the shape of almost any critical container." As the Count predicted: "My revenge has just begun! I spread it over centuries, and time is on my side."

2. *I AM LEGEND*
(RICHARD MATHESON, 1954)

Talk about classic opening lines: "On those cloudy

days, Robert Neville was never sure when sunset came, and sometimes they were in the streets before he could get back."

Matheson's powerful story of a world completely overrun by vampires has been adapted into the films *The Last Man on Earth* (1964) and *The Omega Man* (1971), and was the inspiration for George Romero's *Living Dead* trilogy. The plot works on a simple reversal: Instead of vampires being the alien outsiders, the human Neville is. As the last survivor, he spends his lonely days and besieged nights rationally attempting to sort the science from the superstition. Matheson turns the idea of otherness on its head when Neville comes to realize that normality is a relative concept and finally accepts his own extinction.

3. *SOME OF YOUR BLOOD*
(THEODORE STURGEON, 1961)

This psychoanalytic detective story about a disturbed young soldier in a military ward is one of the most compelling and unusual in all of vampire literature. It is also one of the few which allude to the overlooked attraction of menstrual blood. (Dr. Jean Youngson, president and founder of the Count Dracula Fan Club, assures us that it was based on a true story.) The novel is structured as the medical file of one George Smith, a quiet, backward loner who has suffered an inexplicable breakdown, and contains the patient's written account of his life, transcripts of therapy sessions and off-the-record letters between two psychiatrists. After some surprising test results, the doctors carefully crack George's code and persuade him to fill in the holes in his personal history; slowly we begin to see the

murder, mutilation, and blood drinking that were
there all along. Sturgeon's great humanity shines
through in both George's sensitivity (so different
from the fiendishness we are used to in modern serial-
killing sociopaths) and the wisdom and compassion
we would like to believe all psychiatrists possess.

4. SALEM'S LOT
(STEPHEN KING, 1975)

Who could forget that paperback cover? No title,
just the pitch-black embossed face of a little girl with
red blood dripping from her dainty fangs. Hell, I was
scared of the *book*, never mind the story! King's second novel is a combined homage to *Dracula*, a literary
take on horror comics and pure King terror-in-your-
own-backyard. While the catalytic evil of the vampire
plague comes from without in the person of Barlow
the "king vampire," it fans the flames of lesser, every-
day sins within the typical townspeople.

In *Danse Macabre*, King says he avoided the sexual factors of vampirism, feeling they would be
redundant in our sexually permissive age. But the
subplot that burned most strongly into my horny
teenage mind featured oral sex and one bloodsucker
returning to save a long-suffering wife with his
undead love. I also remember a number of erections
and bites experienced as kisses alluding to the
attraction of evil. (Of course, EC Comics used to
turn me on, too, so maybe it's just me.)

5. INTERVIEW WITH THE VAMPIRE
(ANNE RICE, 1976)

Finally, the vampire's side of the story. Rice uses
the sensual nature of vampires to exaggerate the

loneliness, suffering, and ecstasy of the human condition. Her creatures' heightened senses suggest various altered states (she admits that she was greatly influenced by Carlos Casteneda) and their acts of penetration imply eroticism ("the boy pressed against him, sucking hard, his own back arched and rigid, his body rocking back and forth"). Her dynamic trio of graceful, androgynous characters are unforgettable: Lestat, the callous killer; Claudia, the "eerie and powerful seductress" with her perfect little doll body; and sensitive Louis, mourning his lost human nature as he stares at a bleached skull.

Rice made the legend her own by redefining the vampire in human terms and dispelling the ancient myths. When Louis and Claudia travel to Eastern Europe, they find the Old World vampires to be mindless, animated corpses, stumbling along the ruins in rotting grave clothes. Even the Grand Guignol players in the Théâtre des Vampires fail to provide Louis with an excuse for his condition. In Armand's words: "The only power that exists is inside ourselves . . . "

6. *THE VAMPIRE TAPESTRY* (SUZY MCKEE CHARNAS, 1980)

Charnas puts the vampire psyche under the lens of psychoanalysis to compare animal instinct with intellect and raw appetite with artistic passion. Vampire Dr. Edward Lewis Weyland is an arrogant cultural anthropologist forced to undergo therapy in order to retain his university post. At first impatient with his psychiatrist's attempts at role-playing, body work, and affirmations, he slowly becomes interested in the self-revelations these methods provoke. He stops short, however, of projecting himself onto his victims, knowing that the predator/prey distinction must be upheld if he is to survive. But some identification with his "livestock" seeps through, disturbing him enough to seek the solace of his long sleep.

Like the characters in the book, we also want to make a dent in the vampire's irresistible aloofness, to warm his cool blood. Weyland's final feelings of connection to our race are not a weakness but the acknowledgment of the symbiotic bond between the hunter and the hunted, the lover and the beloved.

7. *THE HUNGER* (WHITLEY STRIEBER, 1981)

It's hard not to compare this one to its excellent film adaptation. Catherine Deneuve *was* Miriam—hauntingly beautiful and fierce. But while David Bowie's rapid on-screen aging effectively illustrated John Blaylock's tragedy, it didn't match his fury or the despair in the matching chimpanzee scene in the book. Everybody feels immortal at a certain level, but poor Blaylock had already lived hundreds of years and had grown secure in his mastery over mortality.

The true horror of Miriam is her sense of superiority. She can weep, suffer nightmares, and declare her unending love till the bats come home, but she will never make it up to John and her other former lovers, whose shriveled husks remain shamefully stashed in her quietly rustling attic. Her promise to love and keep them forever turns out to be a curse. Ultimately, Miriam's majesty is dwarfed by Sarah's true love for Tom. In the end, Miriam's selfishness endures, but Sarah's humanity transcends.

8. *THE DELICATE DEPENDENCY* (MICHAEL TALBOT, 1982)

This novel is truly the last word in vampire worship. Rich with luxurious descriptions, it wraps itself around the reader like an overstuffed velvet chair in an opium-scented chamber. Talbot's vampires are an evolved race of sensual beings who revere the artistic and scientific achievements of the human race. The book's story line follows one Dr. Gladstone, whose idiot savant daughter has been abducted by the vampires. The opulent furnishings of the lavish Parisian mansion where he is imprisoned celebrate the organic overkill of Art Nouveau style, climaxing in the "suffocating beauty" of an intense greenhouse swelling with intoxicating orchids.

The vampires reveal themselves to be the original Illuminati, benevolent caretakers of knowledge and history, preserving "lost" treasures of the world and protecting us from ourselves. The mixture of science, art, and magic and the deified passion of these idealized immortals make this novel an absolute favorite among many vampire fans.

9. *THE LIGHT AT THE END* (JOHN SKIPP AND CRAIG SPECTOR, 1986)

Enough already with sophisticated, sonnet-spouting bloodsuckers! This seminal splatterpunk novel takes a hard, mean look at the legend: "Not your penny-ante, long-suffering darkness of the mind, mind you." Rudy starts out as a spike-haired graffiti artist punk, and his acquisition of fangs makes him more dangerous, but no less of an ass-hole than before. His romantic nihilism doesn't give meaning to anyone's life, it just makes mincemeat out of them.

This was the first vampire novel to fully utilize
New York's bright lights and dark shadows. The
authors revel in an NYC of splatter film festival
massacres, vampire winos who spike bag ladies, and
tabloid headlines that scream "SUBWAY PSY-
CHO!" But within that big, bad city dwell people
who make the difference between heaven and hell
by forming their own tight community. On skates
and on foot, Skipp and Spector's ragtag group of
oddballs turn Manhattan into a giant D&D game
board. The messengers and their friends travel the
city's veined network of subways and streets, communicating by maps, phones, and beepers as they
attempt to flush the disease from its system. No
superiority of evil here; New York's got its own
problems.

10. *LOST SOULS*
(POPPY Z. BRITE, 1992)

With this novel, the entire genre of the damned
received an energizing transfusion. Brite takes the
vampiric themes of estrangement and love of the
dark and perfectly grafts them onto an underground
punk subculture, casting a spell in wet lace and
smudged eyeliner. These mutated vampires prefer
their blood tinged with liquor, junk, and Crucifix
blotter acid. Her New Orleans–set tale takes us out
of the decaying mansions and into the streets, bars,
and herbal shops. Beautifully written in syringe-
sharp language, this novel has the reader smelling
the hot, spicy clove cigarettes and tasting the green
flowing magic of sticky-sweet chartreuse.

Lost Souls plugs into the longing of suburban
youth to escape mediocrity. Misguided and obsessed
with death, these displaced kids cultivate a uniform

vampirish look by which they recognize kindred spirits. Traditional families no longer work for any of them; fortunately, they find the freedom to form new tribes and make up their own minds as to what constitutes evil. The fringe has always been the vampire's natural habitat, and as long as culture has a sharp cutting edge, vampires will be close by the wound, licking up the blood.

IN SEARCH OF
THE REAL DRACULA

RAYMOND McNALLY

MY SEARCH FOR Dracula began in 1958, while I was
watching Bela Lugosi in the 1931 movie on TV's *Creature
Features*. I suddenly began to wonder whether the story
could have a basis in reality, and started to notice certain
things suggesting it did.

First of all, the movie sets Dracula's home in
Transylvania, a place which was not made up by some
Hollywood filmmaker; Transylvania was, and is, a real
geographical location. Today, that state forms part of
modern-day Romania; just as the U.S. is made up of fifty
states, so Romania consists of Transylvania, Wallachia,
and Moldavia. The towns of Klausenberg (called Cluj
today) and Bistritsa, both of which are mentioned in the
novel, also really exist.

In the novel, English real estate agent Jonathan Harker
(in Tod Browning's 1931 *Dracula*, the character is
Renfield) meets Count Dracula at the Borgo Pass. I went
to a map of Romania and found the pass, located just
beyond the town of Bistritsa. That did it for me! I reasoned that if all the places were real, there had to be

something to the Dracula story. It could not all have been invented.

Since Transylvania had been dominated by Hungary for about a thousand years, I began by asking Hungarian scholars whether there had ever been a Hungarian leader named Dracula. I got nowhere for quite a while; they told me I was wasting my time, that I would never find out anything about a real Dracula, and that the story was entirely the product of Stoker's wild imagination. They lectured to me that this is a vampire story, and since vampires obviously do not exist, the story is just fiction. But I persisted; I have always felt that when people say you are not going to find anything, you will probably discover the opposite.

I checked the railroad time schedules in the novel and found them to be absolutely correct for that era—down to the very minute. The book's historical references also seemed to be close to the facts from the actual Eastern European past. I already knew about the existence of an authentic fifteenth-century manuscript in the archives of St. Petersburg which referred to a Romanian ruler named Dracula and depicted his atrocities. But most Russian scholars thought that the story was a historical novel, a blend of fact and fiction.

Finally, I stumbled upon a footnote in an obscure philological journal which stated that there was indeed a Romanian ruler called Dracula, known for his extreme cruelty, who had reigned during the fifteenth century. But that was all—only two or three lines were written about him. I checked the standard encyclopedias, but found nothing other than references to Stoker's vivid creation.

So I began to learn the Romanian language and planned a research trip to Dracula Country. Believe it or not, I was awarded an official government scholarship from the United States, in order for me to go over and study Dracula. I believe that this must have been one of

the only times that the government financed vampire
research. But I didn't feel guilty, because government
money has been spent on worse things than vampires!

In 1969, I traveled to Romania and spent a year inves-
tigating the real Dracula. He was better known there by
his nickname "The Impaler," after his fondness for that
form of execution. Impalement is a lost art, so a few words
of explanation are in order. Impaling someone basically
means that you stick them up on a stake like a popsicle.
There are many ways to do this, such as through the chest
or even through the mouth. But the classic method is to
place the victim on the ground, spread-eagled, then tie
each of the victim's feet to a different horse. One then
prepares a huge stake or pole strong enough to hold a
human body on it. The stake should preferably be
rounded at the end—not pointed, since one does not want
the victim to die quickly. The stake should also be oiled,
so that it can be easily inserted into the victim's anus. As
the stake is inserted, the horses move slowly forward.
Once the stake has been firmly lodged inside the victim's
body, one cuts the bonds holding the feet to the horses.
The unfortunate victim is then hoisted up on the stake
and gradually sinks further onto it, dying slowly from
exposure to the elements.

There are obviously easier and quicker ways to kill
someone, but this torture method has a secondary purpose beyond causing death: Like crucifixion, impalement
is a lasting example to those left behind of what can happen to the disobedient. Needless to say, law and order
reigned over the country in Dracula's day.

There is a definite historical connection between
Dracula and Transylvania. Vlad Dracula was actually born
there in the year 1431, in the lovely town of Sighisoara;
although he would later rule in southern Romania,
Dracula kept up his contacts with the Transylvanian
towns throughout his entire life until he died in 1476. He

signed his name clearly and distinctly as "Dracula" on two manuscripts to the citizens of the town of Sibiu in Transylvania.

The name "Dracula" has its origins in the Order of the Dragon, which was conferred on Vlad's father by the Holy Roman Emperor, King Sigismund, at Nurenberg Castle in 1431. He thus came to be known as "Dracul," and Vlad was so proud of his father's coveted honor that he proclaimed himself "Dracula," meaning "son of he who had the Order of the Dragon." "Dracul" is also a common Romanian word for Satan, however, and Vlad later came to be thought of as "son of the devil." The Order had as its primary insignia the dragon or winged serpent—a common symbol for the devil in Romanian folklore and art. The order was not evil, but when Dracula's father returned to Romania from the West and was wearing the dragon symbol on his cloak and shield, the peasants thought that he had thrown in his lot with the devil. Hence, Dracula's father is commonly known in Romanian history as Vlad "the Devil."

Long before Stoker, the historical Dracula was the subject of horror stories that were best-sellers in his time. Back in the late fifteenth century, people were as interested in horror as they are today. In that age, monks would tell these stories and copy them down to entertain others during those cold nights in monasteries. One of these tales recounts how Dracula used to like to dine surrounded by dead and dying corpses—establishing a connection between the historical Dracula and the vampire character. The Romanian prince was what doctors today call a "living vampire"—a clinical term referring to patients who drink human blood. Dracula evidently enjoyed dipping his bread in the blood of his victims, which he would gather in bowls at his dinner table. He would then slurp down the bloodied bread—part of his high-protein diet.

Dracula once invited the poor and the sick to a great banquet and gave them plenty to eat and drink. Then, when they were full of food and wine, he asked if he could do anything more for them. They expected a great gift, so they yelled, "Oh, lord, if we could only be relieved of our daily cares." "Very well," Dracula said. He ordered his henchmen to bolt the doors and windows of the banquet hall, trapping the outcasts within, and set fire to it. All inside were burned alive. Then Dracula declared, "I only did what they asked me to do. They wanted to be relieved of their daily cares, and that is what I have done. Now they don't have to worry about where their next meal is coming from. I've sent them to heaven!"

Some foreign ambassadors once came to visit Dracula and failed to take off their caps in his presence. He chastised them, "Why have you dishonored me so? Everyone must bare their heads in my presence." The ambassadors replied, "Lord, it is our custom never to bare our heads in the presence of any man." "Very well," Dracula responded. "Be brave. I wish to confirm you in your customs." And he ordered his henchmen to come and nail the caps to the ambassadors' heads. Then Dracula shouted, "Go home this way and tell your master that he should keep his customs in his own land. But when he sends ambassadors to me, they had better go along with my customs."

Sometimes Dracula would show a streak of black humor. Once a nobleman, who was dining with Dracula amid the impaled victims, could not stand the smell of decomposing bodies, so he held his nose. Noticing this ill-mannered behavior, Dracula asked, "Why are you holding your nose?" When the nobleman answered, "Because I cannot stand the stench from the rotting corpses," Dracula replied, "Very well, I shall solve that." He had an extremely tall stake brought out, and impaled his guest on it. Then the man on the stake was hoisted up far above the other sufferers, and Dracula shouted at him, "There! Now you are way up in the clean air where you can catch fresh breezes blowing and you don't have to worry about smelling those rotting corpses down here anymore."

One day, while Dracula was walking through his capital city of Tirgovishte, he spotted a male peasant who was wearing a torn shirt. Dracula asked the fellow, "Do you have a wife?" to which the man replied, "Yes." "Well," Dracula ordered, "Take me to her." The peasant did as he was told. When Dracula met the woman, he asked, "Are you healthy?" She answered in the affirmative. Then Dracula turned to her husband and asked, "Did you sow the grain and reap it this year?" and the peasant replied, "Yes." Dracula turned to the woman and said, "Look, he sowed the grain and reaped it; you should see to it that he does not go around in a torn shirt." So Dracula had her taken prisoner, and he cut off her hands and impaled them in the city square as a lesson to lazy wives. In short, Dracula was one of the first male chauvinists!

Dracula once had a fine gold cup set up in a prominent place by a brook of cool water, and many came to drink. Each person dutifully returned the gold cup to its proper place after drinking; no one dared steal it, because they knew that Dracula would impale them on the spot. He was an extreme law-and-order man, and during his reign no one dared to steal, for he punished both minor and major crimes with impalement. He reasoned that if people got away with the smaller offenses, it would not be long before they committed serious ones.

Dracula did not want any potential heirs around who might challenge his absolute reign. One time, when he was in a black mood, his mistress foolishly thought that she could cheer him up. She told him she was pregnant, since she assumed that he would be happy to hear the news. He wasn't. He said to her, "This cannot be," seized a knife and slit her all the way up her body, so that "the whole world could see where his fruit lay." In this way, he headed off any young rival to the throne, since illegitimate sons could succeed as well as legitimate ones; Dracula's own father had been illegitimate and yet had gained the throne.

A key to Dracula's strange behavior can be found in his difficult childhood. He had been raised as a Christian in Transylvania, but his father left him as a hostage among the Turks when the boy was only thirteen. Suddenly, young Dracula found himself amid a people whose language and religion of Islam he did not understand. Dracula's father and mother returned home, abandoning the boy in Turkey, where the sultan held him as a kind of insurance that Dracula's father would not attack his people. Young Dracula was shipped off by the sultan to the castle of Egrigoz, thousands of feet up in the inaccessible mountains of Asia Minor. (Following clues in ancient Turkish chronicles, I was able to locate this castle in Asia Minor; it was the first time that any scholar had ever found the place, even on a map. I went there personally to find the ruins of that castle prison which had once held Dracula, and saw it with my own eyes.)

While Dracula was held captive there from 1444 until 1448, the horrible news reached him that his father had violated his promise to the sultan and had gone to war against the Turks—with full knowledge that in so doing, he was deliberately risking his son's life. The father even wrote about this fact in a letter to Transylvanian townsmen. This terrible betrayal must have taught Dracula that life is cheap. Luckily, but no thanks to his dad, the sultan chose not to kill Dracula in retaliation, but continued to use him as a pawn in diplomatic negotiations and plans.

Vlad Dracula finally seized power in southern Romania with Turkish support in 1456 and ruled until 1462, a relatively short reign. But in that time, he managed to have some 100,000 people killed, according to the bishop of Erlau (a fairly impartial witness). Considering that the entire population of Dracula's realm was only 500,000, Vlad surely ranks as one of the greatest mass murderers in history, on a scale with Hitler and Stalin. But because Dracula fought a crusade against the Turks during the same six years of his reign, his crimes were often excused; some said, "He was cruel because the times were cruel." Even Pope Pius II admired and supported Dracula as a great warrior against the infidel Turks. But there is every indication that the historical Dracula was a sadistic killer on a par with Jeffrey Dahmer and Charles Manson, and should have been denounced as such. Even after 1462, when he was imprisoned, Dracula could not give up his bad habit of impaling; unable to get his hands on people, he caught mice in his cell, tortured and impaled them on little sticks. He bribed his jailers to buy him birds from the marketplace, then plucked the feathers off them and watched them run frantically around his cell. When he tired of that entertainment, Dracula skewered them.

It was the Hungarian King Matthias who had Dracula captured and imprisoned in Budapest—not for his cruelties, but to cover for his own sins. Matthias had spent some 40,000 gold coins, which Pope Pius II had given to him to transmit to Dracula's crusade against the Turks. The king had letters forged in which Dracula supposedly swore allegiance to the sultan, and so was able to declare Dracula a traitor to the Christian cause. Thus, the king had a pretext for pocketing the 40,000 gold coins meant for Dracula.

By 1476, Matthias decided to put Dracula back on the throne of southern Romania. During a battle with the Turks toward the end of that year, Dracula dressed up in a Turkish soldier's uniform in order to get a better look at the battle scene. He ran into some of his own troops, who supposedly did not recognize him in the Turkish outfit and shot arrows into him. Taking up his lance, Dracula killed five or six of them, but was hopelessly outnumbered; the soldiers fired more arrows into him, and he died. His warriors cut off his head and gave it to the Turks as a trophy of victory, because the Turkish soldiers still deeply feared the man they called the "Impaling Prince." The sultan displayed Dracula's head on the ramparts of his Topkapi Castle in Constantinople, but Romanian folklore has it that Dracula never truly died, and will come to rule again in time of great need.

The Dracula historical legend, which was very popular during the late fifteenth and sixteenth centuries, fell into oblivion until the nineteenth century. It was then that Irish author Bram Stoker decided to resurrect the Romanian prince as the vampiric Count Dracula. At first, Stoker was going to call the main character Count Wampyr—which, of course, would have been a dead giveaway and would have killed the novel's initial suspense. Fortunately, while vacationing, Stoker came across a book by William Wilkinson which described several of the deeds of the historical Dracula. Stoker became fascinated with the prince, and thus changed the name of his novel's main character. The author figured that, since the real Dracula was so frightening in life, he would be much more so undead.

The novel makes historical references to Vlad Dracula's military campaign against the Turks, his resolute will to fight, the treachery of those around him, etc.—but most people ignore these while reading the novel. The irony is that Stoker did not invent the history at all. As for the book's vampire folklore, Stoker derived this material from the work *The Land Beyond the Forest* by Emily Gerard. What he used in the novel is actual mythology that is still believed in Transylvania, such as the power of garlic and the cross to ward off bloodsuckers, the vampires casting no reflection in a mirror, etc.

Stoker's only true invention in his novel was his linking of the historical Dracula with the authentic Romanian folk-lore.

The belief in vampires is still very much alive and well in Transylvania, as the following experiences bear witness. At the foot of Castle Dracula, which I located for the first time in the town of Poenari in Romania, I met a young gypsy woman named Tinka who told me that her father was a vampire. Thirty years before, he had died and was laid out for viewing for three days. But at the end of that period, the villagers noticed that rigor mortis had not set in; his skin was still pliable, and his cheeks bore a ruddy complexion—true signs of the vampire, the undead. Tinka told me that she knew what had to be done, but she could not bring herself to destroy the body of her dear father. But the villagers had no such compunctions; they took a wooden stake, plunged it into the heart of the corpse and drove it through the bottom plank of the wooden coffin into the ground to keep the body from walking. (It is, in fact, not enough to drive the stake into the corpse, as is seen in some Hollywood movies; one must pound the shaft through the corpse and into the ground underneath, pinning it to the earth as in a butter-fly collection. Then, if you are still worried that eventu-ally some idiot might come along and pull out the stake, you should burn the body after staking it.)

While I was traveling through Transylvania, I came across a funeral procession at the town of Rodna near the Borgo Pass. I naturally stopped to see, and a local peasant informed me that they were burying the body of a young girl who had killed herself. I knew that someone who commits suicide in Transylvania is a candidate to become a vampire (as are very cruel people, witches, werewolves, those who die unbaptized, and those born with a caul; the seventh son of a seventh son is also doomed). The Rodna villagers put her coffin in a very shallow grave, not more than two feet deep; at first I did not understand why, but I found out the reason after the official religious ceremony. The villagers came back to the cemetery, dug up the coffin from the shallow grave, and plunged a wooden stake through the heart and into the ground beneath the deceased.

As we look at the wishy-washy characters who fill the world around us, it's no wonder that many of us admire Dracula. He's consistent; you know what to expect from him. Dracula may be evil, but that is easier to handle than some typically vacillating leader of our day. Today, he would not need to impale people to frighten others into obedience; he could simply let the scoundrels and public liars expire on their own sound bites. Sadly, they don't make them like him anymore; as the title of an old Romanian poem puts it, "Dracula, Where Are You Now That We Need You?"

DRACULA UNSEEN

DAVID J. SKAL

BRAM STOKER (1847–1912), best known today as the author of *Dracula*, was a prolific but part-time fiction writer who spent most of his days and nights managing the affairs of the celebrated Victorian actor Henry Irving. He wrote eighteen books, nearly all now forgotten (two besides *Dracula*—*The Lair of the White Worm* and *The Jewel of Seven Stars*—have been adapted as films, the latter as *Blood from the Mummy's Tomb* and *The Awakening*). Exactly how and why Stoker wrote *Dracula* is largely a matter of conjecture; although he could write voluminously, he never described on paper the actual process of writing. His surviving notes for *Dracula* (written between 1890 and 1895) reveal some plot mechanics and reference sources, but provide no insight into his personal fascination with the topic. However, from the time of his earliest published efforts, Stoker was attracted to the fantastic and macabre, and was influenced by the work of fellow Dubliner Joseph Sheridan Le Fanu, whose sensuous novella *Carmilla* laid the groundwork for vampire fiction as we know it today.

The plot of *Dracula* was heavily reworked between the time of Stoker's notes (which he seems to have jotted down during one of his many visits to America with Irving's company; some are written on a Philadelphia hotel's stationery) and the time of the book's publication. The name Dracula was something of an afterthought; Stoker originally intended to call his novel *The Un-Dead* and his vampire "Count Wampyr." He thought better of it, however, after library research brought to his attention the bloodthirsty exploits of Vlad the Impaler, the Fifteenth-century Wallachian warlord whose cruelty earned him the sobriquet "Dracula," meaning "son of the devil" in Romanian.

Many of Stoker's original plot elements were extremely awkward, and the final book gained from their deletion; some, however, were quite fascinating, and it is a shame they were never used. In one bit of inspiration that seems like a deliberate variation on *The Picture of Dorian Gray* by Oscar Wilde—whom Stoker knew well— Dracula's portrait would have been impossible to paint, the image always turning out to be someone else's. Likewise, Dracula couldn't be photographed, except as a kind of skeletal X-ray (an invention of the 1890s). Although it seems like a period piece today, *Dracula* was a very contemporary novel for its time, full of up-to-date technology.

Two substantial cuts were made in the final manuscript. The first was an entire opening chapter detailing Jonathan Harker's encounter with a female vampire on his way to Castle Dracula (after Stoker's death, this fragment would be anthologized as a self-contained short story, "Dracula's Guest," later the inspiration for the film *Dracula's Daughter*). The second major deletion is the castle's total, spontaneous destruction as its five-hundred-year-old inhabitant crumbles into dust. "As we looked, there came a terrible convulsion of the earth . . . " Stoker wrote. "The whole castle and the rock and even the hill on which it stood seemed to rise in the air and scatter in fragments while a mighty cloud of black and yellow smoke, volume on volume, in rolling grandeur, was shot upwards with inconceivable rapidity." It has been suggested that Stoker cut this dramatic finale in order to save the location for a possible sequel.

Dracula received favorable but somewhat condescending reviews. The *Daily Mail* recalled the stories that circulated about Mrs. Ann Radcliffe, one of the first Gothic novelists, to the effect that she locked herself in a secluded room, feasting on raw beef to get in the proper writing mood. "If one had no assurance to the contrary," wrote the *Daily Mail*, "one might well suppose that a similar method and regimen had been adopted by Mr. Bram Stoker while writing his new novel." *Dracula* sold well and went into several printings during Stoker's lifetime, but it did not make him wealthy. Stoker and his wife had a taste for social climbing, and quickly spent what they earned.

Critics have spent a great deal of time speculating on the psychological, and especially the psychosexual, motives that compelled Stoker to write *Dracula* in the first place. There are, however, some intriguing hints that the novel might not be entirely a reflection of his own mind. In a 1932 letter, H. P. Lovecraft claimed to have known "an old lady who almost had the job of revising 'Dracula' in the early 1890s—she saw the original ms., & says it was a fearful mess. Finally someone else (Stoker thought her price for the work was too high) whipped it into such shape as it now possesses."

If Stoker was impatient with the mechanics of novel-writing, it may have been because he had another goal for which the novel was only a preliminary step. He was convinced that the tall, commanding, mesmeric Irving would be the ideal embodiment of his vampire nobleman, and he spent many frustrating hours trying to convince Irving that *Dracula* would make a lucrative stage drama for the Lyceum.

Stoker imagined Irving's Dracula as a combination of Mephistopheles, a favorite role of the actor's, with characteristics drawn from the actor's many showy Shakespearean villains. But Irving, Stoker later said, only laughed at the suggestion. Stoker even managed to hijack the Lyceum stage for a lengthy dramatic reading of the book—officially for "copyright" purposes, but more likely as a last-ditch attempt to convince Irving that *Dracula* was stageworthy. He cast Edith Craig, the daughter of Irving's leading lady Ellen Terry, as his heroine Mina; Tom Reynolds, one of Irving's most popular character actors, played Van Helsing; and, standing in for Irving, a mysterious "Mr. Jones" took the role of Dracula. It is likely this actor was Whitworth Jones, an imposing Victorian performer then active in London.

But Stoker never saw *Dracula* properly dramatized during his lifetime; it fell to his widow, Florence, to oversee the next step in the Count's evolution. Plunged into genteel poverty after her husband's death, Florence guarded the *Dracula* copyright jealously; it was virtually her only source of income. Her eight-year-long battle to destroy every existing print of the plagiaristic German film *Nosferatu* is well-known, but she also halted an unauthorized stage version in Canada. Harry Clarke, the incomparable Poe illustrator, wanted at one point to create a deluxe illustrated edition of the novel. Florence, however, would not agree to his publisher's terms, and book collectors everywhere were thereby denied a macabre masterpiece of graphic art.

Florence was not the only obstruction to would-be adaptors of *Dracula*. As a story, the book presented all kinds of technical difficulties. It was organized as a compilation of letters, diaries, and other documents written by many different characters; its action was spread from London to Transylvania and involved many spectacular outdoor scenes impossible to reproduce on any stage. And the most horrifying scenes were so gruesome—the staking and decapitation of Miss Lucy, or Dracula breast-feeding Mina with his own blood—that it was almost impossible to imagine the British censors permitting them to be presented in any recognizable form.

Florence Stoker finally entrusted the dramatic rights in 1924 to Hamilton Deane, a traveling actor/manager whose parents owned property adjacent to her late husband's family home in County Dublin. It was Deane more than any other person who created the "modern" image of Dracula, more out of necessity than inspiration. Deane realized that the only practical way to scale down *Dracula* for the theater was to adopt the tried-and-true conventions of a drawing-room mystery melodrama.

The persona of Dracula, therefore, would have to be radically reinterpreted as the charming sort of character who would be invited into a drawing room in the first place. Stoker's vampire was a cadaverous old man with hairy palms and pointed ears, more likely to smash his way through the window as a werewolf than to knock at the door. He is largely an offstage presence throughout the novel, avoiding "normal" human interaction. And, while the Count grows younger as he drinks blood, he never becomes attractive.

Deane, therefore, had to reach back beyond Stoker's Dracula to the Lord Byron-inspired vampire image that had been immensely popular in stage melodrama a hundred years earlier. Deane recreated Dracula as a suave Mephisto with impeccable manners, a continental accent, and, of course, the ever-present swirling cape.

Deane wanted to open his version of *Dracula* with an eerie stage tableau of the count's castle in the moonlight, the figure of Dracula slithering facedown from a high window, his cloak (with the aid of a concealed wire frame) assuming the shape of huge bat wings as he descended. The ambitious effect proved too awkward and costly for touring, and Deane had to be content to use the image on his posters only. Other cuts, however, were the result of official order. The Lord Chamberlain's office (England's official dramatic censor) refused to allow Dracula's death to be staged as graphically as Deane had wanted. He had prepared a dummy chest for the vampire, filled with realistically spurting blood. But in order to obtain the necessary license from the censor, the actors were required to stand between Dracula's coffin and the audience, effectively blocking the view of the bloodsucker's demise. Later, however, Deane had a trick coffin constructed along the lines of a magician's cabinet—Dracula was made to "disappear" before the audience's eyes in a nonoffensive cloud of dust.

Raymond Huntley, the veteran character actor best known to American audiences as the family lawyer on television's *Upstairs, Downstairs*, was the most celebrated of the English stage Draculas. He played the role thousands of times, but had plenty of company. Other British Counts included Frederick Keen, John Laurie, Keith Pyott, W. E. Holoway, and Edmund Blake (an actor whose mouth had a weird glint because of a prominent gold front tooth). When the flamboyant American publisher/producer Horace Liveright contracted for the American stage rights (and a script completely rewritten by John L. Balderston), he offered the twenty-two-year-old Huntley the lead. Huntley, unhappy with the terms and also a bit sick of the role, turned Liveright down, thereby inadvertently making a star of an expatriate Hungarian actor named Bela Ferenc Dezso Blasko—otherwise known as Bela Lugosi.

Lugosi spoke almost no English, but Liveright didn't mind that he learned the role phonetically; he wanted his Broadway Dracula to look and sound as otherworldly as possible, and the bizarre inflections helped. Another Liveright inspiration was having Lugosi use makeup with a weird green tint. After out-of-town tryouts in Hartford and New Haven, Liveright's *Dracula* opened in New York in October 1927. It was a major hit, launching two national tours which, by 1930, had earned over $2 million. Huntley was persuaded to cross the Atlantic for the tour, and, while Lugosi's photos were frequently used for publicity, it was Huntley's characterization that most American audiences saw—Lugosi's leg of the tour was limited to the West Coast, while Huntley performed in virtually every major city from Boston to Denver. Victor Jory played the role in Minneapolis and Pasadena, in a bizarrely stylized makeup somewhat reminiscent of Max Schreck's in *Nosferatu*. Courtney White, Frederick Pymm, and even the famous tennis star Bill Tilden took the cape for a whirl during this period. (The stage play continued to be performed even after the release of the 1931 film version; a revival played briefly on Broadway within a month of the film's release.)

Following endless indecision, Universal Pictures finally bought the screen rights to *Dracula* rather than see the property go to MGM. Universal hoped to entice Metro star Lon Chaney, Sr. to return to the site of his two greatest triumphs, *The Hunchback of Notre Dame* and *The Phantom of the Opera*, in a lavish adaptation. The Pulitzer Prize-winning novelist Louis Bromfield was hired by Universal to adapt *Dracula* to the screen, but the studio soon became disenchanted with his efforts. Bromfield, it seemed, was a bit *too* ambitious; he restored the Transylvania sequence and added many effective touches (such as Dracula's women being costumed in the attire of three *different* centuries as they approach Harker in his room.) Bromfield's attempt to integrate the stage play into the film script was less successful, but he accomplished the task, giving Dracula a Jekyll-and-Hyde aspect. As "Count De Ville," he was the romantic drawing-room vampire of the legitimate stage, but when the bloodlust overcame him, he would revert to the cadaverous, ancient satyr originally described by Stoker. Ultimately, however, the studio went with a script by Garrett Fort and Dudley Murphy that more directly mirrored the stage version.

Unhappy with director Tod Browning's cut of the film, Universal trimmed about ten minutes from *Dracula* to speed up its funereal pace. The deletions, now lost forever, included the staking of Lucy, some comic business with Renfield and the maid, Dracula preparing his earth-boxes for departure, and so on. In Massachusetts, censors demanded additional cuts of the now-ludicrous close-ups of a beetle and an opossum scrounging around the crypts. According to a close acquaintance of Browning's, the director was still grumbling about the studio cuts twenty-eight years later, when the film was first released to television.

Almost everything cut for the English-language version, however, was retained in the simultaneous Spanish-language edition filmed on the same sets by producer Paul Kohner and director George Melford. Long thought to be a lost film, its meticulous restoration was finally undertaken by Universal in 1991, utilizing the incomplete original negative and supplementary footage from the Cinemateca de Cuba in Havana. The restored Spanish *Dracula*, far more atmospherically produced than the familiar Lugosi version, is now available on MCA Home Video.

Dracula was a big moneymaker for Universal, but the studio did not revive the character for a dozen years. Part of the problem was the rise of the state censor boards in the early thirties. Universal prepared several different treatments of *Dracula's Daughter*, in which the Count himself was a character, but the idea of a seductive male monster was too much for the professional puritans of the time. They suggested, among other things, that the studio make clear that the young girls dragged screaming to Castle Dracula were only intended as "dancing partners" for the Count's guests, rather than as his jugular prey. The scriptwriters finally gave up and eliminated the character of Dracula altogether—and the studio paid off Lugosi, who had been announced as the film's star.

Lugosi himself dreamed of a big-budget remake of *Dracula* during the 3-D craze of the fifties, and even encouraged his fans to mount a letter-writing campaign to Universal. Unfortunately, the studio was more interested in its newfangled monsters, like the Metaluna mutant from *This Island Earth* and *The Creature from the Black Lagoon*, to seriously consider the project. But the idea of Lugosi, in Technicolor and three-dimensional bat-form, swooping over the heads of Polaroid-goggled audiences, is still one of the most delirious, if unproduced, versions of *Dracula* imaginable.

After the success of Hammer Films' *Dracula* cycle in the fifties, sixties, and seventies, and the hit Broadway revival of the Deane and Balderston stage play in 1977, the larger studios once again considered *Dracula* a viable property. Although it was Universal who beat the competition to the screen (with its plush 1979 version starring Frank Langella and directed by John Badham), provocative script treatments were also developed by directors Roger Vadim and Ken Russell.

Vadim's Dracula, with a screenplay by Matthew Bright, was the freest of the unproduced adaptations, updated to 1970s London where Mia Stewart, the great-granddaughter of Jonathan Harker, meets the dashing Alexis Hanyadi, who has been sleeping for a century in an antique chest (his anachronistic taste in clothing is shrugged off as a fashion tic). Alexis/Dracula likes to drink blood from breasts instead of necks whenever possible; Mia, meanwhile, has frequent flashbacks of the fifteenth-century atrocities of Vlad the Impaler. Among the unique features introduced by *Vadim's Dracula* is the concept of the Renfield character as a schizophrenic woman.

Ken Russell's 1978 screenplay of *Dracula*, derailed by the Langella film, presented the Count as an opera buff entranced by a young diva, Lucy Weber, who is dying of leukemia. A supernatural patron of the arts, Dracula has used vampirism to prolong the lives of deserving but doomed artists through history. Russell's treatment takes strikingly visual approaches to classic sequences. During Dracula's sea voyage to England, the panicked sailors have no idea what force is killing them off—until they look up at the mast, from which Dracula hangs in his cape, bloated like a leech. Perhaps Russell's most perverse touch of all is having Jonathan Harker wrap a rosary around his fist, then use it as a knuckle-duster to defang one of Dracula's seductive, devouring brides.

One of the great pleasures for Draculaphiles, of course, is savoring the number and variety of plot variations that directors and screenwriters have devised around Stoker's core narrative. Rewriting, updating, and embellishing *Dracula* was originally just a practical and financial necessity for Hamilton Deane in the theater. In the ensuing years, it has become almost a spectator sport in the movies, and budgets large enough to fund Deane's theater for five hundred years encourage the process.

As we have seen, Dracula at his inception was a shapeshifting character about whom Bram Stoker himself had many second thoughts. His unending ability to adapt and change form—literally, cinematically, and supernaturally—may well explain why Dracula is one of the champion fictional creations of the past century, and a leading contender for the next.

VAMPIRE CLASSIC:
I Am Legend

CHRISTOPHER KOETTING

"I WANT FIRST to assure you that I am not insane. I want next to bring you with me to the year 1976. I am the last man left upon the earth. I don't know how much longer I can go on. Every night they surround my last stronghold, these vampires from another world, and I can hear them in the darkness screaming obscenities. I have killed so many of them and still they come. How long before they get to me? Only this I know—I will never wake to the sound of another human voice."

So reads the back cover of a novel published by Gold Medal Books in July 1954. Beneath this blurb is a photograph of an intense young man and this caption: "Read this novel. Watch this young writer. You may be in at the birth of a giant." The novel is *I Am Legend;* the writer is Richard Matheson. And to say that readers were witnessing the "birth of a giant" would be a classic understatement.

Lauded by Harlan Ellison as "one of our most consistently original and masterful creators of imaginative literature," Matheson is without a doubt one of the most prolific and diverse writers this country has produced, and *I Am Legend* may be one of the most influential works of fantasy written in this century, a fact acknowledged by many well-known writers and filmmakers, including:

Stephen King: "When I read *I Am Legend* I realized that horror . . . could appear in the suburbs, on the street, or even in the house next door."

Dean Koontz: "[*I Am Legend* is] the most clever and riveting vampire novel since *Dracula.*"

Brian Lumley: "A long time ago I read *I Am Legend*, and I started writing horror about the same time. Been at it ever since."

George A. Romero: "[*Night of the Living Dead* was first] written [as] a short story, an allegory inspired by . . . *I Am Legend.*"

All of these men were intrigued by the same question asked of countless readers—what would you do if you were the last person left alive on the face of the earth? A mysterious plague in the aftermath of a limited atomic war has killed your family, eradicated the population and destroyed civilization. Horrific as these circumstances are, there is something worse: Victims of the plague do not rest after death, but return as bloodthirsty vampires, waiting for you every night outside your fortified house, howling for you to come out. By day, you hunt them; by night, they hunt you. What caused this scourge upon the land? What makes the dead walk and seek human blood? What will the future bring—death, or a life of total isolation? These are the questions that Robert Neville, *I Am Legend*'s protagonist, asks himself daily; these very questions keep the reader turning the pages, sharing Neville's paranoia, grief, and desperation, sharing his search for an answer.

There's another, basic question: What prompted Matheson to write such a tale? "When I was a teenager, I saw Bela Lugosi as Dracula," he says. "I thought that if one vampire was scary, then it would *really* be scary if the whole world was full of them." Matheson modeled Robert Neville after himself—a common Matheson technique. "All my stories were *me* set in a very unusual, frightening situation. I just imagined how *I* would act if I were in that world full of vampires."

The story is set in Los Angeles more than twenty years following the book's 1954 publication date. Endless dust storms and insect infestation follow in the wake of war, spreading a deadly germ of unknown origin. "Setting things in an atomic world was kind of *de rigueur* in the fifties," Matheson says. "There were all sorts of movies like *Them!* and *Beginning of the End* that linked radiation with mutated insects, so that may have played on my mind when I wrote about the bombings and the insects that carried the plague. The fifties were definitely the 'Age of Anxiety,' and the future my children faced really concerned me." However, Matheson expressly denies that the story was written as an allegory. "If you try to do something like that, you go right down the toilet," he says. "You become pedantic and boring. I never try to impose social commentary on my stories—I just tell the story."

An allegory it may not be, but *I Am Legend* can certainly lay claim to being the first to meld the superstitions and myths of the vampire with modern knowledge of physiology and psychology. Neville's pursuit of answers leads him to some interesting conclusions about vampires that debunk traditional Transylvanian thinking: Vampires are the result of a germ, not of damnation; they are impervious to bullets due to a mutated body seal, not supernatural power; the vampires' fear of holy objects is actually the result of their *own* superstitions from previous life, while "hysterical blindness" keeps them from gazing upon their own reflections.

The addition of raw science to horrific fantasy is one of the book's main appeals, giving it a learned and realistic feel. Thus, Matheson's main goal in writing *I Am Legend* should come as no surprise. "What I had in mind was to create the first science-fiction vampire novel, and it's really the most scientific of all my books. Even though I'm known as a fantasy author, I'm very realistic in my writing. I'll take a single fantastic idea—like everyone in the world is a vampire—and then ignore the fact that it is fantasy and act as if it's a realistic story. I consulted a doctor, did a lot of my own research—everything in there was accurate for the time. In fact, the library Neville visits is the same library where I did *my* research, right down to the books he reads."

In the midst of his scientific investigation, Neville discovers something else—there are others who have not succumbed to vampirism. He encounters Ruth, a spy for a "New Society" of infected survivors who have found their own way to resist the plague's effects, and don't want to include in their fraternity the man who has inadvertently killed some of their members. This New Society has been established to deal not only with the vampires and the reorganization of civilization, but with another aberration—Neville himself.

Matheson's reasoning behind this is simple: "The men in the black suits that come for Neville in the end are really the *1984* types. The New Society would have to be a cold, fascistic order to get things rolling again. Neville isn't a part of this order; his having to die and make way for the New Society is inevitable." In this final tragic irony, Neville will die at the hands of the very companions he had so longed for, and in the process, will become like the vampires themselves—the stuff of legend. "I had the title of the book before I started writing it," remembers Matheson. "I had to fight for it—my publisher wanted to call it *I Am a Legend*. But I knew how Neville would end up, and that he would no longer be a person or an individual. He'd simply join the pantheon of folk tales, the only place where he could find any sort of belonging."

Fittingly, Neville *does* live on in the literary and cinematic pantheon; the forty years since *I Am Legend*'s publication have given rise to a plethora of vampire invasions and assorted holocausts. The generation of horror authors who grew up with *I Am Legend* have paid homage to it in everything from a Los Angeles incursion by the undead in Robert McCammon's *They Thirst* (1981) to the struggle between Harry Keogh and an army of vampires for the fate of the world in Brian Lumley's *Necroscope* series (1986–1991); from Stephen King's tale of vampirism engulfing a town called *'Salem's Lot* (1975) and of a devastating plague forcing a battle of moral forces in *The Stand* (1978) to a brood of indestructible vampires on the attack in William Hill's *Dawn of the Vampire* (1991).

Filmmakers have likewise benefitted from Matheson's pioneering efforts. Similarities to *I Am Legend* can be found in *Invisible Invaders* (1959), which features alien-reactivated corpses besieging humans hiding in a cave, and Terence Fisher's *The Earth Dies Screaming* (1964), in which a test pilot returns to find an England of zombies and alien robots. George Romero's *Night of the Living Dead* (1968) revolutionized the genre, but its plot of flesh-eating reanimated corpses overrunning survivors in an isolated farmhouse is a deliberate nod to Matheson.

With the legions it has sired, *I Am Legend* was undeniably an influential work, though the book's own existence has not been as consistent. Though it went through thirteen editions between 1954 and 1980, it has been out of print since, and a good copy of the Gold Medal first edition—which cost 25 cents in 1954—can run between $75 and $150. But in 1995 Tor Books reprinted *I Am Legend* as part of a series of Matheson titles. That same year, Gauntlet Publications also issued a signed limited hardcover edition. A whole new generation will at last have ready access to one of the most seminal works in the fantasy genre, a boon to those familiar with Matheson's book only through the two films that directly acknowledge its inspiration.

With its vivid illustration of a nightmarish world, *I Am Legend* is an extremely visual novel which would require little effort to translate to the screen. Nevertheless, it was three years before Matheson received an offer to film the book. The phone call came from his New York agent in mid-1957, offering him an all-expense-paid trip to England to work on the screenplay for Hammer Films. September of that year found him crossing the Atlantic on the *Queen Elizabeth*, anticipating the opportunity to bring *I Am Legend* to celluloid life.

Hammer's star producer, Anthony Hinds, was on the lookout for properties in keeping with the company's successful *The Curse of Frankenstein* (1957), and his introduction to *I Am Legend* was love at first sight—"I remember reading the book and thinking it was fantastically good," he says today. Hinds offered Matheson $10,000, passage, and a fifty-pound-a-week allowance; it was too good to pass up, though Matheson's presence in England was probably due less to his talent and more to company head James Carreras's desire to keep an eye on his investment. "Since it was the first thing I'd done for them, I don't think they were sure of me and wanted me in arm's reach," the author muses. Carreras met Matheson at the Waterloo train station, where the young writer smiled uncertainly for the trade press cameras, there to cover the arrival of the man who would author "one of the most hair-raising films ever made," according to executive producer Michael Carreras.

The script Matheson wrote was entitled *The Night Creatures*, and while the premise and spirit of the book were preserved, the dictates of filmmaking forced substantial alterations. The story now had no distinct dateline, no mention of a war. It was set in Canada instead of Los Angeles, and the third-person narrative structure was changed to first-person monologue. Much of Neville's research was condensed, certain character relationships bolstered, and the ending changed to allow Neville to join the New Society by virtue of his blood's antidotal value.

"I enjoyed being in England very much; if I'd believed in reincarnation at the time, I'd have thought that I'd come home," says Matheson, who returned to his real home in November 1957. *The Night Creatures* continued to move forward, with Val Guest, fresh from the helm of two popular *Quatermass* films, named as director. In keeping with Hammer's policy of obtaining prior approval, the script was submitted to the British Board of Film Censors (BBFC); Hinds and Michael Carreras knew there would be some trouble, but felt confident that any objections could be accommodated. They could not have been more wrong. With the then-recent firestorm of criticism over *The Curse of Frankenstein* (including a suggestion that it be classified for "Sadists Only"), as well as the Board's own reluctant approval for its follow-up, *Horror of Dracula*, the BBFC were in no mood to be generous to the Hammer thorn in their side.

In interviews with Denis Meikle for his book on Hammer Films, *A History of Horrors*, the late Carreras remarked on the shock Hammer felt at BBFC Secretary John Nicholls's response: "He flatly turned us down. I couldn't believe it. That was one of the best scripts we'd ever had. They just said, 'We will not allow you to make this picture.'" The response from the Motion Picture Association of America in December 1957 was equally discouraging: "This present script is in danger of resulting in a finished picture which could not be approved by this office."

With the threat of a ban in both England and the U.S., Hammer had no choice but to cut their losses and drop the project. "When we couldn't make the picture, we were lucky enough to have Robert Lippert [with whom Hammer had coproduced films between 1951 and 1955] buy us out," Carreras said, "so we didn't completely lose. I'm sure he didn't pay the full amount, though; he never paid the full amount for *anything*."

Whatever his investment, Lippert first announced his intention to film the book in 1959 as he was negotiating for the script (at which time he intended to call the film *Naked Terror* for Fox release). In August 1962, he followed the lead of many a Hollywood producer taking advantage of lower costs and government subsidies available in Rome, and his company—Associated Producers—entered into a coproduction arrangement with Italy's Produzioni La Regina to facilitate the shoot. The ubiquitous Vincent Price was named to star, and after several title changes, what became known as *The Last Man on Earth* emerged, credited to director Sidney Salkow, with whom Price had only just finished the American horror anthology *Twice-Told Tales*.

In fact, sources say that the largely Italian cast and crew were guided by local director Ubaldo Ragona, with Salkow only on hand to supervise the U.S. version. In any event, Matheson, who had previously been courted by Lippert to revise the *Night Creatures* script with talk of Fritz Lang at the helm, was forced to watch his book receive cut-rate treatment and his script rewritten by William Leicester. Deciding to make discretion the better part of valor (and wanting to retain residual rights), Matheson had his screen credit attributed to "Logan Swanson," a composite of the maiden names of his mother and mother-in-law. "What I don't know about what happens to films I write would fill volumes," Matheson says, "and this was no exception. It was an intensely disappointing experience when I finally saw it."

For all its budgetary limitations, the black-and-white

Last Man on Earth remains a fairly faithful adaptation of Matheson's novel. Although the protagonist Morgan is a scientist, a change which downplays the painstaking research process so vital to the novel's drama, many indelible scenes from the book are well translated: the burning of Neville's daughter in a hellish mass grave, the return of his wife from the dead, the New Society's assault on his fortified home, and the vampires that surround it. However, the film's release was slow in coming; it wasn't until April 1964 that *The Last Man on Earth* was unveiled by American International Pictures. For AIP, the film was merely an easy programmer—and another chance to exploit their Price franchise—and the company made no mention of it in their tenth-anniversary publicity that summer. Once it had served its purpose, *The Last Man on Earth* went to join the lengthy roster of AIP-TV offerings, while the film rights to Matheson's book remained dormant with Lippert for another five years.

In January 1970, Lippert finally relinquished his hold on *I Am Legend* to no less than Warner Bros. and Charlton Heston, and fans of the book hoped that it would finally get the big-screen treatment it deserved. The movie was shot late that year from a script by the writing team of John William Corrington and Joyce H. Corrington, supervised by Heston, who had first been introduced to the novel by Orson Welles during the filming of *Touch of Evil* in 1958. This script initially bore the novel's moniker, but by the time the film was released in summer 1971, the title change to *The Omega Man* was a harbinger of other major alterations.

The fact that the opening titles only credit "*a* novel by Richard Matheson" as the source material is telling, and indeed, Matheson had virtually no involvement in the project, save a throwaway $2,500 royalty check. Although sparse traces of his novel remained, the Corringtons and Heston jettisoned the main instrument of the book's terror—the vampiric hordes—and concentrated instead on the New Society as Neville's primary adversary. Furthermore, in an obvious effort to be topical and "with it," they embellished "The Family" (à la Manson) with cultlike features—hooded robes, mirrored sunglasses, albinism equalizing whites and blacks—and gave them a warped but charismatic leader named Matthias. They also added a jive-talkin' female lead (Rosalind Cash), and threw in a commune of flower children for good measure. Such liberties with the story won a large audience in 1971, but dated the movie so severely that it is almost impossible to take seriously today.

Heston's out-of-print journal, *The Actor's Life*, paints a picture of a troubled production, marred by a temperamental director in the late Boris Sagal, an ill-at-ease costar in Cash, and a nervous studio in Warner Bros. Heston also concedes to a botched depiction of The Family: "We failed badly with the whole concept of this part of the film." All this internal strife no doubt contributed to *Omega Man*'s shortcomings, and it makes Heston's comment about *The Last Man on Earth* rather ironic: "I can't see how such a soporific film could've come from such a promising piece."

As in the tale behind many a "promising piece," *The Omega Man* had many Hollywood luminaries attached to it at various times along the way. Walter Mirisch was to have been its producer, but was replaced by Walter Seltzer. Diahann Carroll was considered for the female lead, but her salary was too high for a modest production. Heston wanted Sam Peckinpah to direct, but he was occupied with *Straw Dogs*. William Peter Blatty was brought in to polish the script, but with *The Exorcist* still a year from publication, his name didn't warrant screen credit.

When the film was finally completed, Heston waxed philosophic on the fruit of his labors: "This is another of a not-very-long list of films I have more or less personally

conceived, and this may turn out to be the best of them."
Seven years later, however, his comments reflected a more
objective appraisal: "This picture doesn't please me that
much now, and neither does my performance in it."
Matheson wasn't much impressed, either. "It was so far
removed from my book, I don't know why they bothered," he says. "It was no more *I Am Legend* than *Little
Miss Marker.*"

In the twenty-five years since *The Omega Man*, many
have tried and failed to bring a faithful version of *I Am
Legend* to the screen. Dan Curtis made serious attempts in
the 1970s to do the book justice, but to no avail, as did
The Waltons producer Lee Rich. As recently as 1989,
Carreras himself tried to get things moving again, but his
problems were the same encountered previously by Curtis
and Rich. "No one can make *I Am Legend* because
Warners is sitting on the rights to it. I had some new
ideas that would've brought the picture up to date—like
making the survivor a woman—but Warners just wasn't
interested." Fortunately, a faithful version of the book *did*
appear in 1991 in the form of a four-part graphic novel-
ization from Eclipse.

Matheson has expressed interest in a whole host of tal-
ent to film his book—from directors on the order of
Robert Wise and Roman Polanski to actors like Jack
Palance and Harrison Ford—but until this year, no one
seemed able to untangle the maze of legalities and bad
karma. Tracy Tormé, writer and coproducer of *Fire in the
Sky*, almost pulled off this coup, informing Matheson of
his intention to produce a definitive version of *I Am
Legend*. But most recently, Warner Bros. hired Carlo
(*Fluke*) Carlei to direct a big-budget remake, scripted by
Mark Protosevich.

In reflecting on the lasting impression *I Am Legend* has
made on the genres of science-fantasy and horror,
Matheson states simply, "I am, of course, gratified by the

book's reception and longevity. When I wrote it, I had no idea it would cause such a stir among readers, much less that it would endure as long as it has; but then, are creative people ever able to gauge the ultimate potential of anything they create? I never have. I'm always surprised." However, to those who have read *I Am Legend* over the last forty years, it is no surprise. Nor will it be a surprise to those who discover this landmark work in the forty years to come.

THE *NECROSCOPE* SAGA

JAMES ANDERSON

ALTHOUGH HE WAS BORN exactly nine months after H. P. Lovecraft's death, Brian Lumley denies being the reincarnation of the acknowledged master of horror fiction. Yet, like Lovecraft's stories, Lumley's work goes beyond the stereotyped trappings of horror to touch a nerve and capture an audience of devoted fans who appreciate a well-crafted plot and a good scare.

In 1988, with little fanfare, Lumley's *Necroscope* introduced the concept of "Deadspeak" to American readers of horror fiction in the character of Harry Keogh, a man who could communicate with the deceased and make friends with the "Teeming Masses." Seven novels and close to two million sales later, "Deadspeak" and the *Necroscope* series have become household words in the world of horror, spawning comics, graphic novels, model kits, and a board game. And the books themselves keep getting better and better, with the most recent, *Bloodwars*, bringing the series to a satisfying conclusion.

While Lumley is without question one of the most successful and popular writers in the genre, his success, while dramatic, has not come overnight. Born in northeast England and the son of a miner, he received the lowest marks in his English class in 1946. In fact, when he mentioned to his teacher that he might like to write, he was advised to follow his father's footsteps in the mines. And at fourteen years old, his father told him that "there was no money in words." Instead, he went to technical school and then joined the army, where he served in Berlin and Cyprus. It was during this time that he began to read, especially during night duty along the Berlin Wall.

"I was in Germany when the Wall was built," he recalls. "Berlin was like a goldfish bowl—you couldn't move anywhere. It had the second highest suicide rate in the world, second only to Japan. In Berlin, they committed suicide by trying to escape across the Wall.

"That was a good setting for writing escapism, to get away from the real world. I bought an August Derleth collection of short stories and thought that instead of sitting along the Wall waiting for an incident, I'd use my time wisely and write this kind of thing."

He bundled up three of his stories, single-spaced and written on the front and back of the paper with the pages not numbered, and sent them by surface mail, rolled up in a paper tube, to Derleth at Arkham House. Despite the fact that Lumley had "done it all wrong," Derleth recognized his talent and bought two of the three stories for *The Arkham Collector*. The third was sent back for revisions, and then purchased as well. "I can still imagine him taking the stories out of the roll and having to nail them down to the desk to read them," Lumley laughs.

"The Cyprus Shell," published in 1968, still reads well today and has been reprinted in *Fruiting Bodies and Other Fungi* (Tor, 1993). Lumley blames the story for his allergies to seafood—after one reads it, oysters may never look appetizing again!

Heavily influenced by Lovecraft, many of Lumley's early works were "Cthulhu Mythos" imitations, which didn't endear him to some Lovecraft scholars. His early

Lovecraftian novels involve Titus Crow, a member of the Wilmarth Foundation, who has devoted his life to exterminating remnants of Cthulhu and his minions from the Earth, where they have been imprisoned by the Elder Gods.

Lumley originally wrote these stories for his own enjoyment and satisfaction, and as a tribute to Lovecraft and the Mythos, which he sees as an elaborate game that the author devised and shared with friends and fellow writers. "Nowadays, anyone who tries to write a Lovecraft story is going to come under fire from certain Lovecraft 'authorities,'" the author says. "But in his lifetime, Lovecraft invited others to play, such as Clark Ashton Smith, C. M. Eddy, Robert Bloch, all his revision clients. How the modern gang can say there are no Mythos stories except those written by Lovecraft is beyond me. I think he would be delighted with modern writers who play his game."

Lumley still enjoys writing a Lovecraftian story when an idea strikes him. The four-volume "dreamscape" series (*Hero of Dreams*, *Ship of Dreams*, *Mad Moon of Dreams*, and *Iced on Aran*), based upon Lovecraft's dreamquest stories, is a more modern rendition of the idea, featuring a hero who becomes trapped in a dreamworld that includes lighter-than-air islands, gigantic sentient trees, and fantastic adventures. While some Lumley fans may recognize parts of the dreamworld from the Titus Crow novels, the new series reads much more like modern fantasy, with characters that are more interesting and believable.

Although Lumley has suffered at the hands of some critics, he is more concerned with the opinions of his readers and is content to "let the royalty checks speak for themselves." He compares a few critics to children playing in a schoolyard: "The majority of the reviewers who criticize us for having added to, expanded upon, or explored in depth the Cthulhu Mythos are the people who can't. Isn't it always the truth, the kid who can't play the game is the one who runs away with the ball?"

While Lovecraft inspired his early writings, Lumley's style has evolved into something different, compelling and distinctive. "What a lot of people forget is that when I first started to write in 1967, and for the first thirteen or fourteen years of my writing career, if you want to call it that, it wasn't a career at all. It was a hobby, because I was a full-time soldier. That was my business. Writing was something I did in my spare time. Everything I wrote during this period was for me."

He left the army in 1980 and decided to write full-time. "Twenty-two years of being a soldier taught me that there had to be better things in life," he says. At this point, he realized that if he wanted to make a living as an author, his work would have to be modern and commercial. "It wasn't that I eschewed Lovecraft so much as I had to appeal to the general public, which a lot of Lovecraft stories no longer do. Lovecraft wouldn't have dreamed of entering a pub in his life—my people hang out in wharfside taverns." His first "commercial" novel, *Psychomech*, was published in England in 1984, and the *Psychomech* trilogy was released by Tor in 1992 after *Necroscope* had already become popular in the United States.

Necroscope was, without a doubt, Lumley's breakthrough book. "I think there comes a time in a writer's life when you wake up one morning and say, 'I cracked it with that one and now I'm never going to write another duff one'—and we all write duff ones. I knew immediately that *Necroscope* was the one, even before it began selling."

The inspiration for *Necroscope* came when Lumley's father died and he wished he could speak to him again. The idea wouldn't go away, and evolved into the character of Harry Keogh, the man who can talk to the dead. Because of his powers, Harry is able to tap into the universal knowledge of humankind, and learns how to travel throughout time, space, and alternate worlds via the Mobius Continuum. Harry encounters a vampire named Thibor Ferenczy in *Necroscope*, then battles another vampire, Yulian Bodescu, in *Vamphyri!* In *The Source*, Harry travels into an alternate world where bloodsuckers are the dominant creatures, and which serves as the setting for his *Vampire World* trilogy: *Blood Brothers*, *The Last Aerie*, and *Bloodwars*.

"I never use an outline," Lumley admits of his writing process. "I paint myself into a corner. I like to think that if I don't know how a book's going to end, then the reader can't *possibly* figure it out.

"In *Necroscope*, for example, I had built the story up and, with fifty pages left to go, Harry hadn't discovered the Mobius Continuum yet. I wondered, 'How the hell am I going to get him to the heart of Russia and out of England in one leap?' So that's how I did it—in one leap, through the Mobius Continuum. I had him teleport, for God's sake! Now, that sounds impossible, but it worked. And that's the kind of thing I like—if I can give myself some work to do, then I'm giving my readers something worth reading."

The entire *Necroscope* series, while it appears to have been planned out in advance, came into being much like Harry Keogh's invention of the Mobius Continuum— through inspiration and creative accident. *The Source* was originally planned as a different series entirely, but with similar creatures, which is why Harry doesn't appear until a third of the way through the book. But by the end of the third volume, Lumley realized he had a series and was already planning a fourth book.

"That is why we finish the story with the Dweller feeling someone's eyes upon him, looking up and seeing that his father is still watching him," the author explains. "But it's only his father, so he doesn't worry. Of course, what Harry is thinking is, 'I'm going to cure him. I wonder if I can get rid of that leech? I wonder if I can get rid of that vampire in him?' Which led on to *Deadspeak*.

"Because I really enjoyed writing the books, there were several places, usually when we were at the point of a gory happening, that I would remind the reader that this is fun," Lumley continues. "In *Vamphyri!*, Yulian Bodescu's auntie says to him as he is about to stuff his uncle into the furnace in the cellar, 'Oh, no, don't kill him *again*.' Some hard-core horror readers might complain that this ruined it for them. But these are deliberate touches of humor, because the books are supposed to be entertaining."

Lumley introduces the vampire world in *The Source*, wherein Harry, the Dweller, and some human heroes defeat the vampire lords. *Blood Brothers* begins the *Vampire World* trilogy and, by introducing Harry's sons, ushers in the "next generation" of *Necroscope* books.

While vampires might be a staple in horror fiction, Lumley's bloodsuckers make Bram Stoker's Dracula look like a Boy Scout. The Wamphyri Lords can grow over eight feet tall, read minds, and reshape their faces and bodies into monstrous forms. Lesk the Glut, for example, has lost an eye and half of his face in battle, which he keeps covered with a huge leather patch stitched to his jaw and head. However, he has regrown the missing eye on his left shoulder, which he keeps bare.

These creatures not only have superhuman strength, but can manipulate the flesh and protoplasm of their victims like putty to build hideous monsters that obey their immortal masters. These giant, dragonlike flyers and living war machines with dozens of armored heads, arms, and tentacles defend the Wamphyri strongholds, natural castlelike stacks lined with armored skin tissue and heated by huge gas-producing monsters. The vampire lords terrorize the human population and engage in terrible battles amongst themselves.

Not only are Lumley's bloodsuckers more brutal and

savage than the traditional model, their mythology is more believably thought out, despite their fantastic appearances and powers. The vampire lords are not supernatural creatures, but aliens from another world. According to this concept, the vampire leech grows in the swamps of this planet, then "infects" other creatures. An infected wolf becomes a werewolf, and an infected human becomes a vampire. The parasite grows within its host, giving the creature incredible powers and virtual immortality while taking over the host's mind and will. Earth's vampires emigrated from a small "greyhole" connected to the vampire planet and centered in the secluded mountains of Romania.

"You can do more with a vampire than you can with a werewolf, a ghoul, or a zombie," Lumley explains. "The werewolf only has his fun once a month, and ghouls and zombies are slow and really aren't much fun. If you're going to choose one of the bunch of standard monsters and do it differently, then you've got to choose the vampire."

Lumley has plans for two future books in the *Necroscope* series, which will bring the total to ten volumes. These books will be about the lost years (between Volumes II and III) and events that occurred while Harry Keogh was looking for his wife and son, but which he can't remember. And although Lumley has turned down offers for the film rights to the series, he expects that a *Necroscope* movie may happen "when the right producer comes along." The author is also developing an entirely new series based upon a concept as interesting as the *Necroscope* idea, but which he isn't ready to reveal until the books are written.

"A horror story should be entertaining as well as horrifying," Lumley says, when asked about his success. "A lot of modern writers forget that. They believe that if it's full of blood and gore and guts and entrails, then it's a horror story. But if it doesn't entertain, it's a *horrible* story." He also credits his popularity to his combining of numerous different genres in his novels, which encompass horror, science fiction, fantasy, and even espionage fiction. "I reckon that *Necroscope* works for the same reason that John Carpenter's *The Thing* works, and for the same reason that *Alien* works—because they cross genres. They're science-fiction horror stories."

Lumley works from the credo that "if it doesn't please me, it won't please the reader" and tries hard to stay in tune with his fans. He attends a number of conventions each year to sign books and meet his fans, who have consistently grown in numbers, making him one of the most popular genre authors today. But unlike many of today's writers, who aim to be "mainstream," Lumley still considers himself a horror author and likes it that way. "A good story is a good story no matter what genre it's written in," he says. "And the authors who write good stories will be remembered, while the dregs will go spiraling down to the bottom." Rather than be buried in the stacks of mass-market books by authors such as Danielle Steel and Judith Krantz, he feels comfortable in the horror section, with Stephen King's books to the left and Robert McCammon's to the right. "People know where to look for me," he says.

With some twenty books in print and more to come, it seems that Lumley's place is secure beside that of his predecessor, H. P. Lovecraft. While he may not be the reincarnation of the old gent from Providence, his work is, indeed, something that the master would have enjoyed and been proud of.

ANTHONY TIMPONE is the editor of *FANGORIA* magazine. He is also the writer of *Men, Makeup and Monsters* (St. Martin's Press) and the editor of *FANGORIA's Best Horror Films* (Crescent Books).

DARE TO ENTER

The World of Darkness™ is a trademark of the White Wolf Game Studio.

MAIL TO: **HarperCollins Publishers**
                P.O. Box 588 Dunmore, PA 18512-0588

Yes, please send me the books I have checked:

❑ WRAITH: SINS OF THE FATHERS by Sam Chupp 105472-0 . . . .$4.99 U.S./$5.99 Can.
❑ MAGE: SUCH PAIN by Don Bassingthwaite 105463-1 . . . .$4.99 U.S./$5.99 Can.
❑ VAMPIRE: DARK PRINCE by Keith Herber 105422-4 . . . .$4.99 U.S./$5.99 Can.
❑ VAMPIRE: NETHERWORLD by Richard Lee Byers 105473-9 . . . .$4.99 U.S./$5.99 Can.
❑ VAMPIRE: BLOOD RELATIONS by Doug Murray 105674-X . . . .$5.50 U.S./$7.50 Can.
❑ VAMPIRE: BLOOD ON THE SUN
        by Brian Herbert and Marie Landis 105670-7 . . . .$5.50 U.S./$7.50 Can.
❑ WEREWOLF: WYRM WOLF by Edo van Belkom 105439-9 . . . .$4.99 U.S./$5.99 Can.
❑ WEREWOLF: CONSPICUOUS CONSUMPTION
        by Stewart von Allmen 105471-2 . . . .$4.99 U.S./$5.99 Can.
❑ WEREWOLF: HELL-STORM by James A. Moore 105675-8 . . . .$5.50 U.S./$7.50 Can.
❑ STRANGE CITY edited by Staley Krause and Stewart Wieck 105668-5 .$5.50 U.S./$6.50 Can.

SUBTOTAL . . . .$_____
POSTAGE & HANDLING . . . .$_____
SALES TAX (Add applicable sales tax) . . . .$_____
TOTAL . . . .$_____

Name _____
Address _____
City _____ State _____ Zip _____

Order 4 or more titles and postage & handling is **FREE!** For orders of fewer than 4 books, please include $2.00
postage & handling. Allow up to 6 weeks for delivery. Remit in U.S. funds. Do not send cash. Valid in U.S. &
Canada. Prices subject to change.   http://www.harpercollins.com/paperbacks   P027

Visa & MasterCard holders—call 1-800-331-3761